William Holden Hutton

S. John Baptist College

William Holden Hutton

S. John Baptist College

ISBN/EAN: 9783337402259

Printed in Europe, USA, Canada, Australia, Japan

Cover: Foto ©Andreas Hilbeck / pixelio.de

More available books at **www.hansebooks.com**

University of Oxford

COLLEGE HISTORIES

S. JOHN BAPTIST COLLEGE

BY

WILLIAM HOLDEN HUTTON, B.D.

FELLOW, TUTOR, AND PRECENTOR, AND FORMERLY
LIBRARIAN, OF S. JOHN BAPTIST COLLEGE; EXAMINING
CHAPLAIN TO THE LORD BISHOP OF ELY

LONDON
F. E. ROBINSON
20 GREAT RUSSELL STREET, BLOOMSBURY
1898

Printed by BALLANTYNE, HANSON & Co.
At the Ballantyne Press

TO

OUR PRESIDENT,

REVERED AND BELOVED.

PREFACE

During nearly the whole of their existence, until the changes which resulted from the Universities of Oxford and Cambridge Act 1877, the Colleges of Oxford have been so closely bound to the Church of England that the study of their life may properly be regarded as a part of ecclesiastical history. A great experiment in education, one of the chiefest works of the Church, they have undergone many changes and modifications, internally and from without, as the currents of doctrine and feeling have ebbed and flowed. In their social life, as in the way in which they have responded to the intellectual ideal they represented, they serve as examples, sometimes painful ones, of the way in which the Church has carried out her mission. Times of energy and sloth, of decay and revival, are represented in them as in the Church at large. They are often a picture in little of the wider body to which they belong. A College which like S. John's was founded at the very crisis of the reforming movement in England deserves the special attention of the student of Church history; and it is for this reason that I have not hesitated to turn aside for a while from the investigation of the English Reformation which occupies such leisure as I can obtain, and to put together notes which I have made from time to time on the history of the College to which it is my happy privilege to belong.

This book does not pretend to be a complete history of the College. My utmost hope is that it may serve to direct attention to points of special interest, and to existing materials of great value, which may be utilised at some future date, possibly by myself, more probably by some one hereafter better qualified for the task. In writing it I have endeavoured to bring into special prominence what has not hitherto been printed or exists only in very rare books. No history of S. John's has till now been written, so that in some parts I have had to break new ground. But few Colleges have had among their *alumni* antiquaries more devoted to the study of all that belongs to their history, and the work of all subsequent investigators has been greatly lightened by the labours of Rawlinson, Holmes, and Derham. After the MSS. in the College, the chief sources of information are the collections of Rawlinson and Tanner. These I have examined, and with them all other MS. materials in the Bodleian Library. The printed authorities for the history of the Colleges are well known and need no special mention here.

I feel sure that I shall not please everybody, either by what I have said or by what I have omitted to say. I will only state, in reply to the criticisms I anticipate, that since I was forced to be brief, I have intentionally treated the history of the last two centuries much less fully than the earlier years.

I desire to express my sense of the courtesy which allows me to reprint here some pages contributed to the *Guardian*.

W. H. H.

CONTENTS

LIST OF ILLUSTRATIONS

PRESIDENTS OF S. JOHN'S COLLEGE

1555.	ALEXANDER BELSIRE
1559.	WILLIAM ELYE
1563.	WILLIAM STOCKE
1564.	JOHN ROBINSON
1572.	TOBIE MATTHEW
1577.	FRANCIS WILLIS
1590.	RALPH HUTCHINSON
1605.	JOHN BUCKERIDGE
1611.	WILLIAM LAUD
1621.	WILLIAM JUXON
1633.	RICHARD BAYLIE
1648.	FRANCIS CHEYNELL
1650.	THANKFUL OWEN
1660.	RICHARD BAYLIE, *restored*
1667.	PETER MEWS
1673.	WILLIAM LEVINZ
1698.	WILLIAM DELAUNE
1728.	WILLIAM HOLMES
1748.	WILLIAM DERHAM
1757.	WILLIAM WALKER
1757.	THOMAS FRY
1772.	SAMUEL DENNIS
1795.	MICHAEL MARLOW
1828.	PHILIP WYNTER
1871.	JAMES BELLAMY

CHAPTER I

THE ORIGIN OF THE COLLEGE

THE Oxford Colleges to-day, when we look at them in their historical aspect as illustrations of the life of the nation and representations of its aspirations at different stages of its development, fall naturally into three classes. There are first the medieval colleges, of different dates, but all founded, it may be roughly said, in the same spirit. The close connection of the colleges with the Church, and in some cases with monasticism, is the distinguishing feature of the medieval foundations. They have many great names: perhaps the greatest, judged from this standing-point, is that of William of Wykeham, whose influence continues into the second period.

The Renaissance and the Reformation, in England only different and continuous aspects of the same great movement, claim the second class for their own. Bishop Foxe, Cardinal Wolsey, King Henry the Eighth, " the sole and munificent founder of Christ Church " as some University preachers still generously call him, and the rich burgesses and country gentlemen whom the social changes of the time endowed with property that had been beforetime, perhaps, in better hands, are those

A

whom we remember when we see the foundations of the sixteenth century.

The third period is a long one, and it includes the Stewart foundation of Pembroke and the splendid memorial to the Tractarians in the person of their most persuasive and popular leader. Whether or no Keble College is the advance guard of a series of modern foundations it would be rash to attempt to prophesy. Apparently, the fountain of beneficence is choked, if it be not dried up.

The College of S. John Baptist belongs to the second of the three classes. It is closely associated with the English Reformation. It may, indeed, be said that it serves as a perpetual memorial of the continuity of the national Church, of which, through its most critical period of change, the founder was a pious and consistent member.

Mr. J. R. Green who, it must be admitted, sometimes, to the delight of his readers, sacrificed accuracy to picturesqueness, once characterised the Oxford Colleges of the sixteenth century thus: " If Christ Church was the last and grandest effort of expiring medievalism, if Trinity and S. John's commemorated the reaction under Philip and Mary, Jesus by its very name took its stand as the first Protestant College." It would be hard for an able historian to compress more error into a single sentence. For our purpose it is sufficient to trace the circumstances which brought S. John's into being, and to illustrate, as we proceed, the relation of its foundation to the stormy history of the time.

Oxford at the middle of the sixteenth century was strewn with the relics of religious houses dissolved and decayed. Great churchmen had stepped in, with the State and its prodigal head by their side, to visit, to amalgamate, to suppress the smaller societies which had been bound more or less closely to the monastic ideal. The lesson which Morton and Warham and Wolsey had taught was easily learnt; and when the dissolution of the monasteries came in 1539, the revenues and the property of houses now extinguished were seized, more readily than their buildings were found useful for purposes of religion or learning. It was not easy to know what to do with the old monastic buildings. They were practically useless to private owners, who had no taste for an arrangement of bedchambers as extensive and intricate as a rabbit warren, and less inclination to live in public in a large hall or say their prayers with dignity in a private chapel. Thus, many of the old houses, whose memory we owe to the gigantic labours of the Oxford antiquaries of the Stewart age, utterly perished, and left not a rack behind. Their buildings disappeared from the earth, and it is a pleasing task to our antiquaries to discover a trace of their sites. Others were happily saved from destruction just in time, and it is to British merchants that we owe their preservation. S. John's College in this way arose from the past of a monastic house.

In the fifteenth century there had been no worthier primate of all England and no wiser benefactor to sound learning than the good Archbishop Chichele. Among his Oxford foundations was that of a small house outside the city, which he dedicated to S. Bernard of Clairvaux.* He had observed that the scholars of

* This account is based upon S. John's MSS. and Anthony Wood.

the Cistercian order, English, Welsh, and Irish, who came to study in the University, had no dwelling-place belonging to their order where they might stay, for Rewley Abbey was "a Cistercian monastery, and not a college for students from Cistercian monasteries elsewhere." Their living separately in the different halls and inns made it impossible for them to perform the obligation of their order as to the saying of offices and the like, and in consequence they did not so often take advantage of the University education as did other orders. "This, then, the Archbishop considering, desired King Henry VI. that he might perform some acceptable thing to God in helping or contributing towards the necessities of these holy Cistercians in building them a place where they might gain humane and heavenly knowledge." The King's letters patent (March 20, 1437) gave leave to erect a college to the honour of the B. V. M. and S. Bernard "in the street commonly called Northgate Street, in the parish of S. Mary Magdalene without Northgate." The Archbishop held about five acres therein of the King *in capite*, but only two acres, including the land leased from Durham College, were in possession of the new house. The buildings at first erected faced west and south. They still remain but little changed in their outward aspect. Over the great gate is the statue of S. Bernard. Below the west building is a fine vaulted cellar, which some believe to have been originally the refectory of the monks.

The house prospered. Its members came from many

City of Oxford, vol. ii,, in the admirable edition of the Rev. Andrew Clark, Oxford Historical Society, 1890, pp. 305 *sqq*.

Cistercian houses at home and abroad; and though, strictly speaking, the Bernardines were a variety of the greater order and wore a black gown over their white habit, while the Cistercians were "white monks," the distinction in Oxford at least was but nominal. They were governed by a "Provisor" under the Chancellor of the University, who was their Visitor. The names of several of the Provisors have been preserved,* and it seems possible that the last, Philip Acton (*circa* 1535), had some connection with the foundation which took the place of his house.†

The hall was built in 1502. Its original open-work roof, which extends to beyond the fireplace, is still preserved under the ceiling which was put up, probably, when the hall was enlarged. The chapel was built later. It was consecrated in 1530 by Robert King, Abbat of Bruer and Thame and last Abbat of Osney, who was titular Bishop of Rheon, "supposed," says Anthony Wood, " to be in the province of Athens," and suffragan to the Bishop of Lincoln, in whose vast diocese Oxford lay.

The monks had a garden eastwards, part of which was bought from University College and part leased from Durham College, the house of the northern Benedictines which adjoined S. Bernard's on the south.

Something of the appearance of the College may be gathered from the following description:

"According to a survey taken of Durham and S. Bernard's Colleges, *temp.* Henry VIII., the eastern side

---

* See Ant. Wood, *City of Oxford*, ii. 308–309.

† Thomas, Bishop of Bangor, whose will was dated 10 May 1533, left £20 for the repairs of S. Bernard's College. (For this further reference I am indebted to Mr. E. H. Stapleton, scholar of the College).

of the quadrangle was intended for a library and chambers, but seems to have been left unfinished. The walls were then rough, and considerably high, extending 112 feet in length, which is the admeasurement of the opposite side.

"The breadth of the library and chambers was to be nineteen feet within the walls.

"The windows, twenty-five in number, on the side facing the quadrangle, were secured with iron bars; but nothing is said respecting glass.

"On the east side were twelve windows, with iron bars also.

"The chambers on the south and west sides of the quadrangle, about eighteen in number, are described as measuring from 22 feet to 26 feet in length and 18 in breadth, with a study or studies to each; and over the hall and entry thereto was a fair chamber, in length from east to west 41 feet, and in breadth 27.

"The chapel was 80 feet by 27; the hall 30 by 27, and underneath a cellar or buttery of the same dimensions.

"The kitchen was 42 feet by 27. There were three altars in the chapel, as in the old chapel of Durham College; with seven windows: and every window had six lights, or divisions, well glazed; the great east window behind the high altar having fourteen fair lights, with the appurtenances well glazed also." *

After the dissolution in 1539 the College, with all its buildings, gardens, enclosures, &c., excepting the bells and lead (which, it is to be presumed, the King sold to his own profit), were granted by Henry VIII. to his new house of Christ Church in 1546. In the five years

* "MS. penes Ed. transcribed from the original in the chapter-house at Westminster": Ingram's *Memorials of Oxford*, vol. iii., p. 8, footnote.

that intervened, it seems that some of the monks had continued to live in the buildings. Wood found traces of them, at least from 1537 to 1540. The property, it would seem, was considered to be of little value, " worth to farmers but twenty shillings per annum ; by which we may understand how this place was undervalued, and therefore sold, I believe, as they used to say, ' for Robin Hood's pennyworths.' " *

Of the old associations much remains to those who have entered upon the heritage of the Bernardines. Chapel, hall, the tower which holds the muniments, the bursary, and many fine sets of rooms are visible links between us and our monastic predecessors. It is possible, but unlikely, that some of the vestments † now kept in the College library may have belonged to them. There is also among the MSS. a link between the College property in north Oxford and the days of S. Bernard's house. It shall speak for itself : ‡

" John Manfield, Alderman of Calice, son and heir of Hugh Manfield, sometime citizen and stockfishmonger of London, and Agnes his wife, daughter and heir of John Steynton, sometime of Oxon, and Alice his wife, doe appoint Robert Heth of Oxon, brewer, to deliver for him to John Staynbourne, Provisor or Prior of S. Bernard's College, and the Fellows and Brethren there, full seisin and possession of an acre and a half of land in Walton

---

* MS. *History of S. John's College*, by Joseph Taylor, LL.D., 1606. The phrase has been used by Wood, who copied Taylor, *City*, ii. 310.

† See p. 245.

‡ I use Dr. Rawlinson's note—cp. Appendix in Fourth Report of *Historical MSS. Commission*, p. 468.

field.   'Videlicet in cultura quæ vocatur 'le Buts' contra
Putmede, et dat penultima die Augusti I. Edward. IV.'"

It is like enough this land was part of the property
Sir Thomas White bought "for Robin Hood's pennyworths"; and that is, except the ground within the
College walls, all that has descended from S. Bernard's
house to the College of S. John Baptist.

CHAPTER II

THE FOUNDATION OF THE COLLEGE

THE scanty lands of S. Bernard's house did not long
lie waste or the monastic buildings remain untenanted.
The literary influences which transformed the England
of the Lancastrians into the England of the Tudors
and the Reformation were nowhere more strongly felt
than among the lawyers, merchants, and public officials
of the age. The scramble for wealth which disfigured
the reign of Edward VI., and the general feeling of
insecurity about the state of the *Ecclesia Anglicana,*
prevented any foundation of societies for the promotion
of true religion and sound learning in Oxford between
the death of Henry VIII. and the accession of Mary.
But no sooner was Henry's elder daughter on the
throne than two colleges were founded by two friends
within two months on the sites of two adjacent
houses. Sir Thomas Pope, who had already bought
the property of Durham College, received letters patent
on March 1, 1555, to found Trinity College, Sir
Thomas White on May 1 to found S. John's.

The history and personality of the Founder are
interesting. Thomas White was the son of William
White, a clothier, of Rickmansworth. His mother
was Mary, daughter of John Kebblewhite of South

Fawley, Bucks. His father, shortly before his birth in 1492, had moved to Reading. It was probably at the Grammar School of that town, founded by Henry VII., that he had his first schooling; and he endowed the school when he became rich with two scholarships to his Oxford College. But he must soon have gone to London, for he tells us himself that he was brought up "even almost from infancy" there, and therein "gathered the greater part of such goods and commodities which by God's permission and mercy he enjoyed; therefore, to no one was he tied in so sure a bond of friendship as the Londoners."

He was apprenticed at the age of twelve to Hugh Acton, a merchant tailor, and prominent member of the company. That the last Prior of S. Bernard's College was one Philip Acton, who flourished in 1535 (the name Acton was on the window of the room opposite the present Bursary in 1574, Wood says), suggests the hypothesis that it was through some family association that White was later drawn towards S. Bernard's, but it is only a plausible conjecture. Hugh Acton died in 1520, and left his industrious apprentice £100. William White died three years later, and then Thomas, with his scanty patrimony and his hundred pounds, set up in business as a tailor, for himself. The story of his life, at least till his later years, is one which has often served like Dick Whittington's for a moral to the 'prentice lads. He did all that Hogarth's good boy did except marry his master's daughter—and yet even that he may have done, for the surname of the Avicia, whom S. John's College commemorates in its Founder's prayers and its after-dinner grace, is unknown. He

prospered rapidly.   In 1530 he was first Renter
Warden of the Merchant Taylors' Company, and their
historian thinks that he was Senior Warden in 1533, and
Master in 1535.

He was a good, religious man, in touch with the
literary influences of the time, and not altogether out
of reach of its superstitions.   Sir Thomas Pope, who
had acquired immense wealth as Treasurer of the Court
of Augmentations, was his friend; and Sir Thomas
More was Pope's friend, as William Roper his son-in-
law was White's.   As a good merchant he meddled
not too much with contentious politics or contentious
religion, but it seems that he was nearly being in
danger of the lion's wrath in 1553, when the Maid of
Kent made him the confidant of some of her indiscreet
"revelations" which King Harry so strictly punished.*
The danger passed over and White took no more part
with religious fanatics of either party.   He remained a
pious man, but he hasted to grow rich.   In 1535 he
was assessed for the subsidy at the substantial sum
of £1000, and in the following year he is found making
large loans in the chief mercantile cities of England
which in later years he often made into gifts, endowing
benefactions for apprentices and the like.   He resided
in the parish of S. Michael, Cornhill, and it was for
that ward that he was elected Alderman on June 17,
1545.   He was not eager to take upon himself what
are now called "civic honours," and the city records
show that he was actually committed to Newgate, and
his shop-shutters were closed by the order of the City
Fathers " so long as he should continue in his obstinacy."

* See *Calendar of State Papers* (Domestic), 1533, p. 587.

A short imprisonment gave him the tamed spirit proper for an Alderman, and in the same year, having "taken upon himself the weight thereof," he contributed £300 to the city's loan to the King. In 1547 he was sheriff of London. In 1553, when Edward VI. lay a dying, he embarked upon a greater venture than London merchants had made for many a day, for he joined in founding the Muscovy Company, which received its charter at the beginning of Queen Mary's reign.

He would have nothing to do with Queen Jane and her rash adherents. It is likely enough that being a man fond, as Machyn's Diary shows us, of the comely ceremonies of religion, of processions, and the dignity of High Mass, he was heartily sick of the ritual changes of the protestant party. At any rate he supported Mary and was one of the first to be knighted when she was firmly seated on the throne. On October 2, 1553, in the Queen's presence, the Lord Steward, the Earl of Arundel, made him knight, and twenty-seven days later he became Lord Mayor of London.

He gave the city a splendid pageant at his inauguration, though his mayoralty was marked by somewhat stringent sumptuary laws for the citizens. He was himself content to give feasts, at funerals and other suitable occasions, such as had never been seen, by honest Machyn at any rate, before. But he had much more serious business. He sat on the commission that tried poor Jane Grey. He received the Spanish envoys, who came to negotiate for the hand of the Queen. When Wyatt's rebellion broke out he showed a prudent promptness. He hastily arrested Lord Northampton in dead of night, and made all ready for the city's defence. It was to him that Mary came when like a true daughter of Harry VIII. she rallied the citizens round her by her appeal to their honour. On January 3, 1554, it was he who repulsed the rebels from the Bridge gate at Southwark. At a critical point in English history it may well be said that it was Sir Thomas White who preserved the constitution and the throne. Then came more work of trying rebels, proclamations for the observance of the Catholic religion, and a state reception of King Philip and Queen Mary. Few mayoralties have been more important than that of the Founder of S. John's.

It seems that no sooner was he freed from the cares of the chief magistracy than he turned to execute what must have been with him, as with his friend Sir Thomas Pope, a long cherished project. He already possessed land in the neighbourhood of Oxford; probably he had been buying up the property of the dissolved monasteries and of impoverished landlords for some time.

A tradition which is recorded by Griffin Higgs, who wrote the Founder's life early in the seventeenth century, states that Sir Thomas had seen in a dream a tree which should mark the site of his foundation. Long he searched for it till one day riding by chance by S. Bernard's College he recognised in a great elm out of whose single root grew three trunks, the tree of his dream. One Triplet, a mason, an old man, is said to have held his bridle while he alighted and gave God thanks for his discovery. More than a century later when Dr. Levinz was President (1673–1697) the tree was shown in his garden as a testimony; and now fabulists show another tree outside the Common Room of which Sir Thomas may have dreamed, but which he can never have beheld with waking eyes.

The site determined, the purchase was easy. The new foundation of Christ Church was not sorry to part with a property, probably useless to itself, to the rich merchant who wished to become a patron of learning. Sir Thomas, says an enthusiastic College annalist in the next century, had already poured over England a torrent of munificence, and now among the many things in which he deserved well of the State this that he did was the worthiest. The old house of the Bernardines became the College of S. John Baptist in the University of Oxford.

The licence of the Crown to "erect the College" was dated, May 1, 1555. The foundation was to be set apart for the study of the sciences of sacred theology, philosophy, and good arts. The College was dedicated to the praise and honour of God, and of the Blessed Virgin Mary His Mother, and S. John Baptist. One president and thirty scholars, graduate or nongraduate, were provided for; and Sir Thomas White was given power to make ordinances or statutes.

Thus armed with the royal licence, on May 29 Sir Thomas White issued his deed of foundation fixing the same number of scholars, but promising "more to be added hereafter." He created Alexander Belsire, Bachelor of Divinity, the first President, with three Fellows; and then by an interlineation in the deed John James, B.D., was added. Beyond the property of S. Bernard's

College, the capital messuage and "half his part of one virgate commonly called a grove joining to the said messuage," the College was not liberally endowed in Oxford, but Sir Thomas White gave to it a yearly rent of £36 due to him from the mayor and commonalty of Coventry; and, above all, the manors whose names every Fellow to-day knows so well if not from personal inspection at least from their solemn recitation on the now rare occasion of a College dinner; "Long Wittenham, Fyfhyde *alias* dict. Fyfelde, Cumner, Eton *alias* dict. Eaton, Kyngston, Frylsham *alias* dict. Frylford, et Garford."

The new society entered on the possession of its own on June 18, 1555, the President of Corpus Christi College who held half the ground surrendering it. To complete the record of the founding it should be added that by a further deed of March 5, 1558, the numbers were increased and the intention of the Founder was more clearly specified. Theology, philosophy, civil and canon law were declared to be the subjects to which the scholars were to devote themselves; and of the fifty Fellows and scholars, six were to be Founder's kin, two each from Coventry, Bristol and Reading Schools, one from Tonbridge and the rest from the Merchant Taylors' School in London. Twelve scholars were to study Civil and Common Law, the rest Theology, save one only who (lest doctors should differ and patients die) was to apply himself to medicine. There were moreover to be three priests as chaplains, six clerks not priests yet not married, and six choristers. In the same year a benefaction came from another hand. On July 23, 1558, George Owen, M.D., granted to Sir

Thomas White, to be added to the site of the College " three acres of arable land without the north gate, parcel of the manor of Walton." In 1559 the president and scholars obtained an acre on the other side "in the furlong called Beaumont."

On January 18, 1567, the Chancellor incorporated the College in the University. By this the foundation may be regarded as complete.

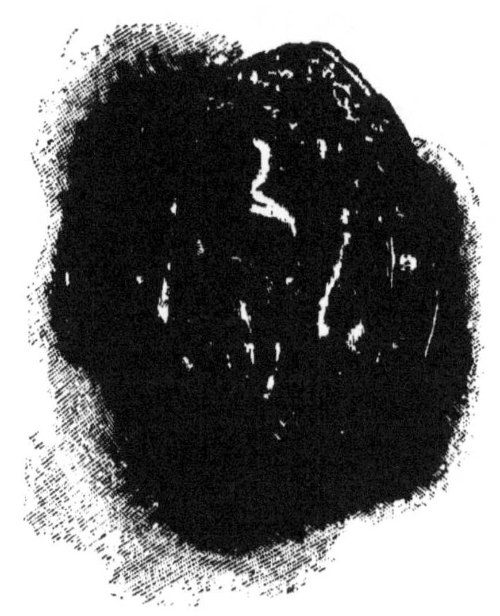

OLD SEAL

CHAPTER III

THE EARLY PRESIDENTS

Sir Thomas White lived twelve years after the foundation of his College. His interest in learning did not cease when he had created S. John's. He took a leading part in the founding of the Merchant Taylors' School, and of Gloucester Hall he made a hall for students under the direction of the College he had endowed. He continued to watch over the College till his death.

The society has fifteen letters of his (five of which are the originals) which show his close interest. They prove that though he loyally followed the Church of England in the changes she underwent, he did not desert his old friends who adhered to the Roman supremacy. Thus in 1566 he wrote that "for as much as Dr. Fecknam* hath written unto me of late for Mr. Bramston that he may remain with him in the Tower for a season" he ordered that this be allowed, in spite of his statutes, and that his fellowship and allowances be continued. "Because," he adds, "Mr. Fecknam is my dear friend whose request I may not deny him."

Again, in the same year, he ordered that " the children of those my prentices which be poor be received, and not the children of those which shall be rich and wealthy

* The last Abbat of Westminster.

B

in no wise." He had given such a preference, and he wished to guard it by the poverty qualification, which Parliamentary commissions in their wisdom have now, for scholarships, utterly abolished. An instance of the preference is to be found in another letter of the Founder's where one Brogden is placed scholar, because his father " was one of my first prentices."

In this connection, it may be well to add that the statutes were always meant to be obeyed, and yet the Founder did not think them beyond mending. In 1560, when he revised their original form, he wrote to the President directing "that they should be sett in the librarie, and a lock to be sett on the librarie dore, and every one of the fellows to have a key, that he may come to reade and knowe my statutes, and note in them ought he thinketh in them might be reformed."

Four Presidents in succession governed the College while the Founder lived. Alexander Belsire B.D., once Fellow of New College, was canon of Christ Church and incumbent of many livings when Sir Thomas named him in his deed of foundation. While he was President, he held the benefices of Tingewell, Buckinghamshire, and in Oxfordshire, Westwell, near Burford (a Christ Church living) and Hanborough (of which the Founder gave the patronage to the college). He held the office of President only for four years, and was then deprived. It has been asserted that the deprivation was due to the religious changes, and that the phrase so often found, later in the College annalists' notes, would apply to him, "ex alteratâ religione vel cessit vel amotus est." But the evidence does not support this view, though there is a "propter religionem" in the College register; and whether or not we can consider him a convinced supporter of the Pope's supremacy, there was clearly a more cogent reason for his deprivation, in the fact that he cheated, or was said to have cheated, the Founder of £20.

Among many dismissals of members of the foundation for various offences occurs the Founder's own account of the removal of Belsire; "great causes me moving and especially for that when I had delivered to the said Mr. Belsire three score pounds in cash, and for the College's use, and being required to restore the same, he answered that he owed but £20 and that the other £20 was his own." So the Founder wrote, and then he told how the proof of the debt was brought home, and the prevaricating President was dismissed. The story, which one can only hope is not so discreditable as it seems, is worth telling because of the persistence with which Roman Catholic writers have described his dismissal as for conscience sake and for the supremacy of the Pope.

He retired to Hanborough* "where, living obscurely several years, [he] died in the parsonage house and was buried in the chancel of the church there, over whose grave is, within an arch in the south wall, a plate of brass affixed, whereon is engraved the picture of a man laying along in a winding-sheet, under which is this engraven :

"Obiit ALEXANDER BELSYRE, 13 die Julii ANNO DOM. 1567.

"Over it on one side are these verses :

> "Hoc quod es, ipse fui, mortalis, uterque perinde
> Mortuus, ac fato tu moriere tuo.
> Sic ergo vivas, ut cum moriere, superstes
> Vita sit in cœlis non moritura tibi.

* Gutch, *University and Colleges* i., 543.

"Over the said picture on the other side are these—being the former englished :

> "That thou art now the same was I ;
> And thou likewise shalt suer die ;
> Live so that when thou hence dost wend
> Thou mayst have blysse that hath no end.

"THOMAS NELUS nepos, alumnus, Alexandro Belsyre avunculo, Maecenati suo, sibique et successoribus suis posuit."

Between Hanborough and Westwell, through Wychwood forest, he might ride along pleasantly in his declining days. There was no great town hard by to set spies upon him, for Witney was but a small place, and Burford though larger, was busy with its trade, rather than with search for men who loved not, as their fathers had done, the royal supremacy ; and happily the old man died before the Pope's bull of deposition came to tempt men to be traitors. He died, it need not be doubted, reading the Book of Common Prayer to the people, and praying for the Queen in peace.

The first College register begins on S. John Baptist's Day, 1557. Its records were taken up by William Elye, Master of Arts, who had been Fellow of Brasenose College. He was a much younger man than his predecessor, and had been a graduate little more than ten years, when he was elected by the Founder with the consent of the Fellows. He tarried but four years, when he was deprived for maintaining the Pope's authority. It is clear that he was a more serious Romanist than Belsire. He had disputed with Cranmer before his execution, and had been chaplain to Maurice bishop of

Lincoln. He fled abroad—was he connected with the Archpriest controversy?*—but returned when the land began to be overspread by the Roman missionaries, and was seized according to Act of Parliament as a seminary priest and committed to prison at Hereford. His only benefice in the English Church had been the Rectory of Crick, Northants, since held by many distinguished doctors. The imprisonment of the " recusants," it is clear was not a harsh one, and Elye, like the last Abbat of Westminster, lived for many years. He survived his five successors in the office of President, and died in 1609.

William Stocke, also a Fellow of Brasenose, was appointed in 1563. He had already been Principal of Sir Thomas White's foundation of Gloucester Hall.

Though a believer in the Pope's supremacy, like his predecessor, he was a man of a different habit of mind. He resigned the Presidency after a year, for fear, it is somewhat strangely said, of being deprived, and returned to the headship of Gloucester Hall which he held for ten years longer. He was allowed to retain the lease of a chamber, formerly the Library, in S. John's. It was he who, as Principal of Gloucester Hall in the first year of its existence, had received the body of Amy Robsart and let it rest till the burial at S. Mary's, " the great chamber where the mourners did dine, and that where the gentlewomen did dine, and beneath a great hall being all hung with black cloth and garnished with scutcheons." The nearness of Sir Thomas White's property at Eaton and Fyfield to Cumnor had no doubt made him acquainted with the unhappy wife of Leicester.

* *Cf.* Taunton, *English Black Monks*, i. 250 note.

Stocke certainly did not suffer by his retirement from S. John's. He held many ecclesiastical benefices—so that his Romanism must have been but skin-deep—and in one of them, Sherborne, Gloucestershire, was a near neighbour of the first President at Westwell, while at another, Crick, he was the successor of the second, Elye.

It is clear that the Founder had from the first desired to connect the College as closely as possible with the neighbourhood of Oxford. He settled his own family at Fyfield, in the beautiful old manor house of Edward III.'s day which still stands, and by the church where his predecessors the Golafres and the "rose of Scotland" Katherine Gordon, widow of the impostor Perkin Warbeck, lie buried. He made friends with the "county people." He associated the first President and Fellows of his College with the neighbouring livings. But the experiment seems, as far as the College was concerned, to have been a failure, and he now determined to go far afield for a man who should govern the College according to the true principles of the Ecclesia Anglicana. His choice fell upon a young Cambridge man, John Robinson of Pembroke Hall. He already held two benefices in the Midlands, to which he soon added many more. He was rector of East Treswell, Nottingham-shire, 1556; Fulbeck, Lincs, 1560; Thornton, Yorks, 1560; Great Easton, Essex, 1566-1576; Kingston Bagpuze, Berks (a S. John's living), 1578; Brant Broughton, Lincs, 1575; Fishtoft, Lincs, 1576; Caistor, Lincs, 1576; Gransden, Cambs, 1587; Somersham, Hunts, 1590—truly a goodly list. But this was not all. He was not content to remain among the "inferior clergy." He was Precentor and a Prebendary of Lincoln Cathedral, Archdeacon of Bedford, Archdeacon of Lincoln, Canon of Gloucester; and at last he died in March 1598. The reason of all this pluralism is not far to seek. He was a *protégé* of the Master of Trinity, Cambridge, and had by him been commended to Cecil. There is not much beyond this to say of him. He gave to the College the dignity and stability of opinion which it lacked; and he held office but eight years, from September 4, 1564, to July 10, 1572. On his resignation a greater man took his place. But we must turn back to trace the last years of the Founder. While Robinson was still President he had passed away.

From 1562 it seems that Sir Thomas White had fallen on evil days. The cloth trade had suffered severely, and he was unable to fulfil the obligation of his second marriage contract. His first wife had died in 1558 and had a great funeral. His second was wedded eight months later—Joan, daughter and co-heiress of John Lake of London and widow of White's friend, Sir Ralph Warren. She survived him, but they lived the last years of his life in comparative poverty. The knight had money out at loans, but it was not easy to recover it. He had plenty of landed property, but land which was felt to be insecure was a glut in the market. Besides he had acquired an inveterate habit of giving; and he died, as Mr. Ruskin says the "entirely merciful just and godly person" always must die, in poverty.

If he could not live richly himself he could still settle considerable trusts on the London Livery Companies, on different towns with which he had been connected, and on his own kindred. He completed the arrangements and made his will in November, 1566. At the beginning of the next year, February 2, 1567, he gave further statutes to the College by which provision was made for forty-three scholars from Merchant Taylors' School to be "assigned and named by continual succession." An attempt was made to break the rule within a few years, but it failed, and ever since, the Master and Wardens of the Merchant Taylors' Company with the President and two senior Fellows of the College have yearly filled up the vacant scholarships on S. Barnabas Day.

The later years of the Founder were disturbed, there is no doubt, by dissensions. He was himself present probably when John Robinson was admitted President on September 4, 1564. Certainly he was "·in an upper chamber within the President's Lodge" a few days later, September 15, when Thomas Robinson was admitted a member of the College.* From this time he resided in Oxford, if not in College, but his will showed that he continued his business as a "merchant of the Muscovy" till his death. He took care to provide for his own family, for his wife's "joynter" and for his brother Ralph and his nephew Roger. To these last he bequeathed, with the consent of the College, by whose grant the lease was made, the manor of Fyfield. Ralph White was to hold it for life and Roger for ninety-nine years at the rent of £14 15s. 4d., and of

* Mr. Clode, Historian of Merchant Taylors' Company, thinks that this was the President. But the birthplaces as well as the names are different.

conies to be delivered at the College weekly, four couples from September 1 to Christmas, six couples from Christmas to Candlemas. The lease, a filial acknowledgment of the Founder's generosity, was especially excepted from the Acts 18 Eliz. cap. 6, and 18 Eliz. cap. 11, against long leases of corporate property.

In Oxford he paid the closest attention to the affairs of his College. Not only were the presidents of his choice but he nominated all the earlier Fellows, and made John James B.D., his own kinsman, Vice-President for life. His statutes, which he himself drew up, made minute directions for the election, for the binding of the President to the performance of his duties, and for the ruling of the College. In case of contention not appeased within five days by the President and Deans, it was his order that it be referred to the Warden of New College, the President of Magdalen and the Dean of Christ Church, and when their decision was given all must abide by it. His two last letters, written within a few days of his death, should be inserted in any history of the College he founded. The first is a letter of farewell ; the second shows that he died a loyal son of the Church which he had never deserted.

" MR. PRESIDENT, WITH THE FELLOWES AND SCHOLLERS,

"I have mee recommended unto you even from the bottome of my hearte, desyringe the holy Ghoste maye bee amonge you untill the ende of the worlde, and desyringe Almightie God that everye one of you maye love one another as brethren ; and I shall desire you all to apply your learninge and soe doinge God shall give you his blessinge both in this worlde and in the worlde to come. And further more, if any variaunce or strife doe arise amonge you, I shall desyre you for God's love to pacifye it as much as you maye; and that doinge I put noe doubt but God shall blesse everye one of you. And this shall be the last letter that ever I shall sende unto you, and therefore I shall desyre everye one of you to take a coppye of yt for my sake. Noe more to you at this time, but the Lord have you in his keeping untill th' ende of the worlde. Written the 27 of Januarye, 1566. I desyre you all to praye to God for mee that I maye ende my life with patience, and that he may take mee to his mercye.

> " By mee Sir Thomas White, Knighte,
>   " Alderman of London, and
>   " Founder of S. John's Colledge in Oxforde."

We do not know what was the answer to his letter. On Februrary 2 Sir Thomas White wrote again, expressing his " very desire that the service of Almighty God might be maintained to the uttermost of his power," and choristers appointed for the conduct of public worship. This letter has a special interest, in that it was written within nine days of the Founder's death. It removes the restriction in the election of choristers, and gives a freedom which is still enjoyed.

" Mr. President and Fellows,

" I heartily recommend me unto you being glad to hear of your welfare which I pray God long to continue to God's pleasure and to your hearty desire, viz., for that my very desire is that the service of Almighty God might be maintained to the uttermost of my power, I do therefore, will and require you that the six choristers appointed by my statutes be from time to time chosen and elected by my president for the time being, and for the more part of the ten seniors of my College, of the most aptist and metist that may be had for that purpose without respect of any place or country, so that he be born within England, any statute, letter, decree, or ordinance by me heretofore made to the contrary, in anywise not withstanding, and if it please Almighty God to take me out of this transitory life before I put my hand to my statutes books for the assurance thereof, then I charge you and command you that you, and others that be put in trust by me to make statutes after my decease, do with as convenient speed as may be, make a good and sure statute for the performance of this my will and intent in that behalf, and keep this my letter to declare that this is my very deed herein.

"No more to you at this time but God have you in his keeping, the 2nd day of February, in the year of our Lord God, after the computation of the Church of England, 1566, by me.

"Thomas White, Knight, Alderman of London."

"That the service of Almighty God might be maintained" in the chapel of the College was his last wish. It was there that he directed in his will that he should be buried "with as much convenient speed as might be possible after my decease. . . honestly, without pomp or vainglory."

He died on February 12, 1567, and was buried as he wished. Edmund Campion (M.A. 1564), who had made a speech before Queen Elizabeth at her first visit to Oxford, now spoke his "funeral oration." His coffin was laid in a vault under the altar, where it was found intact when nearly a century later the greatest of those who had enjoyed his benefactions, the greatest of English Archbishops since the Reformation, was laid by his side.

From the Founder's death the troubles of the College began. He had left as visitors of the foundation his executor, Sir William Cordell, Master of the Rolls, and William Roper, the husband of Sir Thomas More's daughter Margaret. They can have had no easy task in allaying religious dissensions, but both would be sympathetic with the Catholic aspect of the English Church. Sir William Cordell gave more material aid in procuring, as it would seem, through his legal influence, the confirmation of the Founder's will in parts contested. "Partly by pious persuasion and partly by judicious delays" the Master of the Rolls carried through the difficult business, and the College received unimpaired the scanty endowments which its Founder had been able to bequeath.

The association with the neighbourhood of Oxford which the Founder had begun by the grant of the Berkshire manors already named was made more close in 1573 by the purchase with money which the Founder had bequeathed of the manor of Walton, from Richard Owen. This included the lands of Godstow, where fair Rosamund was buried, one of the three known Norman abbeys for women. The last Abbess, Katherine Bulkeley, received a pension of £40 a year at the dissolution. Her portrait hangs in the President's house. The lands were granted to Henry VIII.'s physician, Dr. George Owen.

Through this purchase the College has become in modern times the ground landlord of the greater part of the new town which has sprung up in North Oxford.

Of the buildings erected thereon it would be kinder not to speak. It may be anticipated that, according to the style of Victorian house building, they will allow before another century has passed the erection of some worthier architecture on their sites. More interesting to the historian, though not to the Bursar, of the College are the many ancient deeds which came to the College with the manors of Walton Osney and Walton Godstow. They may be here briefly summarised. Probably the earliest is a grant from Robert D'Oilly, the famous builder of the castle, to the church of " S. George in the castle " at Oxford ; it bears his seal, a mailed knight on horseback with sword and buckler.—" Sigillum Rob. de Olleyo." In 1235 another grant : Henry son of Lewis released to Godstow his claim to a house in S. Giles's parish. In another grant of 1282 'Roysia de Oxhay' is mentioned as abbess of Godstow, and in many later documents the names of the abbesses are given as are also those of the vicars of S. Giles's Church.† A deed of the early years of Henry III. is interesting. The grant is as follows :.

"Sciant præsentes quod ego Fulco Basset teneri reddere Philippo Molendinario 32 solidos sterlingorum, quos debeo ei reddere ad festum S. Michaelis proximum post consecrationem Hugonis Foliott Episcopi Herefordensis ; et nisi tunc reddidero, prædictus Philippus tenebit de me et hæredibus meis, illi et hæredes ejus pratum de Biscopeseie, pro una libra cymini annuatim reddendo ad fest. S. Micha. quod pratum autem tenuit de me pro 60

† A complete list of these should be drawn up. The church has been since 1583 in the patronage of the College. It was consecrated by S. Hugh of Lincoln. The consecration cross may still be seen.

den. per ann. hereditarie.   Hiis testibus Roberto Oeini Alured. Hergut, Joh. Padly, etc." *

A grant of 1295 of Mabilia, Abbess of Godstow (whose name was Wafre or Wafri) seems to concern land on which Trinity College now stands. Earlier, Walter de Mapes, the famous archdeacon of Oxford, makes known to all that his villeins in the manor of Walton from the dedication of S. Giles's Church without the north gate shall give their tithes thereto. Many interesting references are made to the holders of houses within the district, and to the names of old dwellings, "Le Burell Hall," "Black Hall" and the like.

By these and similar deeds the property of the abbey of Godstow, with its increase, its leases, and its obligations, may be traced till it came into the hands of the College and of the Earl of Abingdon. The "rectory or chapel" of S. Giles was granted by Henry VIII. June 16, 1546, with all tithes of grass, corn and other matters to John Doylie (the name still survives in Oxford) and John Scudamore, gentlemen. By their grant in 1550 it passed to George Owen of Godstow Esquire, by whose heir Richard it was sold rather more than twenty years later to S. John Baptist College. The deed of sale of the property is February 12, 1573, of the "manor of Walton with all its appurtenances lately belonging to Godstow with all tenements and houses belonging thereto."

One final note may be given from Anthony Wood's MSS.

"In a large roll showing all the lands in Walton or S. Giles Field which did chiefly belong to Osney and

* Mr. Riley's note of this (*Historical MSS. Commission iv. Report*) has a few errors.

Godstow, is mention made of such and such lands in Stadium in Walton, Walton croft juxta Rutherweye. Stadium vocat. le Twenti acres; stadium vocat. Nyne acres; stadium vocat. 5 et north; stadium vocat. middle bradmore juxta Merston way; stadium vocat. old land; stadium vocat. Nether bradmore. Note all lands are within the head of 'stadium.' Whether 'stadium' doth not signify a chief division?" *

The manor of Walton which had belonged to the crown was granted by Edward III. to the abbey of Osney.†

Sir Thomas White was patron of the benefice of North-More. His deed of appropriation, wherein is recited Cardinal Pole's licence, as papal legate, for appropriating the tithes of the rectory and also of the rectory of Fyfield to S. John's College A.D. 1555-6, is in the college archives. The rectory house, it appears, had been leased to William Moore by the founder. He enjoyed it for fifty-five years, till 1612. It was then leased to William Clerk, the College cook. It is doubtful indeed if the benefice ever had a resident rector till 1890, since when a new rectory house has been built. When the parsonage was turned into a farm-house, two rooms, separate from the rest, and part of the old house, were reserved for the rector, a resident Fellow of S. John's, who could ride over to his duties.

---

* Stadia, of course, are furlongs. The correct meaning would be a bundle of arable strips, but by Elizabeth's time "it was quite clear that the term was losing its original meaning, and was often used by the surveyors as the equivalent of 'field,' as used at present." W. J. Corbett on Elizabethan Village Surveys in *Transactions of the Royal Historical Society*, N.S. vol. xi. p. 71.

† Inquisit. 29 Jan. 14 Edw. IV. College MSS.

After the Founder's death more purchases of land were made by his bequests and by the sale of the London property which he had directed. Bagley Wood was purchased in 1583 through William Leech, who married the Founder's niece, acting as agent for the College; or rather the moiety of the wood not belonging to the Norreys family, from Anthony Weekes, who had taken the name of Mason on obtaining the wood from its last possessor.

The other purchases of this period,—and it is noteworthy that in each case a complimentary payment to the wife of the vendor was added by custom—besides those already mentioned, were at Hardwick, South More, Stoke Basset, Warborough, the parsonage at Kirtlington and the chantry house at Fyfield.

The purchase at Warborough brought the College into direct relation with the Crown, with all the expenses thereon dependent.

"Gloves to her Majesty and noblemen during three years' suit in that cause £30. To the Lord Treasurer, in a garter and rich George, £20. To the Earl of Leicester a bason and ewer of silver double gilt, £20. To Mr. Litchfield by Sir Walter Mildmay's order for relinquishing his title in Warborough lands, £20. To Mr. Secretary Wolley and his men for furthering that suit, £13 6s. 8d. To Mr. Maynard for solliciting My Lord Treasurer three years to procure her Majesty's grant under her hand for the same, £10."

It is a large item in the accounts of a poor College.

Enough has been said to show how closely the College was connected with the country outside Oxford. Its interests were preserved at the first by special bursars for each of the manors (as Fyfield and Long Wittenham in the first statutes), and the register shows a very close association, religious as well as secular, with the district.

It is noteworthy that the original statutes contemplate the College kitchen being supplied from the neighbouring farms. It is directed that "gallinæ ex compacto cum tenentibus collegio debitæ inter collegiales distribuantur; sed certo pretio, viz. pro singulis 2d collegio solvendo." A parallel in more modern times is said to have been afforded by a time when the Fellows were often in danger of a surfeit of Bagley rabbits.

CHAPTER IV

SOCIAL LIFE IN THE SIXTEENTH CENTURY

There are some lines in Greene's *Friar Bacon and Friar Bungay* which too eloquently describe the condition of the Colleges in the early years of Elizabeth. Meanly learned the scholars of S. John's were certainly not, if they obeyed to any serious extent the Founder's statutes. Meanly fed no doubt they were, but they were strictly ruled.

Emperor.

Trust me, Plantagenet, these Oxford schools
Are richly seated near the river-side:
The mountains full of fat and fallow deer,
The battling pastures lade with kine and flocks,
The town gorgeous with high built colleges,
And scholars seemly in their grave attire,
Learned in searching principles of art.—
What is thy judgment, Jaques Vandermast?

Van.

That lordly are the buildings of the town,
Spacious the rooms, and full of pleasant walks;
But for the doctors, how that they be learned,
It may be meanly, for aught I can hear.*

* Old English Drama, edited by A. W. Ward, 3rd ed. p. 80.

From a Photo by the]

Among the famous Caxtons in the library of the College, is the *Magnus et Parvus Chato.* On its first page is a picture which tutors are accustomed to point out to the parents of their pupils as illustrating the difference between the discipline of the Universities to-day and the stern rules of the first foundation. There the teacher sits comfortably in a high-backed chair and is armed with an extremely formidable birch. The contrast is, perhaps, too painful to-day; but the memories of the past may please by their very incongruity with the present.   There is a passage from a sermon of one Leaver at S. Paul's-cross, preached a few years before Sir Thomas White founded his college, which has been too often quoted to escape quotation again.   The students, he tells us, would rise between four and five, and study till ten.   Then they dine—

"Content with a penny piece of beef between four, having a pottage made of the same beef with salt and oatmeal, and nothing else.   After their dinner they are reading or learning till five in the evening, when they have a supper not better than their dinner, immediately after which they go to reasoning in problems or to some other study till nine or ten ; and then, being without fire, are fain to walk or run up and down for half an hour to get a heat in their feet, when they go to bed."

Some gleanings, almost at random, from the statutes of S. John's may serve to make a brighter picture.

We begin with an observation that the Founder hoped to give his College at least a freedom from noise.   It is sometimes thought to-day that the natural exultation of spirits among young men is fittingly expressed in vocal and instrumental music at hours when the scholar studies and the man of sense is asleep. Such a thought did not enter the mind of Sir Thomas White. S. John's was not to be a nest of singing birds. "Aves cantatrices" were expressly not to be nurtured within its walls; and, as a corollary, the Fellows were forbidden to catch birds in the garden, though not outside. So in the same way " cantica in privatis cubiculis " were forbidden ; but singing, at certain times, was permitted in hall. All immoderate clamours in private rooms were banned; yet honest conversation, "cum moderato silentio," sometimes before the fire in hall, or elsewhere, for the purpose of enlarging the mind (if thus it be allowed to translate the words " animum largandi causâ") was followed. And in the bedchamber how modestly and quietly should the chamber fellows behave. In no way should they disturb their neighbours by immoderate clamour, laughter, noise, song, leaping, or the striking of musical instruments. And football was utterly forbidden—" pila pedalis prohibita." The order that Latin was to be spoken, especially by the seniors with the juniors, would no doubt stay some clamours that find more ready outlet in the vulgar tongue. No immoderate laughter was suffered at any time. Yet holidays there were and recreation. On feast days, after a refection to the scholars and Fellows, songs were to be sung, and there were other " honesta solatia," for poems, histories, and miracle plays were recited. " The miracula mundi," or " mirabilia," might be the subject of the talk by the fire in hall in the time after dinner, which would be to many the happiest hour of the day; but no card-playing on any account—" the game of painted cards " was strictly forbidden. There are minute regulations as to the chamber-companions, very necessary if the young folk were not to be bullied, and the elder bored. The "convictores "* (commoners), scholars, Fellows, and choristers seem equally to be bound by these rules. In the same room, so far as it be convenient, juniors were always to be with seniors, for the benefit of their good advice, and when they were over sixteen years they had the privilege of separate beds. The President was to order each chorister or scholar to sleep with a Master or bachelor Fellow, that he might serve him in all things lawful and honest. But no Fellow was compelled against his will to receive any scholar, chorister, or commoner under his care, but only at his choice. The scholars were not to be personally afflicted in body or mind ; and indeed before long there arose a question whether one could hold his scholarship who had " a very crushed and deformed leg, as some take it." Strangers were not to be brought into college, except under strict conditions, and all were to be accounted such to whom " commons " were not assigned by the statutes—save twelve, or, at most, sixteen commoners. The janitor, who must be vigilant and circumspect (and who was also barber), would exclude them easily, for the great gate was never to be wholly opened, save by the order of the President or Vice-President. Females, too, must never enter to any one in his room, except by the leave of the President previously given, save for a short time a mother or sister and their servants. Horrid indeed would have been the

* This was at first the correct term at S. John's. Other colleges use *alumnus*, or *commensalis*, and the latter word is found in the seventeenth century at S. John's. Their number, at first strictly limited by the Founder, was before many years much extended.

thought of maidens at lecture, with trim note-books and wind-blown hair.

The porter's duty was to shave the President and Fellows, and the undergraduates if they needed it—as well as to keep the gate ; long hair should not be worn, and no man might inordinately nourish a beard. Of food and commons we hear little, but there is mention of a great " bibesia " which is explained to be a drinking in hall after meals, after the accustomed manner of the University. These were the days before common-rooms; later ages withdrew in some solemnity to their port.

In hall during meals there was Bible-reading—the reading, too, of other good books. The chief enactments, indeed, regulate the religious life of the society. Confession was obligatory four times a year, or punishment followed from the President. All were to be present at Mass, and great stress was laid on the distinctness with which the Divine Liturgy should be said. On the great festivals, and on the feasts of the B.V.M. and S. John Baptist, the President must always say Mass. No one might say Mass outside college for money. The servants were to be present in chapel, and there were special rules for the observance of Sunday, and for the holding of theological disputations.

There are minute directions as to the position and power of the President, the Deans, the Bursars, and the Fellows. Two Bursars at least were contemplated—the " Bursarius sylvestris " and the " Bursarius equitans." The former was to be also " custos sylvarum." The riding Bursar figures frequently in the early accounts. No doubt to him alone was it permitted to hunt, for to the Fellows generally there was an order that none might keep or nourish any kind of hunting-dog, nor might any member of the College carry arms. The President's powers were very great, and they were exercised subject solely to appeal to the Visitors. The Bishop of Winchester, on the decease of the founder's friends, Sir William Cordell and William Roper, was to be permanent Visitor of the College; but rules were laid down lest his visitations should be frivolous or vexatious. The President was always to be a Fellow or late Fellow, or, if such could not be found worthy, a Canon of Christ Church.

The Fellows were divided into three classes. First came the ten senior gradutes in divinity, arts, and law; then the twenty next in order; then the last twenty; making the fifty contemplated in the foundation. The salary of a Fellow varied according to his class. A Fellowship was vacated either by becoming a monk, or by marrying, or by taking business outside Oxford, or by entering on the possession of private property or an ecclesiastical benefice above the value of £10, so soon as it be known to the President, Vice-President, and two of the Fellows. The government of the College was practically in the hands of the President and ten seniors, but it seems to have been expected that for their decision to be binding on the rest it must be unanimous. The " Convention," it was later ordered, was to consist of a complete number of Seniors, not a bare majority. The election and duties of the scholars are no less carefully provided for, and there are many regulations as to the choristers. These are to be chosen from the City of London, and, when elected, to remain till their voices break. They are to be instructed in grammar and good authors ; they are to wait in hall and have food like the servants.   The castigation of them is to be committed to the President and Vice-President, and they are to have fitting tonsures.

Most important after the chapel in the life of the College stood the library. Most of the early Fellows gave books and manuscripts. Of this much might be said, but here it may suffice to note how strict were the rules about the lending of books. A stringent, but most wholesome, order, that any one who loses a library key is to replace the lock and all the keys at his own cost, should be reinforced to-day.

Among the officials of the College, the teaching belonged to the readers in Greek, in rhetoric, and the like. Of the law Fellows, one every third year was to be Vice-President, and the canonists were always to be sub-deacons, rising after a time to the priesthood. There was to be one physician among the Fellows, and he was not of necessity to be a priest.

It may be said that there is little of special interest in these statutes. They resemble those of the earlier colleges and show for how distant a posterity the great William of Wykeham had legislated. This is true. Sir Thomas White, founding a college in 1555, thought he could make little improvement on the statutes of earlier and greater founders. But in that very fact there is much significance which we may again emphasise. Sir Thomas White was a living representative of the continuity of the English Church. To him there seemed no breach of the past. Founding his college under Philip and Mary he could yet rule it by the same statutes under Elizabeth. If the early Presidents and Fellows asserted the Pope's jurisdiction when the English Church denied it, they must go. But the College went on with the same statutes, and the Founder watched over it till his death in 1567, and in his last letter provided for the continuance of Divine service in the chapel which had been consecrated for the monks of S. Bernard.

None the less do the statutes witness to the disturbance of the times. The direction for the preaching of the Fellows in the Church of S. Peter in the East at Oxford during Lent is to be accounted for by the great deficiency in the city when Sir Thomas White founded his college. It is said that in 1563 there were but two preachers before the University, and these were of a puritanical habit of mind. There is a quaint tale of Mr. Taverner of Wood Eaton, being High Sheriff of the county, and a layman, giving discourses in S. Mary's stone pulpit. "Fine biscuits," he called them, "baked in the oven of charity, carefully conserved for the chickens of the Church, the sparrows of the Church, and the sweet swallows of salvation."

The salaries fixed by the Founder are worth adding here as illustrating the position which his foundation was intended to take.

To the President for his wages, commons, and livery* was allowed £20. To ten Masters of Arts, or senior Fellows, for the same, "£8 to every of them," to twenty Bachelors of Arts £5 10*s.* to each; to twenty scholars, £4 10*s.* each; to three chaplains, £7 each; "to three singing men, whereof one to be an organ

* Gutch, *Collectanea Curiosa*, i. 191.

player, £6 13s. 4d. each; to six choristers, £4 6s. 8d. each." With the servants the phrase is only "for his wages and livery." The chief cook received £5, the under cook £3 6s. 8d., the head butler, £4; the under butler £2; the manciple, £4; the porter £4, and Mr. President's man £1. To the barber for wages, £1; the launder, £1 6s. 8d. Then came the steward of the Courts, £1; the Vice-President, £2; the Dean of Divinity, £1 6s. 8d.; the Dean of Arts, £1 6s. 8d.; the Greek Reader, £3 6s. 8d.; the Rhetoric Reader, and the Logic Reader, the like; the two Bursars, £2 13s. 4d.; the Steward of the kitchen, £1 6s. 8d. For the Gaudy days were allowed £10; for "detriments" (? decrements), £3 6s. 8d.; for strangers, in hospitality, £8; for almsmen, £3 10s. For candles was set apart £2; for the carriage of wood, £7; for mplements, £6; to the woodman, £1 6s. 8d. The sum total of all the aforesaid charges is £456 10s.

In the thirty-fourth year of Elizabeth's reign the College was rated for her entertainment at £400, standing seventh on the list of colleges.*

Further details on some of the points of interest suggested in the statutes may be gleaned from the Bursary books of 1584 and 1587. The earlier shows the rents received from London houses and from Gloucester Hall. The London property was soon sold by the Founder's directions, for the purchase of agricultural estates. The ownership of Gloucester Hall was not uncontested. It was conveyed to the College March 23, 1560, by William Dodington, and thereupon let to William Stocke, Fellow (President 1563–64), for twenty years;

* Gutch, *Collectanea Curiosa*, i. 191.

but a claim of the Bishop of Oxford to the land was constantly causing troubles.   An accomplished member of Worcester College has thus compressed the tedious dispute: "The Bishop of Oxford, in 1604, revived his claim to the Hall, maintaining that the surrender to the Crown [it had been allotted in 1542 to the Bishop for his palace] had not been acknowledged by Bishop King, and duly enrolled in Chancery; and to try his right he 'did make an entry by night, and by water, and did drive away the horses depasturing on the land belonging to the said Hall.'   He failed, however, to make good his claim against S. John's College."* Among the S. John's muniments are "divers writings concerning the bishoprick transcribed upon a quarrel had between S. John's College and the Bishop concerning the Hall."   It was by Laud's persuasion that Bancroft resolved to build a palace at Cuddesdon, thus finally ending the dispute.†

In the year of the founder's death, Queen Elizabeth visited the University.   On Thursday, September 5, as she was on her way to hear disputations at S. Mary's she was struck by a large map of the colleges, which was hung outside the church.   This was the work of Thomas Neale, the Regius Professor of Hebrew, and John Bereblock, who took the degrees of B.A. 1561, and M.A. 1566, from S. John's, and was afterwards a Fellow of Exeter.   Neale was a nephew of the first President of S. John's, and it was natural that the map

* *The Colleges of Oxford*, pp. 429-430.
† *The College Register*, vi. 22, contains the consent of Sir Jonathan Trelawney, Bishop of Winchester, to the alienation of Gloucester Hall in order to its being turned into a college, Nov. 3, 1713.

should find, afterwards, a resting-place in S. John's. It remained there till Sir Thomas Lake begged it in 1616, and gave it in return £20 towards the restoration of the buildings. Bereblock's picture of the College represents the present front quadrangle alone, without the cook's buildings, the Library, or the archway entrance to the inner court.

By the end of the sixteenth century the College had assumed the character and appearance which it retained till the days of Laud, its second founder. In 1576 Sir Christopher Brome, Knight, sold to the College all the piece of ground lying on its west front, containing, in length from north to south, 208 feet, and in breadth from east to west, 44 feet. The terrace, which is, by University custom, still counted as within the College,* was enclosed with a wall and outer gateway, both of which may be seen in engravings of the end of the eighteenth century. The high gate has gone, but the wall still remains, though the public footpath is now allowed to pass between the terrace and the College gate. It was suggested by Dr. Ingram that "the next liberal step on the part of the Society will be the removal of the wall altogether ; by which the front would lose nothing in grandeur of effect, and the elm avenue would be less interrupted." This was written in 1837, but the "next liberal step" has not been taken.

The original President's lodgings were completed in 1597 ; they face the outer quadrangle. In the same year the old library, which forms the south side of the inner quadrangle, was built. The east window erected

---

* On it an undergraduate, if he is impolite enough, which is un-likely at S. John's, may defy the Proctors.

in 1598 records the help of the Merchant Taylors'
Company and contains one of the earliest portraits of
the Founder.   The stone and timber used for the building of the library came from the ruins of the ancient
palace of Beaumont, in which Richard I. was born.*

Such was the College in the forty years following its
foundation.   It remains to say something of the earlier
Fellows.   Among them the religious difficulty made the
union which the Founder so touchingly urged long
difficult of attainment.   Of many of them the College
annalist writes "alterata religione aut cessit aut
amotus est."   John Bavant, the first Greek reader in
the College, the tutor of Gregory Martin and Edmund
Campion, ended his days in the castle of Wisbeach, and
with him Ralph Windon and Leonard Stopes. Gregory
Martin (M.A. in 1564) became tutor to the Duke of
Norfolk's son, then passed over to Rheims and was
prominent in the production of the Rheims Bible.

Edmund Campion, who was Martin's contemporary,
was one of the earliest and most courageous of the Jesuit
missionaries, stood firm when his colleague Parsons fled,
and was executed at Tyburn in 1608.   Of him more
hereafter. Thomas Bramstone, one of the earliest Fellows,
received the Founder's leave to reside with John
Feckenham, the last abbat of Westminster, became a
priest, and died abroad.   John Bereblock was "peritis-
simus in arte delineandi": of his picture of the colleges
"which did usually hang in Mr. President's lodgings"
we have already heard.   Henry Shaw, of a later generation than those mentioned above, also "went over

* Leonard Hutten's *Antiquities of Oxford*, in Oxford Historical
Society's *Collectanea I*.

to Rome" and was imprisoned in Wisbeach Castle. William Wiggs, a brother Fellow, in the same incarceration, is said to have been stabbed "a quodam generoso." With them was John Meredith who also "defended the Pope's jurisdiction." Of others, one Thomas Wright became a lunatic, and Thomas Denham, who took service like many another adventurous spirit in Ireland, was drowned in a bog. Another Fellow, Timothy Willis, became an ambassador of Elizabeth's to Muscovy. As famous was Richard Latewar who became chaplain to Charles Blount, Lord Mountjoy, afterwards Earl of Devon, in which post he was succeeded by Laud. He was a clever literary personage, whom the College histories speak of with reverence. His epigrams especially are noted; but every one wrote epigrams in those days. He was struck by a shell during the Irish campaign of Lord Mountjoy, and was buried in the cathedral of Armagh, but a monument describes his merits and virtues in the College chapel.

Not all the Fellows were noteworthy in such ways. The annalist tells of one who was Bursar, became a papist, embezzled the college money and fled. He found employment under an Austrian Archduke.* Not unconnected with this may be the reduction of the College expense in 1577 and the reduction of the chapel foundation. These difficulties continued under the first president appointed after the Founder's death. To his rule we must now turn.

---

* Georgius Russell, Ll.B., Bursarius Collegii parum fidelis abiit non sine solvendo, postea mutata religione Archidux Austriae fecit stipendiarium.

CHAPTER V

STRUGGLES WITH POVERTY

With Sir Thomas White's death the College begins a
new chapter of its history. John Robinson, the last
President whom he had chosen, did not linger on the
barren soil. But in appointing a successor the College
acted as the Founder would have wished. It chose a
young man already eminent in the University.

Tobie Matthew, Archbishop of York, who was
elected July 18, 1572, and resigned May 8, 1577,
demands a longer notice than his predecessor. He was
already a prominent man when the Founder chose him,
and he lived to reach a high position in Church and
State and to support in the world, there can be no
doubt, the College the headship of which had been one
of his first steps on the ladder. He was only thirty-eight
when he became President, but he was already Canon of
Christ Church, Prebendary of Salisbury, and Public
Orator in the University ; and a few months after his
election he became also Archdeacon of Bath. He had,
some years before, attracted the attention of Queen
Elizabeth, and so his fortune was made. He had been
ordained in 1566, when he was only twenty, "at which
time he was much respected for his great learning,
eloquence, sweet conversation, friendly disposition, and

the sharpness of his wit."* He took part in a "disputation in philosophy" before Queen Elizabeth in S. Mary's Church on September 3 of the same year. " Qui oratione perpolita ac numerosa illa quidem totius Academiæ gratias illi ageret, atque benigne conservaret collegium quod pater inchoavit frater ornavit soror auxit, rogaret."† "He was one of a proper person (such people, *cæteris paribus* and sometimes *cæteris imparibus* were preferred by the Queen) and an excellent Preacher."‡

The appointment of Tobie Matthew was a sign of the intimate connection which the Founder had designed between his new College and the *Ædes Christi*. The Presidents were always, said his statutes, to receive institution from the Dean of Christ Church, and this rule descended till the present century.

Matthew was elected on July 17, 1572. As President, the fifth since the foundation seventeen years before, he had to struggle with the difficulties of a poor and divided College. In 1573 he tried on the ground of poverty to win release from the annual obligation to elect scholars from Merchant Taylors' School.§ Happily he was unsuccessful, or the connection that has been so great a benefit to the College, and greater to the school, might have lapsed. He took the degrees of B.D. December 10, 1573, and D.D. June 1574. He resigned the headship on May 8, 1577, having been appointed to the Deanery of Christ Church.

---

* Wood, *Athenæ Oxonienses*.

† Acts done at Oxford on the occasion of Queen Elizabeth's visit in 1566, ed. Plummer, Oxford Historical Society.

‡ Fuller, *Church History*, p. 133.

§ His letter, and the details of the dispute that ensued, in Wilson's *History of Merchant Taylors' School*.

In his short tenure of office he had certainly done much for the College. It is probable that he had some hand in assuaging the religious difficulties. Edmund Campion, the brilliant scholar who had preached the funeral sermon of the Founder, was already set on submission to Rome. It was under Matthew's presidency that he left the College, and when he published the *decem rationes* in 1581, it was Matthew who first answered him in Oxford. In a Latin sermon before the University, October 9, 1581, he defended the Reformation, appealing chiefly to the teaching of the Lord and of the primitive Church, and refraining from any defence or quotation of Luther.

From the day he left S. John's his promotion was rapid. He passed from Christ Church to Durham as Dean, then as Bishop, and he died Archbishop of York. A humourist who delighted to spread a rumour of his own death and watch the scramble for his offices, he became the Government agent in the rule of the northern shires. James took to him as kindly as Elizabeth, had him by his side at the Hampton Court Conference, and trusted him to repress among Papists and other dissenters of the northern shires all " schismatical tricks." His reports to the King and Cecil are some of the most valuable accounts of the condition of the north at a time when Roman missions were strong.

He is chiefly noteworthy all through his life for the talents which made him a good head of a poor college. He was a man of business and a statesman as well as a theologian, a prominent example of those political ecclesiastics whom the Reformation changes naturally produced. But his chief fame in his own day (save perhaps as the father of the clever pervert Sir Tobie Matthew) was as a preacher.   A passage from Thoresby is worth quoting:

"By the favour of the late excellent Abp. Sharp, I had the perusal of his Diary or journal, wherein he hath left a catalogue of his own handwriting of the several times & places when and where he preached, to set down which would be to transcribe the Villare of the County Palatine, scarce any town but had him in their pulpit and some places very often."

During the time he held the Deanery of Durham (eleven and a half years) he preached 721 sermons—in some years sixty, some seventy or eighty.

"We sometimes find him preaching twice a day (which he called not prating as some affect to do) especially when he found no preaching Minister there, but rarely omitted every Sunday and holiday except when sickness or some inevitable cause hindered."

His contemporaries bitterly regretted that his sermons were not published.   Some still remain in MS. in the Bodleian and at S. John's.

"'Tis much to be lamented that those sermons that were so passionately desired by persons of the greatest quality, so acceptable to the judicious, and so crowded after by Persons of all ranks, should not have been published, such especially as were upon extraordinary occasions & made such impression on himself as to make him give thanks for Divine Assistance."   Great & continuous as were his labours as a preacher, "yet for all his pains on preaching he neglected not his proper Episcopal Acts of Visitation, Confirmation, Ordination and the like.   He confirmed sometimes 500 sometimes 1000 at a time yea so many that he has been forced to betake himself to his bed for refreshment. At Hartlepool he was forced to confirm in the church-yard. At such times he often preached to instruct them more fully in the duties of Christianity that they were now more solemnly obliged to."

Such an account of the fifth President seemed necessary since he held office at so critical a time, and it was his influence doubtless which set the College on its prosperous course.

Scarcely less important than the Presidents were the Visitors. William Roper, whom the Founder had appointed with Sir William Cordell, to fulfil that office, died in 1578. The appointment had been disputed by the Bishop of Winchester, July 1571, but the Court affirmed the Founder's intention. Roper represented the opinions which Sir Thomas White had held: a true Catholic, yet not without sympathy with the reformers, he remained, in spite of the barbarous murder of his great father-in-law by Henry VIII., attached to the national church. He held the post of prothonotary of the King's Bench till within a few months of his death. His own copy of the English Works of Sir Thomas More was given or bequeathed to the College Library, where it still remains.

Sir William Cordell lived till May 17, 1581, and was a vigilant overseer of the College interest. Several of his letters to the President severely comment on the College debts, the immoderate riding expenses and the like.

The pecuniary difficulties in fact were the greatest obstacles which Tobie Matthew and his wise critic, the Master of the Rolls, had to remove.

It is sad evidence of the poverty of the College that on October 12, 1577, by "general consent of the Fellows" as the Register records, the "removal of the Quire, chaplain, clerks and choristers" was ordered in College meeting.

For some time the endowment for the scholars was far from adequate. Sir Thomas White had left little, and the College was certainly not rich enough to make up the deficiency. The President and Senior Fellows could not even afford at their own costs to journey to London for the election, and the Merchant Taylors' Company agreed to contribute (as they still do) to the expense. The first election of scholars was on S. Barnabas Eve 1572. In the next year the College was obliged to make efforts to reduce its expenses. Tobie Matthew wrote to the company that "for lack of ready money it is miserable to see how the poor scholars of our house this dear season are pinched. We are also, partly from coldness, partly from want of room, constrained to overloft all chambers in the College." It was a plea for suspension of the scholarship election that year. The Company would not hear of it, and the Master and Wardens pointed out shrewdly enough that such a course would stifle new benefactions. "Ye are wise enough to consider and godly enough to grant," they wrote, " that the not executing of the godly devices of such as have heretofore given their goods therefor is the great discouragement, yea rather hindrance of many (in these days of racked consciences) why they do not follow their predecessors' like godly and charitable precedents, which pernicious evil we hope and wish that both by word and deed you will show yourselves to condemn."

But the difficulty continued. The Visitor, Sir William Cordell, decided in 1574 that the College should only be required to elect so many scholars as "from time to time they shall be able to maintain." In 1577 the Company lent the College £100, by which the President wrote "our College is discharged of many old debts and delivered of many shameful reproaches, divers poor men satisfied, your children our scholars and our diet far bettered by the help of ready money to buy our victuals."

The difficulty was partly met by Walter Fish's endowment in 1580, but for many years the pinch of poverty was felt. Asking for a grant for the scholars in 1584 the President wrote: "It will set an edge on the minds of your scholars, when they shall have wherewith to provide them books and other necessaries for the back and the belly, the want whereof is now so great in the most part of your scholars chosen from your school, having either no friends or such poor friends as cannot help them ; that some of them do lose their time for lack of books, others pressed for lack of apparel, others hazard their place quarterly in the College for that they have not to pay for their meat and drink they spend in the house over and above the Founder's allowance, and other some are of extreme misery and penury constrained to leave the University, and to cast off study and betake themselves to some other trade or life or to a worse course not so commendable to themselves nor so profitable to the common weal."

In 1591 the College expenditure exceeded its revenue by £167. In 1593 the accounts stood thus:

Expenses	.	.	.	£702	9	3
Receipts	.	.	.	535	6	8½
"Exceedings"	.	.		£167	2	6½

In those days certainly the Presidents needed to be good beggars.

In the next year, owing to an under-cook being added, and needing his livery like the others, matters were worse.

Expenses	.	.	.	£709	7	5
Receipts	.	.	.	535	6	8½
"Exceedings"	.	.		£174	0	8½

The financial position of the College is well worth examining in detail. It can best be perceived by reading the receipts for batells, the payment of salaries, and some typical specimens of College expenses, such as " reparationes " (a larger term than repairs nowadays) and " equitantes " (the riding charges on which Sir William Cordell commented so severely to Tobie Matthew).

RECEPTIONES PRO BATTELLIS SOCIORUM.,
1° Termino finito ad Festum Natiuitatis Dñi : 1583.*

Mr. President	.	.	.	v^s	ix^d	ob qr
Mr. Vice-Præsident	.	.	xiiij^s	vij^d	
Mr. Reade .	.	.	.	iiij^s	iij^d	qr
Mr. Rixman	.	.	.	v^s	iij^d	ob
Mr. Lee .	.	.	.	iiij^s	ij^d	
Mr. Nashe .	.	.	.	v^s	iij^d	qr
Mr. Aubrye	.	.	.	v^s	ix^d	qr
Mr. Gwine	.	.	.	ix^s	iij^d	qr
Mr. Sprott .	.	.	.	iiij^s	vj^d	ob qr

* *i.e.*, from Michaelmas 1582.

Mr. Wighte	. . .	ij^s	ob qr
Mr. Denham	. . .	iij^s ij^d	
Mr. Rauens	. . .	v^s vij^d	
Mr. Potecary	. . .	xv^s xj^d	qr
Mr. Perin .	. . .	v^s vij^d	ob qr
Mr. Dixon .	. . .	iiij^s x^d	
Mr. Webb .	. . .	xx^s j^d	qr
Capellanus	. . .	iij^s viij^d	ob qr
Ædituus .	. . .	vij^d	
Sr. Gittens	. . .	iiij^s ix^d	
Sr. Belfeelde	. . .	xv^d	
Sr. Faucett	. . .	vj^s j^d	ob
Sr. Bearblock	. . .	xj^d	ob
Sr. Millard	. . .	xvij^s ij^d	ob qr
Sr. Oburne	. . .	xvij^s iij^d	ob qr
Sr. Shingleton .	. .	ij^s xj^d	qr
Sr. Kighte	. . .	v^s vij^d	ob
Sr. Speene	. . .	xj^s iij^d	qr
Sr. Smythe	. . .	iiij^s viij^d	qr
Sr. Buckeridge .	. .	ix^s vij^d	
Sr. Finmore	. . .	viij^s xj^d	ob qr
Sr. Childerly	. . .	ij^s vij^d	ob qr
Sr. Addams	. . .	xiiij^s vj^d	ob qr
Sr. Rainsbie	. . .	vj^s ij^d	qr
Withington	. . .	viij^s vij^d	qr
Burgesse .	. . .	viij^s ix^d	ob
Lattwar .	. . .	vj^s x^d	ob
Cook .	. . .	iij^s j^d	qr
Wall .	. . .	viij^s iiij^d	
Firmin .	. . .	vij^s vj^d	ob
Gunter .	. . .	iij^s vj^d	ob
Cromwell .	. . .	viij^s	ob
Walldron .	. . .	vij^s vij^d	qr
Leeche .	. . .	xj^s vj^d	ob

Hanlie	iij[s]	iij[d]	qr
Capell	vij[s]	x[d]	ob
Sprott	vj[s]	xj[d]	qr
Aldworthe	viij[s]	ij[d]	ob qr
Linbie	v[s]	viij[d]	ob qr
Searchfeelde	iij[s]	vj[d]	qr
Waterhouse	x[s]	viij[d]	ob qr
Wall, Jn.	vij[s]	xj[d]	ob qr
Lee	iiij[s]	·ix[d]	ob
Hutton	iij[s]	xj[d]	ob
Servus Præs.		v[d]	ob
Servus Præs. 2[dus]		vj[d]	
Obsonator			ob
Promus		xiiij[d]	
Sacrista		v[d]	ob qr
Janitor		ij[d]	
Coquus	ix[s]	viij[d]	
Subcoquus	vij[s]	v[d]	
Coquus 3[us]		v[d]	

Sūma xix[li]   xij[s]   iij[d]   ob qr

RECEPTIONES PRO BATTELLIS
Conuictorum 1° ter. 1583

dccre.		com :	bat :	gau :	Chamber.
	Mr. Russell				
	Mr. Kiblwhighte	iij[s]	j[d]	ob	xvj[d]
	Mr. Huchinson	o	o	o	
ij[s]	Mr. Reade	xxix[s]	iij[d]	qr	xvj[d]
	Mr. Smythe	ij[s]			
ıj[s]	Mr. Paulett	xlvj[s]	viij[d]	ob qr	xvj[d]
	Mr. Hungerford		xviij[d]		xvj[d]
	Mr. Hungerforde		xviij[d]		xvj[d]
ij[s]	Mr. Dugdall	xxvj[s]	v[d]	qr	xvj[d]
ij[s]	Perrin	xxxij[s]	iiij[d]		xvj[d]

ij^s Gryffethe	xxxiij^s	x^d	qr	xvj^d
Webb	ix^s			
Amerste		xvj^d		
xij^d Baines	xxj^s	ij^d	qr	xvj^d
ij^s Bateman	xxxij	v^d	ob qr	xvj^d
ij^s Corham	xxxviij^s	ij^d		xvj^d
Haukins		xvj^d		
ij^s Shakerly	xxviij^s	viij^d		xvj^d
ij^s Horner	xxxiiij^s	iiij^d	ob qr	xvj^d
ij^s Prise	xxxij^s	vij^d	ob	xvj^d
ij^s Charleton	xxxj^s	x^d	qr	xvj^d
ij^s Marshall	xxviij^s	xj^d	ob	xvj^d
xij^d Foule	xvj^s	iij^d	ob	xvj^d
xij^d Gunter	xiiij^s	vij^d	qr	xij^d
Nashe	vij^s	vij^d	ob	xij^d
Lodge		ix^d	ob	
xij^d Harvie	xviij^s	viij^d	ob	xij^d
xij^d Cocke	xj^s		qr	xij^d
xij^d Bayly	xviij^s	iiij^d	ob qr	xij^d
xij^d Sheldon	xvij^s	iiij^d	ob qr	xij^d
ij^s Merser	xxvj^s	v^d	ob	xij^d
	Sūma	xxx^{li}	ij^s	ob
	Cubicula	xxx^s		

Solutiones Stipendiorum 1° ter. 1583

Mr. President	v^{li}	
Mr. Vice-President	xiij^s	iiij^d
Mr. Reade	xiij^s	iiij^d
Mr. Rixman	xiij^s	iiij^d
Mr. Lee	xiij^s	iiij^d
Mr. Nashe	xiij^s	iiij^d
Mr. Aubrye	xiij^s	iiij^d
Mr. Gwin	xiij^s	iiij^d

Mr. Sprott	xiij^s	iiij^d
Mr. Wighte	xiij^s	iiij^d
Mr. Denham	xiij^s	iiij^d
Mr. Ravens	vj^s	viij^d
Mr. Pottycary	vj^s	viij^d
Mr. Perrin	vj^s	viij^d
Mr. Dixon	vj^s	viij^d
Mr. Webb	vj^s	viij^d
Capellanus	xiij^s	iiij^d
Sr. Gittens	vj^s	viij^d
Sr. Belfelde	vj^s	viij^d
Sr. Faucett	vj^s	viij^d
Sr. Beareblock	vj^s	viij^d
Sr. Millarde	vj^s	viij^d
Sr. Osburne	vj^s	viij^d
Sr. Shinglton	vj^s	viij^d
Sr. Kite	vj^s	viij^d
Sr. Speene	vj^s	viij^d
Sr. Smythe	vj^s	viij^d
Sr. Buckeridge	vj^s	viij^d
Sr. Finmore	vj^s	viij^d
Sr. Childerly	v^s	viij^d
Sr. Addams	v^s	viij^d
Sr. Rainsbee	v^s	viij^d
Withington	iiij^s	
Burgisse	iiij^s	
Lattware	iiij^s	
Cooke	iiij^s	
Wall	iiij^s	
Firmin	iiij^s	
Gunter	iiij^s	
Waldron	iiij^s	
Leeche	iiij^s	
Cromwell	ij^s	vj^d

Hanly	ij^s	vj^d
Capell	ij^s	vj^d
Sprott	ij^s	vj^d
Aldworthe	ij^s	vj^d
Linbee	ij^s	vj^d
Searchfelde	ij^s	vj^d
Waterhouse	ij^s	vj^d
Wall	ij^s	vj^d
Lee	ij^s	vj^d
Hutten	ij^s	vj^d
Sr. Vi Præ. duo	x^s	
Obsonator	$xiij^s$	$iiij^d$
Sacrista	v^s	
Promus	v^s	
Janitor	v^s	
Coquus	xvj^s	$viij^d$
Subcoquus	x^s	
Coquus 3us	xv^s	
Vice præ.	x^s	
Decanus Theolog.	vj^s	$viij^d$
Decanus Juris Civil.	vj^s	$viij^d$
Decani Artium duo	$xiij^s$	$iiij^d$
Burs. duo	xx^s	
Lector Juris Civil.	xxv^s	
Lector græcus	xxv^s	
Lector Rhetor.	xxv^s	
Lector Philoso.	xxv^s	
Lector Dialec.	xxv^s	
Custos Siluarum	x^s	
Tegulator	vj^s	$viij^d$
Tonsor	v^s	
Lotrix	$viij^s$	$iiij^d$
Clericus Compoti	x^s	
Faber lignarius		xx^d

Expensæ intra & extra

Collegium 1° ter: 1583.

Imprimis paide to Mrs. Mathews for saulte, pottes, trenchers, and other suche thinges spent for one wholle yere ending the ixth of November 1583	iij^{li}		
Item for Candels from Midsomer to the Audite 1583		xxvij^s	
Item sett on in Battels geuen to twoe poore men		v^s	j^d
Item a sugar loafe		xiiij^s	viij^d
Item gloues sent to Mr. Recorder of London		vj^s	viij^d
Item scouringe of vessell			xx^d
Item for wine for the cõmunion on Allholloudaye			x^d
Item geuen in rewarde to Godyere Mr. Owens man for searching of rowles in his Mr's custodye		v^s	
Item for saulte		xvj^s	
Item for engrossinge the last yers accountes in parchment			xx^d
Item for hay spent for three shepe before the laste Audite			iiij^d
Item to Jones for goinge to Fiffelde for Mr. Whites rent			vj^d
Item to Sr. Faucett for meat for the pigions			vj^d
Item to twoe poore men putt on in the Buttery book 11^a hebd.		ij^s	ij^d

Item for waxe to the sealinge of the Accquittance sent vp to Mr. Radclyffe . . .			iij^d
Item to Goodwiff Webbster putt on in the Buttery book before the Audite		xxxviij^s	
Item for fryes for the fowre ser-servantes liueries . . .		xx^s	
Item for a baskett in the chit-chen			vj^d
Item to Mr. Vice præ. for Mr. Præsidentes & his ferryinge over Bagbrookhiue going to viewe Bridgis growndes .			iiij^d
Item wax for the sealinge of Mr. Sweates lease & Prickettes .			vj^d
Item to Mr. Præsident wch he bestowed at Abingdon vppon Mr. Yates & 4 or 5 woodmen wch tooke paynes wth him to survaye Bagly woode . .		v^s	
Item geven in rewarde to him y^t brought Phelps boore .			iiij^d
Item in Sonsinge drink for the brawne.			x^d
Item hay for the Sheepe . .			x^d
Item to the Smythe for a Gird-yorne & ij spittes weighing xxiiij^{li} at 3^d the pownde .		vj^s	
Item to the poore woeman for keeping the Inner Courte & ye base courte for Christmas quarter		ij^s	vj^d

Sūma   x^{li} xvij^s ij^d

Reparationes 1° ter 1583.

Imprimis for drawinge of timber from Highe bridge	iij^s	vj^d
Item for lathe for the lofer of the pigion house		vj^d
Item for a loade of lime . . .	xij^s	
Item to the Smythe for mendinge of lockes and kayes about the colledg	ij^s	vj^d
Item for squaring of timber at Eaton	v^s	
Item to Androse an to an other for squaring timber	ix^s	
Item to Andros for v dayes and a half more	v^s	vj^d
Item for boordes for Mr. Denhams studdye and workmanshipp there .	v^s	iiij^d
Item for carryag of vj boatloads of timber from Eaton	xv^s	
Item for carriage of vij loads of timber from the same place . . .	xvij^s	vj^d
Item for ashes for the chitchen plompe		xvj^d
Item to a carpenter for v dayes worke about the lofer of the pigion house	iiij^s	viij^d
Item for timber for the lofer . .	iiij^s	x^d
Item for halfe a hundren & v foote of boords for y^t lofer	iiij^s	vj^d
Item for slatting of y^t lofer . .		xxj^d
Item for a boulte to the hall dore .		vj^d
Item for mending the iron of the plompe in the groue . . .		vj^d
Item for charges of building a newe windowe in Lattwarrs chamber and making footstepps to every chamber dore	xxx^s	

Item for a desk for the readers in the haule . . . . . . } ij[s]

Item to Jhon Herberte simoninge certaine loose stones in the newe gate . . . . . . } iij[d]

Item for mending the lock & a keaye for the store house dore over the citchin wth a hinge and a foote for the skillett . . . . . } xij[d]

Item to Jhon Herbart for repairinge the rainge in y[e] citchen . . . } xij[d]

Sūma vj[l] v[s] ij[d]

Equitantes 1° ter 1583.

Imprimis Mr. Præsidentes charges in Michaelmas tearme . . } viij[ll] 6[s] ij[d]

Item the coste of the Colledg sutes the same terme . . } viij[ll] 14[s] 2[d]

Item Mr. Præsidentes and Mr. Bursars charges to survay Mr. Herls lande . . . . } iiij[s] ij[d]

Item to Mr. Præsident towardes the keping of 3 geldinges . } l[s]

Item to Mr. Vice præsident & the ij bursars towardes the keping of their geldinges . } xvj[s] 8[d]

Sūma xx[ll] xj[s] ij[d]

Nothing more clearly shows the position of the small and struggling College, its local interests and at the same time the way in which it endeavoured in state and dignity to take its place among the older Colleges, than these accounts.

These difficulties belong especially to the presidencies of Matthew and his successor. Under the latter also religious disagreements caused no less vexation.

Tobie Matthew resigned on May 8, 1577.

He was succeeded by Francis Willis, who had been one of the earliest scholars, and had vacated his fellowship by marriage. In him the association with the neighbourhood of Oxford was kept up, for he held the benefices both of Cumnor and Kingston Bagpuze. He was already Canon of Bristol, and in 1587 he became Dean of Worcester. He was elected on May 15, 1577, and resigned on June 2, 1570. Under him the building was continued and he is said to have paid for the upper part of the library. He was succeeded by Ralph Hutchinson, who had been Fellow since 1570. He was Vicar of Charlbury, Oxon (which, like Kingston, was in the College patronage). A peaceable scholar, he guided the College well in times of poverty, and added to it some lustre as one of the translators of the Bible. He had been nominated to his scholarship by Joanna White, the Founder's second wife, and he was the last of the Presidents whom Sir Thomas can himself have known. His monument, now in the Baylie Chapel, was painted, as Wood says, " to the life in doctoral formalities," and praises him for his vigilant care of the studies, and his munificent support of the building of the College. In his days flourished the most brilliant light of the first age of the foundation, in describing whom the enthusiasm of the annalists bursts all bounds. Dr. John Case, theologian, philosopher, musician, was a student, as his grim portrait in the College hall shows, of anatomy, but he was no less a poet, a student

of political theory,* and a " painful preacher." He
was an Oxfordshire lad, born at Woodstock, and, as a
child, was a chorister of New College and Christ Church.
He was elected to a scholarship at S. John's in 1564.
He married the widow " of one Dobson, the keeper of
Bocardo prison," and then became what in modern
days is called a " coach." He had the University's
licence to teach philosophy and logic in his own house;
and it has been said, though evidence is not forthcoming,
that his instruction was chiefly given to Roman Catholics.
Certainly he did not desert the national Church, and
he died a Canon of Salisbury. His fame was made as a
commentator on Aristotle. One of his books, the
" speculum moralium quaestionum in universam ethicen
Aristotelis," 1585, was the first book printed in Oxford,
by the University press given by Leicester. The
" Sphæra Civitatis," 1588, was so highly valued as a
manual of political philosophy, that in 1590 every
Bachelor of Arts was ordered to buy one on taking his
degree. No less skilled was Case in music, vocal and
instrumental. His studies of natural science are commemorated in the grim picture of him in the College
hall, which shows him examining a skeleton, and bears
an hour-glass and other " emblems of mortality," with
the mottoes appropriate to his position. Of this, and
of his benefactions, more hereafter. He is to be
remembered as one of those who gave the College fame
in its early years, and who kept up the tradition of
Catholic Anglicanism.

He died on January 23, 1600. His tomb, now in

* His *Sphæra Civitatis* has an interest of its own in the history of
political science.

the Baylie Chapel, has a magniloquent inscription and a bust.   The former exhausts the virtues and the sciences in recording his praise.   As a physician, he was beloved alike by rich, mean, and poor ; and he died holily, as he had lived well.   " Cujus scripta extant logica, ethica, œconomica, in octo libb. ; physicorum encomium, musicæ encomium, apologia Academiarum, rebellionis vindiciæ, quae nondum tamen in luce prodierunt." It is not likely that the modern world will ask for his unpublished works.

With the end of the sixteenth century the tide had turned in favour of the College.   It was still poor, but it was beginning to be famous.   Men of wit resided in its walls ; sons of statesmen were taught by its tutors. The Earl of Shrewsbury sent two of his sons in 1564 ; in 1572 young Lord Strange was matriculated, and two of the Stanleys.   The good deeds of Sir Thomas White had found imitators in the City of London.   It became a fashion to bequeath endowments to what had begun to be considered a merchants' College.

A list of some of the early benefactions illustrates at once the poverty of the College and the generosity of the Londoners, and of its own richer members.

John Case himself gave a hundred pounds to purchase land to increase the endowment of two fellowships. Mrs. May gave an endowment for a Divinity Lecture, of which Laud was the first reader.   Sir Richard Lee, 1608, gave endowment for a scholar ; John Rixman, formerly Fellow, £100 for the College discretion.   But the merchants form a more magnificent list ; and the College records gratefully acknowledge the generosity of Walter Fish, Citizen and Merchant Taylor (part of whose endowment, for " five poor scholars of the College that are most like to bend their studies to Divinity," is still preserved for its original purpose) ; Hugh Henley, Citizen and Merchant Taylor.; George Palin (whose name, in the person of an eminent descendant, is still warmly received at College gaudies) Citizen and Girdler ; Thomas Paradyne, Citizen and Haberdasher ; Sir Robert Ducie ; Sir William Craven and Geoffrey Elwes, Aldermen of London ; and Master George Benson, also a Citizen. A new era of munificence begins with Laud.

Turning back from finance to religion we may notice two of the earlier members of the College who left her walls and the English Church.

Edmund Campion was one of the ·first scholars of the College, appointed by the Founder on the request of the Grocers' Company. He became, it is said, a special favourite with Sir Thomas, and he accepted the religious changes of Elizabeth with a mind as ready as his. " As a mere layman," says his modern apologist, " he had no particular call to certify himself more securely on so very inconvenient a point."*   He studied philosophy, he says himself, for seven years, and theology for about six. He became a notable orator, welcomed Elizabeth, and wept over Amy Robsart in rhetoric as flowing. His speech at the Founder's funeral was considered a masterpiece. He called upon the city towns to bewail him, recorded his charities, and eulogised his domestic virtues. The core of his commemoration comes in such words as these:

* *Simpson's Life of Campion* p. 4. Of the accuracy of this interesting biography some idea may be obtained by observing that in it William Roper is called "the descendant of Sir Thomas More."

" For the last ten years he has devoted all his thoughts, his money, and his labour to us. When he was away from Oxford his heart was there. Awake or asleep of us only did he think. As soon as the last and fatal palsy struck him, he sent for one of us. The President was away, and I was sent instead. When he saw me, the old man embraced me, and with tears spoke words which I could not hear dry-eyed, and cannot repeat without tears. . . . He begged us not to pray for his recovery. Nothing vexed him more than wishes for a renewal of health."

Campion retained, for several years, his association with the University. He was Proctor 1568–69, was ordained and became a noted preacher. But he left Oxford the year after his proctorship, one of those no doubt whom the Pope's bull against Elizabeth forced to a painful choice. He joined his friend Gregory Martin abroad, and S. John's saw no more of him.

Of another convert to Rome, John Roberts, an interesting life has recently been published.* Many of the earlier Commoners of S. John's were from Wales, and Roberts would be far from lonely when he matriculated in 1596. He was a friend, probably, of Laud's chamber fellow, John Jones. He would know Laud and Buckeridge, and perhaps also Cuthbert Mayne the College Chaplain, who was also to suffer by the harsh penal laws as a traitor. Roberts stayed hardly more than a year in Oxford. He went to London to study at Furnival's Inn, and before long deserted the Church. It is impossible to tell whether or not he was influenced

* By an English priest, the Rev. R. P. J. Camm (Dom Bede Camm) 1897.

in S. John's towards Rome ; but the tide of secession had ceased, before his time, to affect the College.

The record thus far is typical of the fortunes of the new foundation of the Reformation age. Everything depended upon the intelligence, and the harmony, of the first members. The temptations to desert the English Church and " adhere to the Pope's jurisdiction " were constant; the missionary enthusiasm of the Jesuits, in spite of their intrigues and squabbles, was contagious. S. John's had the great advantage of the care of a Founder whose attachment to Catholicism, and whose personal piety, could not be doubted. To him the changes in the constitution of the English Church, if not all wholesome, did not appear to be vital. He remained to show that a plain man could live and think no harm without damage to his faith from

<blockquote>" silken sly insinuating Jacks."</blockquote>

He endeavoured to gather round him men of the like sober mind, who should give themselves to true religion and sound learning. In Tobie Matthew, with his intense activity, plain churchmanship, and simple devotion to duty, he found a worthy successor; and there were others to hand on the trust. It is well to remember, when some profess to consider the continuity of the English Church a modern theory, that Sir Thomas White and his College form a practical illustration of it. The College did not lose by the secession of some of its members. Campion may well have been regretted, for his sincerity and his quick wits ; but for the others the picture of Wisbeach Castle drawn by Father William Weston, who was himself imprisoned there for many years, and of its clerical inmates as given up to "whoring, drunkenness, and dicing" suggests that the College may have been the better for their departure. The stability of the new College was tested by its misfortunes. It survived them, and in the seventeenth century it rose to be the most important body in Oxford.

From a Photo by the]　　　　　THE HALL.　　　　　[Oxford Camera Club

CHAPTER VI

OLD CHRISTMAS IN S. JOHN'S

WE may now turn aside from the chronological survey of the College history to touch upon a characteristic incident of its social life, the winter festivities of the seventeenth century. The cynic who traces all pictures of the old English Christmas to the sentimental imagination of Charles Dickens and Washington Irving belies at least the persistent tradition of the Universities. Even now at Oxford there lingers much quaint ceremonial in some of the colleges—and at Queen's one may follow the boar's head decked with rosemary on Christmas Day, and take from the bursar his needle of thrift on the first night of the New Year. These are survivals of a much more elaborate cycle of feastings, which the Reformation hardly touched, and only the grim nightmare of the Great Rebellion and its University Commissioners destroyed.

Christmas at the beginning of the seventeenth century was in Oxford a time of high revelry. It was, of course, vacation; but the difficulty and expense of travelling in midwinter, as well as the obligations which many colleges laid on their scholars, kept most of the students at the University during the few weeks between the Michaelmas and Lent terms. At the seat of learning they were, but not at their books. All lectures and exercises, all dissertations and disputings, were suspended. The sober dons themselves yielded to the sweet influence of the time, and became boys again at their sports, and let the lads have their way in all quaint diversions and merry pranks.

This time of revel took the place, no doubt, that had been filled by the ceremonies connected with the feast of the boy-bishop, so common in pre-Reformation times. On the feast of S. Nicholas or of the Holy Innocents one of the children of the choir in most large churches would assume the mock style and dignity of the Episcopate; his fellows would have leave to join him, and a strange semi-reverent burlesque of the most sacred ceremonies would ensue. The Reformation was, in one of its most prominent aspects, a striving after more reality and solemnity in the treatment of holy things, a reaction against a perfunctory slovenliness such as may still be seen in Italy, even in the very holy of holies. Many observances, in themselves innocent, but which tended to irreverence, were swept away. In this connection comes the proclamation of King Henry VIII. in 1542:—

"Whereas heretofore divers and many superstitions and childish observances have been used, and yet to this day are observed and kept in many and sundry parts of this realm, as upon Saint Nicholas, the Holy Innocents, and such like; children be strangely decked and appareled to counterfeit priests, Bishops, and women, and to be led with songs and dances from house to house, blessing the people and gathering of money; and boys do sing mass and preach in the pulpit, with such other unfitting and inconvenient usages, rather to the derision than any true glory of God, or honour of His saints; the King's Majesty willeth and commandeth that henceforth all such superstitious observations be left and clearly extinguished throughout all this realm and dominions."

The boy-bishop was suppressed; but he died hard. Still in the streets of Oxford on a winter night you meet little urchins trampling through the snow with rags and wreaths and paper decorations, " gathering of money "— the fallen followers, it would seem, of the distinguished boy-bishop of old time.

But while church-mumming perished Christmas plays throve. The revival of learning, coming to its height in England in the days of great Queen Bess, and the Renaissance, with its delight in personal and artistic beauty and love of human life for its own sake, bore fruit in the winter recreations of the student societies, as well as on the great stage of Shakespeare and Burbage. The king had ever his " lord of misrule "—a " master of merry disports " Stow calls him—" and the like had yet in the house of every nobleman of honour or good worship, were he spiritual or temporal." So it was in the Universities and in the Inns of Court. And besides these the lads of the village and the 'prentice boys would gather to play traditional gambols, and now and again to invent new frolics to show in the houses of the great or in the taverns of the city or the country-side. Something of this still lingers in several of the shires; in Mid-Lincoln, and in Oxfordshire too, the plough-boys will come to you of a winter's eve and act S. George and the Soldan, Tom-Fool and Harry Fift, France and Spain,

The Dragon and Admiral Nelson, in strange medley with current topics and old words to very modern tunes.

Two specimens of the Christmas wit of the great age of England lie in manuscript in Oxford libraries. The one, " A Twelfe Night Merriment," which its editor calls " Narcissus," was a few years ago transcribed from the MS. in the Bodleian by Miss Margaret Lee, and brought out by Mr. David Nutt. The other, a much longer piece of work, spreading the record of festival from its conception on All Saints' Eve to its ending on the first Saturday of Lent, was written down by Master Griffin Higgs, of S. John's College, afterwards Fellow of Merton, chaplain to Queen Elizabeth of Bohemia, and Dean of Lichfield, and given for the instruction of future ages to the College Library, where the MS. is still a treasured relic. A few copies were printed for some antiquarian club in 1816.

From these two books we may see very happily what a merry Christmas of the olden time might be in the Universities—what bustle and merriment there was, what largess and luxury, and yet withal what a homely simplicity of pleasant feeling. There is a distinction between the two pieces. *The Christmas Prince*, as the S. John's MS. is called, describes and records a whole series of revels and plays, depending on the custom of choosing a lord of misrule from among the under-graduates who should hold sway during the whole period, often greatly prolonged, of the Christmas festivities.

The winter in which this was played was that of

1607, and the Prince chosen was one Thomas Tucker, a lad of nineteen, who had been some six years at the College, and had taken his bachelor's degree. The custom had died out since 1577, when the famous John Case was chosen for Christmas Prince. The interval of these thirty years had, it seems, been passed with no scholars' play. But in 1602, though they could not find actors in college they could provide a writer who told the story of Narcissus from the third book of Ovid's *Metamorphoses*, in a burlesque English version. The play professes to be acted by "youths of the parish"—*i.e.*, of S. Mary Magdalene, within the bounds of which the old College stands—and seems written in rustical fashion, after the style of Shakespeare's interludes in *Love's Labour's Lost* and *A Midsummer's Night's Dream*, for fit performing by unlearned youths. But this may be only a poetic fiction to disguise the scholar-players. Certainly the 'prentice lads or the choir-boys would need much drilling to play so clever a piece successfully. *Narcissus* does not claim to be a finished work, even of the sort which the plays in the festival of the Christmas Prince afford. It stands by itself too, as a Twelfth-Night revel, with no great preparing before or systematised gaiety after. It is introduced by the Porter of S. John's—one Francis Clarke—who had been placed on the list of *personae privilegiatae* by the University the year before, a young man of a merry wit and popular with scholars, a worthy predecessor of some famous janitors of more modern times. On the feast of the Epiphany, at the end of supper, when by the statutes the scholars might sit round the hall fire—for they had no warmth in their own rooms—and talk of the "*mirabilia mundi*," he enters with plea for Christmas jollity:

> "Christmas is now at the point to be past.
>   'Tis giving up the ghost and this is the last;
>   And shall it pass thus without life or cheer?
>   This hath not been seen this many a year.
>   If you'll have any sport, then say the word.
>   Here come youths of the parish that will it afford.
>   They are here hard by coming along
>   Crowning their wassail bowl with song."

So the lads are admitted, "bearing the bowl and singing the song"—a carousing ditty, with chorus, something after the fashion of worthy Bishop Still's famous lines in *Gammer Gurton's Needle.* The song done and the bowl emptied they betake themselves to the business of the evening:

> "Then we begin, and let none hope to miss us,
>   The play we play is Ovid's own *Narcissus.*"

Certainly the drama does not weary by its length. It is rather of the fashion of those plays which children make. It is all action and its dialogue of the briefest. The dialogue is adapted from Ovid and, in fact, is in most parts a literal translation. There might be many worse exercises for the scholar in his Christmas vacation than this turning the classic poets into his own rhymes. The development of the plot is a curious mixture of sentiment and boisterous comedy. There is the common trick of Echo playing with the astonished clown—the delight in far-fetched rhyme and the humour of incongruous conjunction. Tiresias appears in a Bishop's rochet, and thus he speaks:

> " All you that see me here in Bishop's rochet,
>   And I see not, your heads may run on crochet,
>   For ought I know, to know what manner wight
>   In this strange guise I am, or how I hight;
>   I am Tiresias, the not seeing prophet,
>   Blind though I be I pray let no man scoff it;
>   For blind I am, yea, blind as any beetle,
>   And cannot see a whit, no ne'er so little."

To the fond father and mother of the sweet Narcissus Tiresias gives dark sayings: and to Dorastus and Clinias he prophesies an untimely end. Narcissus himself is something of a lay figure, but he affords an example of the extravagant Renaissance feeling so familiar to students of Elizabethan literature. He is like Sebastian in *Twelfth Night*, or "Mr. W. H., the onlie begetter of these sonnets," the beautiful youth beloved by man and maid alike. The absurdities in which the literature of the time revels when it touches this chivalrous friendship of man for man are neatly satirised in the hyperbolical extravagances of the rustic youths. Sentimental vapourings are mingled with broad burlesque:

Dorastus.

> O thou whose cheeks are like the sky so blue,
> Whose nose is ruby, of the sunlike hue,
> Whose forehead is most plain without all wrinkle,
> Whose eyes like stars in frosty night do twinkle,
> Whose ledge of teeth is far more bright than jet is,
> Whose lips are too good for any lettuce.

O do thou condescend unto my boon,
Grant me thy love, grant it, O silver spoon,
Silver moon, silver moon.

CLINIAS.

Grant me thy love, to speak I first begun,
Grant me thy love, grant it, O golden sun.

NARCISSUS.

Nor sun, nor moon, nor twinkling star in sky,
Nor god, nor goddess, nor yet nymph am I :
And though my sweet face be set out with ruby,
You miss your mark, I am a man as you be.

DORASTUS.

A man, Narcisse, thou hast a man-like figure :
Then be not like unto the savage tiger,
So cruel as the huge chameleon,
Nor yet so changing as a small elephant ;
A man, Narcisse, then be not thou a wolf
To devour my heart in thy maw's griping gulf.
Be none of these and let not nature vaunt her
That she hath made a man like to a panther,
A man thou art, Narcisse, and so are we,
Then love thou us again as we love thee.

But Narcissus will have none of the foolish affection
of the lads.

The maidens meet as scant courtesy as the youths.
Then, with some inconsequence, they betake themselves
to hunting; and there is a capital hunting song. Mis-
fortune comes as soon as Echo is heard mocking, and so
at last Dorastus and Clinias kill each other, and
Narcissus is lured by his own sweet face to drown him-

self in a well—a well like Shakespeare's *Wall*, impersonated
by one of the actors. The dialogue throughout is inter-
spersed with quaint little songs, of which the last is that
addressed by Narcissus to the face he sees in the water,
and answered by the mocking Echo from below:

> "O delicate pretty youth,
>   Pretty youth;
> Take on my woes pity, youth!
>   Pity, youth!
> O sweetest boy, pray love me!
>   Pray love me!
> Or else I die for thee!
>   I die for thee!

The Porter as Epilogue turns the players out of door
and "makes his leg" to the audience. So the quaint
and rustic piece ends. The chief feature of the entertainment undoubtedly is the merry porter, Francis
Clarke, who is like Macbeth's porter without his
drunkenness, a fellow of infinite jest. Miss Lee, in her
beautiful edition of the plays, prints also three speeches
" written for the foresaid porter." In the first he pleads
for pardon of Mr. President for letting the fiddlers into
the hall at Christmas, wherefore he had been sconced
ten groats. We have seen that no strangers were
allowed within the College walls without the President's
leave previously given. In the second he begs of an
unknown Lady Kennedy that her "servant Monsieur
Piers " may join the annual jaunt of the " kitchen-folk."
In the third he pleads for the freshmen: " O that I were
Janus indeed, that I might have two tongues to intreat
for this pitiful crew." It is probably at the end of

their "colting," with all its experience of "fresh fees and drink," and is designed to win their admission into the ranks of the "students of the second year whom they call Poulderlings."

From this Twelfth Night merriment of 1602 we turn to the much more elaborate revels of 1607. On this occasion a beginning was made as early as All Saints' Eve, when it was decided to choose a Christmas lord, prince of the revels, who should have authority "to appoint and moderate all such games and pastimes as should ensue." The College authorities cordially joined in the sports, and the vice-president, one of the Deans, and one of the "ten seniors" (in whose hands, as we have shown, the whole government of the College practically lay) took the votes. Thomas Tucker had one vote above John Towse; he had himself been present at the play in 1602, so that he had some experience of the manner. The next duty was to collect moneys for the expenses. The College itself subscribed as a corporation, and Mr. President (Dr. Buckeridge, afterwards successively Bishop of Rochester and of Ely, who had succeeded Ralph Hutchinson in 1605) and Mr. Laud were among the donors of "subsidies." Juxon figures among the masters of arts, and Baylie (afterwards president) among the bachelors. Among outside benefactors, old members of the College, was Sir William Paddy, the physician to King James.

"For all these subsidies at home and helps abroad," adds the truthful record of Master Griffin Higgs, "yet it was found that in the end there would rather be want (as, indeed, it happened) than any superfluity, and therefore the Prince took order with the bursars to send out

warrants to all the tenants and other friends of the College
that they should send in extraordinary provision against
every feast, which accordingly was performed ; some send-
ing money, some wine, some venison, some other provision,
every one according to his ability."

The merriment began with a Latin play, *Ara
Fortunae*, which is given at length in the MS.   It was
but the precursor of many others, *Saturnalia* (" showing
the first causes of Christmas candles "), *Philomela*,
Philomathes, and *Ira seu Tumulus Fortunae.*   These
all in Latin, and written for the occasion, some well,
some ill, show that there was a memory in the whole
affair of the learned life which the universities professed
to lead and to foster.   The plays, it appears, were
keenly criticised.   S. John's was, as we know, later, in
Laud's time, the centre of dramatic interest in the
University.   Thence came the best plays and the best
actors, and the other colleges were eager to emulate
and to pick out faults.   But if the players were always
eager to pose as scholars, their audiences were not
always satisfied with a learned language.   So to suit all
tastes they were given also several masques in English
in the true old vein of Christmas, and after the fashion
of rustic mummers :—

" The Prince's honest neighbours of S. Giles's presented
him with a mask or morris, which though it were but
rudely performed, yet it being so freely and lovingly
proffered, it could not but be as lovingly received."

So, too, there was a pageant of " the twelve days," the
holy days talking Latin while the working days spoke
English :—

> " Ye see these working days they wear no satin,
> And I assure you they can speak no Latin."

There were also English plays of *Time's Complaint*, the *Seven Days of the Week*, and a wassail in the president's lodging, " where privately they made themselves merry," called "The Five Bells of Magdalen Church," with at the end of all an "English tragedy" called *Periander*. The revellings seem to have spread over the whole University, for " the Prince was solemnly invited by the Canons of Christ Church to a comedy called *Yuletide*. But there," says the chronicler—

" Many things were either ill-meant by them or ill-taken by us ; but we had very good reason to think the former, both for that the whole town thought so, and the whole play was a medley of Christmas sports, by which occasion Christmas lords were much jested at, and our Prince was so placed that many things were acted upon him ; but yet Mr. Dean himself, then Vice-Chancellor, very kindly sent for the Prince and some others of our house, and laboured to satisfy us, protesting that no such thing was meant."

The period of festivity would naturally have ended earlier but that the term was prorogued for a week " because of the extreme cold and frost which had continued full six weeks and better without any intermission." As it was the Christmas plays were not finished till after Ash Wednesday.

Much interesting light is thrown, it will be easily seen, upon the social usages of the time, and certainly the picture of comradeship and good feeling at the Universities is pleasanter than could be furnished by any record of the following century. The tone of the proceedings is entirely of the great age of English history. The plays and the merrymakings breathe of great Elizabeth, not of the Stewarts. The life is free, buoyant, unrestrained, but with no touch of the sentimental animalism of the decadence. It is in 1607 as in 1602 : the student-lads are enjoying themselves a little boisterously it may be, and with all sorts of æsthetic and euphuistic extravagances, but always as scholars and gentlemen. In such a circle it is no surprise to see moving pleasantly the famous Master Laud. He is then but a Fellow of his college. He subscribes twice to the expenses of the Christmas Prince; and in 1603, when he was proctor, the irrepressible Frank Clarke, " who in his brother's behalf did break one's head with a black staff," is made to read a letter to him in a style of mock penitence, which only a man, such as Laud's letters reveal him, who loved a jest, would suffer to be addressed to his grave dignity.

Such were the general features of the period of Saturnalia. The ceremonies of the Christmas dinner itself are worth quoting, as they suggest those still retained in the hall of Queen's :—

" At dinner the Prince being set down in the hall at the high table in the Vice-President's place (for the President himself was then also present), he was served with twenty dishes to a mess, all which were brought in by Gentlemen of the House attired in his Guard's coats, ushered in by the Lord Comptroller and other officers of the hall. The first mess was a boar's head, which was carried by the tallest and lustiest of all the Guard, before whom (an attendant) went first, one attired in a horseman's coat, with a boar's spear in his hand, next to him two pages in taffety sarcenet, each of them with a mess of mustard, next to whom came he that carried the boar's head crossed with a green silk scarf, by which hung the empty scabbard of the falchion which was carried before him. As they entered the hall he sang this Christmas Carol, the last three verses of every stave being repeated after him by the whole company:

I.

The boar is dead,
Lo, here's his head.
   What man could have done more
Than his head off to strike,
Meleager like,
   And bring it as I do before.

II.

He living spoiled
Where good men toiled,
   Which made kind Ceres sorry:
But now dead and drawn
Is very good brawn,
   And we have brought it for ye.

III.

Then set down the swine-yard,
The foe to the vineyard,
   Let Bacchus crown his fall;
Let this boar's head and mustard
Stand for pig, goose, and custard,
   And so you are welcome all."

It will be seen that there is no trace of austerity

about the Christmas celebrations.   It is a far cry to the Puritan horror of the festival of the Nativity.   But at the same time it is to be noted that the fast-days as they come round are rigidly observed.   The whole picture is a very graphic representation of English social life, as the Reformation left it, with customs of gaiety mellowed by time, but purged of all irreverence and brightened by the activity of scholar-minds.

SEAL NOW IN USE

CHAPTER VII

BUCKERIDGE, LAUD, AND JUXON

With the election of John Buckeridge, January 18,
1605, the seventeenth century, the most important time
in the College history, may be said to begin. The
College register gradually assumes a new aspect. The
period of foundation is over. No longer are the books
filled with particulars as to College land and tenements
or copies of earlier title-deeds; the resolutions, the
leases, the internal orders, of a settled society have
taken their place.

John Buckeridge, who was of kin to the founder,
continued his tradition. He was a distinguished theologian, wrote against Bellarmine, and based the studies
of his pupils " upon the noble foundations of the fathers,
councils and ecclesiastical historians." He was chaplain
to Archbishop Whitgift and had, at the time he was
elected President of S. John's, considerable eminence
as a preacher and theologian. Besides several country
livings, he held, from 1604, that of S. Giles's, Cripplegate, and was thus brought into connection with the
London merchants. Another connection, which links
the name of Laud's college to that of the great leader
of the opposing party, may find a place here.

The Cromwell family had sent many members to S.

John's. The daughter of Sir Thomas White's second wife, Joan Warren, married Sir Henry Cromwell of Hitchinbroke.   Her son Henry was elected a Law Fellow in 1581 ; his younger brother Philip, became Fellow in 1594. Both were Oliver's uncles. It was from Sir Oliver, another uncle, that the living of Crick, Northamptonshire, was bought by Sir William Craven, a rich merchant, and bestowed on the College in 1613. In the last years of the sixteenth century it is clear that Buckeridge resided constantly in the College. He was very likely the tutor of the younger brother, as he was of Laud ; and the family association may well have led the great Oliver to S. Giles's Cripplegate, where, on August 22, 1620, he married Elizabeth Bourchier.

Under Buckeridge it would seem that the Oxford conflict with Popery, for the time, died down ; and the theologians of S. John's turned their weapons against Calvinism, now rampant in many of the other colleges. The College at the beginning of the seventeenth century was before all else literary.

Its Christmas plays do not stand alone. Fuller speaks of S. John's as the nursery of many bright wits, and an ode to the memory of Sir Thomas White, prophesies of the College with an evident certainty of fulfilment

> " Their infant bards shall try the golden lyre,
>   And soften into sound the jarring ire.
>
>   *   *   *   *
>
>   From thence shall flow a venerable race
>   Vers'd in each art and form'd with every grace."

Chief among the wits and playwrights was Matthew

Gwynne, for many years medical Fellow of the College, whose tragedy of Nero his companions much admired. He wrote too, we are told, the most diverting epigrams in Latin, English, Italian and French, being (by the College licence) a traveller in foreign parts. His *Vertumnus* was played before King James I., the Queen, and Prince Henry, at their visit in 1605, the year of Buckeridge's election. The account of the reception of the King is worth quoting at length.

At the gate of S. John's

" three young youths in habit and attire like nymphs, confronted him, representing England, Scotland, and Ireland, and talking dialogue-wise each to other of their state, at last concluding yielding themselves up to his gracious government. The scholars stood all on one side of the street, and the strangers of all sorts on the other. The scholars stood first, then the Bachelors, and at last the Masters of Arts." *

Among those who then saluted the king must have been the two future Archbishops, Laud and Juxon.

Two days later, Dr. Gwynne's comedy was played before the King.

" It was acted much better than either of the others that he had seen before, yet the King was so over-wearied [he had had a long day of disputation and feasts] that after a while he distasted it and fell asleep. When he awaked he would have been gone, saying ' I marvel what they think me to be,' with such other like speeches, showing his dislike thereof. Yet he did tarry till they had ended it, which was after one of the clock."

* *Oxoniana*, i. 113.

There is no record of what further intercourse the
King then had with the College men of learning.
Doubtless he relished them better than the College
wits, since it was not long before Buckeridge was made
a Bishop, and Laud, in spite of some distrust the King,
no doubt from his Calvinist sympathies, had of him, a
Dean. James had already a S. John's man to his
physician, and thus he was prepared to look at the
College in its most serious aspect.

Gwynne's wit (such as it was) descended to John
Sandsbury, Vicar of S. Giles's, a poet the most ingenious, who wrote epigrams, tragedies, and " libellos
de insignibus Collegiorum." Christopher Wren was
another of the same party. He was Andrewes's
chaplain, and a good general scholar and a good orator,
says Aubrey. He became Dean of Windsor. His
brother, as Bishop of Ely, was one of Laud's chief
supporters, and his son was the great Sir Christopher.

To these we may well add a few more of the wits
of the next generation. There was Abraham Wright,
a fellow of infinite jest. It was he who welcomed
Charles I. and Henrietta Maria, to the Library, and
acted in the play that night, " Love's Hospital."
He was already a maker of plays. A few years
earlier, an interlude of his, called " The Reformation," was played " before the University," at S.
John's.* In the next year he published his " Delitiæ
Delitiarum," a quaint collection of sixteenth and seventeenth century epigrams. In 1645 he was appointed
to the Vicarage of Oakham, and in 1656 he was elected
Minister of S. Olave's, Silver-street, but he never

* T. Warton's edition of Milton's poems, pp. 602-3.

obtained legal possession of either benefice till the Restoration (when he declined all honours and went to Oakham) because he would not take " the engagement," or any oath to the Government " de facto." It is worth remembering too, that he was one of the earliest critics of Shakespeare. In a MS. book of his are some shrewd comments on the literature of his day, on the plays of Ben Jonson, Beaumont and Fletcher, on the S. John's man Shirley, and on Shakespeare, with short shrewd comments on the plays. In 1656 he published an audacious volume, " Parnassus Biceps, or several choice pieces of Poetry, composed by the best Wits that were in both the Universities before their dissolution, with an epistle on behalf of those now doubly secluded and sequestered members, by one who himself is none." The boldness of publishing a book full of laudation of the Royalist party, and scoffs at the Puritans, is well worth notice. The book shows that Wright had kept up the traditionary interest of the S. John's Fellows in the neighbourhood. There are two poems on the Fairford windows, curious in their glee that there, almost alone, in the neighbourhood the glass had not been smashed by Puritans.

> " Fairford, boast !
> Thy Church hath kept what all have lost,
> And is preserved from the bane
> Of either war or Puritan.
> Whose life is colour'd in the paint.
> The inside dross, the outside Saint."

His poems were audacious, but more audacious still was his collection of sermons, published in the same year.

" Five sermons in Five severall Styles or Waies of
Preaching; First in Bishop Andrews his way: before the
late King upon the first day of Lent; Second in Bp.
Hall's Way, before the clergie at the author's own ordination in Christ Church, Oxford; Third in Dr. Maine's and
Mr. Cartwright's way: before the Universitie at St.
Marie's, Oxford; Fourth in the Presbyterian way: before
the city at Saint Paul's London; Fifth in the Independent
way: never preached."

This book, with a smart preface containing many
apostolic knocks, was published in 1656.

The author mocked wittily at the prevailing mili-
tarism.   Never, he thinks, in old days, did the minister
of the Gospel " preach or pray in Buffe," and " I do not
find in ecclesiastical storie that old Anselme did ever
command a troop of horse, or Nazianzene a regiment
of foot."   His aim was to discredit the " superstitious
idolising of preaching," by showing that any one could
preach as the sects did.

Wright was a *protégé* of Juxon, who had heard him
speak at Merchant Taylors' School the year before he
was elected scholar and commended his elocution.   In
his *Parnassus* he eulogises his patron as the true ex-
emplar of " the temper,"—the attitude of mind which
should belong to the scholar and the priest.   Most
honoured, he declares, is " that good man " (it was
Charles I.'s name for him) in his affliction.

> " And now more great than when you were
>   O' th' Cabinet * to your King, and Treasurer."

But perhaps the most interesting point about Wright

* This is a very early use of the word in this sense, I believe.

is his adoration of Strafford. We have no knowledge
that the great Lord Deputy was ever at S. John's,
though this century has made stories of his spirit walk-
ing with Laud's in the Library; but his fame evidently
occupied the thoughts of the young loyalists at Oxford.
Wright wrote a Latin theme on him, the "Novissima
Straffordii," which swells with praise of the great statesman and hero.*

A contemporary of Wright's, and another player in
the College entertainments, was George Wilde, who was
afterwards Laud's chaplain, vicar of S. Giles's, Reading,
and at the Restoration became Bishop of Derry. It
was his play which was acted before the royal party in
the College Hall in 1636. Laud left him his "ring
with a toadstone in it." He kept up the Church service
during the suppression in a room in Fleet Street.

Wood says that James Shirley, the last of the great
Elizabethan dramatists,

> "A small clear beacon whose benignant spark
>   Was gracious yet for loiterers' eyes to mark,"

was for a time at S. John's. Certainly he was a
Merchant Taylors' boy, but he took his degree at
Catherine Hall, Cambridge. Wood, nevertheless, is
precise, and he adds a quaint story:

> "At the same time, Dr. William Laud presiding that
house, he had a very great affection for him, especially
for the pregnant parts that were visible in him; but then
having a broad or large mole upon his left cheek which
some esteemed a deformity, that worthy doctor would

* Published in historical papers of the Roxburgh Club, Part I.
London 1846.

often tell him that he was an unfit person to take the sacred function, and should never have his consent to do so."

If the story be true, he may have migrated to Cambridge to secure a college recommendation; but it is probable that Laud noted some moral as well as physical deformity. Shirley became a Roman Catholic, and lived till 1666. He was a prolific dramatist, he served in the wars under the great William Cavendish of Newcastle, he taught school; but no later association of his name with S. John's is known. His dramatic interests and his school training may have attracted him to the College, but it is not possible to say with certainty that he was ever a member of it, for no complete list of commoners is preserved.

Another connection there is, more remote, with the drama, which brings the college within a few paces of association with Shakespeare : John Davenant, "oinopolos," as he is styled in the College books, was a benefactor to the library, and no doubt an "ancient friend and ingle" of some of the Fellows. The Davenant family were London merchants. John (1576–1641) was Bishop of Salisbury. His brother Edward was, says Aubrey, "a better Grecian than the Bishop." John, the Oxford vintner, was "a very grave and discreet citizen," and his wife "a very beautiful woman, and of a very good wit, and of conversation extremely agreeable." Robert, their eldest son, became a Fellow of S. John's. He was chaplain to his uncle, the Bishop, and was like his brother William, the companion of the best wits of the day. A friend and companion of Sir John Suckling, he told Aubrey that it was "on the table of the parlour," in his parsonage at West Kingston, that Suckling's tract on Socinianism was written, during a week, it would seem, "of mirth, wit, and good cheer flowing."

It was at John Davenant's house that Shakespeare would "commonly lie" once a year on his journey into Warwickshire; and Aubrey adds: "I have heard Parson Robert say that Mr. W. Shakespeare has given him a hundred kisses." It is like enough that Shakespeare visited the College, where his old friend was well known, and to which his young friend was to come, and perhaps in S. John's he learnt what little he tells of the manners of Universities. In S. John's Shakespeare may have seen Shirley, certainly he must have seen Laud. And it may be from talks with the playwright that the Archbishop drew his humane view of the stage, which came out many years later, at the trial of Prynne.

"I was never play-hunter," he said then, "but I have observed at Court some Puritans to be at a play because they would not be thought Puritans; and for better testimony that they have been there have stood under the candlestick and been dropped on by the candles, and so have carried away a remembrance of the place. If your lordships, after pains taken in the managing of State affairs, grow weary, what is fitter than to take your recreations? But Mr. Prynne will not allow you to see a play—they are, in his opinion, *mala per se.* But I say, take away the scurf and rubbish which they are incident unto, they are things indifferent." *

It is natural in a college with such associations there

* Laud's Works, vi. 236.

should be no sympathy with the prim Puritans who ruled the University in the first decade of the seventeenth century.

"Dost thou think because thou art virtuous there shall be no more cakes and ale? Yes, by Saint Anne; and ginger shall be hot in the mouth, too."

The reaction against Calvinism, which so largely emanated from S. John's, can hardly be described without touching on the province of other college historians, save by confining the story to the work of the Presidents who succeeded Buckeridge. Laud and Juxon have their part in the history of the nation. Here, as far as may be, the record must be confined to their connection with the College.

William Laud was first a commoner, then a Reading Scholar of the College. At Reading he had been born on October 7, 1573, the son of a large clothier. He was a boy when at the coming of the Armada the loyal enthusiam of the country rose to its greatest height, and it may well be that in those impressionable years he learnt the devotion to the throne for which he was afterwards to suffer. He matriculated on October 17, 1589, and at the next Scholarship election, S. John Baptist's Day 1590, he was chosen to fill the vacant Reading scholarship. There is practically no record of his undergraduate days. The rooms he occupied whether as scholar or Fellow are not known. His 'chamberfellow' John Jones became a Romanist through the influence of Father Gerard in 1596, and being with John Roberts, another member of S. John's in Spain, took the Benedictine habit at the Abbey of S. Martino,

Compostella, and was afterwards known as Dom Leander of S. Martino. Of his later dealings with Laud much was said, but the archbishop could easily show that their old friendship implied no Roman leanings on his part.*

We have already seen that Laud had wide sympathies. Fuller perhaps shall tell us best—though he writes of a later date—what manner of man he was.†

"The Archbishop," says he, "was low of stature, little in bulk, chearful in countenance (wherein gravity and quickness were well compounded), of a sharp and piercing eye, clear judgment, and (abating the influence of age) firm memory. He was very plain in apparel, and sharply checked such clergymen whom he saw go in rich or gaudy cloaths, commonly calling them the church triumphant.

"Thus as Cardinal Wolsey is reported the first prelate who made silks and sattens fashionable amongst clergymen; so this archbishop first retrenched the usual wearing thereof.

"Once at a visitation in Essex, one in orders (of good estate and extraction) appeared before him very gallant in habit, whom Dr. Laud (then Bishop of London) publickly reproved, shewing to him the plainness of his own apparel. My Lord (said the minister) you have better cloaths at home and I have worse, whereat the Bishop rested very well contented." ‡

Laud's personal simplicity indeed is an important

* Mr. Ethelred Taunton's interesting book on the Black Monks (1897), which has much about Jones, throws no new light on his relations with Laud.

† I have endeavoured to restrict this account of Laud as much as possible to a supplement to my *Life* (Methuen & Co., second edition 1896).

‡ Quoted in *Oxoniana*, iv. 73.

element in his character, with which we may well start. He sought always the dignity of the Church, his college, the offices he was to hand on to others, never his own.

He was associated, as we have seen, from the first with the High Church party. Buckeridge was his tutor. From him no doubt he learnt to base his study "above the system and opinions of the age," so that Bishop Young when he ordained him "early presaged that if he lived he would be an instrument of restoring the Church from the narrow and private principles of modern times to the more enlarged, liberal and public sentiments of the apostolic and primitive ages." Through College friends too he would have come to know the great Bishop Andrewes whom he ever profoundly reverenced and whose sermons he prepared for the Press. He was early determined to follow the way of that "lumen orbis Christiani." Another association was less happy. No doubt it was through Richard Latewar that he came to know Charles Blunt, whose chaplain he became when Latewar died, and for whom he made that uncanonical marriage which ever after lay heavy on his heart.

Laud served the offices of grammar reader and divinity lecturer in College. He was ordained deacon in 1600, priest in 1601. He was junior proctor in 1603-4, and won a character for being "civil and moderate." Wood tells a story of the year, no doubt from tradition, thus: " *Thou little morsell of justice, prithee let me alone and be at rest*, quoth a drunken fellow, sleeping on Penniless Bench, Oxon, to Laud of S. John's Coll., then proctor of the

University."* The Proctor's Black Book contains no record of punishment in his time. In college it is clear that he also won a character for lenity. The tale of the porter, Frank Clarke, whom he restored to his place in the lodge, witnesses to it.†

The year after his proctorship he took, as the custom was, his B.D. degree, and then he made his first attack upon ultra-Protestantism. His next was in a sermon before the University when he maintained the Catholicity of the English Church. The Vice-Chancellor at once "convented" him. He was saved by the intervention of Sir William Paddy and the Chancellor. Till then he was deemed a heretic, and, as he told Heylin in later days, a man was suspected of heresy who spoke to him in the streets. Oxford has always been sensitive of a too keen orthodoxy: quite a modern story tells of an undergraduate suspected of Romanism (not at S. John's) because he said the responses in chapel. But from this day Laud came into the outer world, as chaplain to Bishop Neile of Rochester, and as incumbent of several livings. In 1608 he became D.D. In 1610 he resigned his Fellowship, to devote himself entirely to parish work.

But he was not long to be absent from the University. On May 1, 1611, Buckeridge on his appointment to the see of Rochester resigned the Presidentship of S. John's. He "laid a good ground" for Laud's "succession . . . thereby to render him considerable in the University."‡

The history of Laud's election§ is a most dramatic

* Clark, *Wood's Life and Times*, ii. 234, note.
† See *Narcissus* (edited by Miss Lee, 1893) supplement, pp. 35–36.
‡ Heylin, *Cyprianus Anglicus*, p. 60.
§ See Appendix to this chapter.

one.   He did not seek the post himself.   He lay sick, as he said years after, in London, and was neither able to go down nor to write to his friends about it.

There was a "bitter faction against him."   The Archbishop of Canterbury, Abbot, once Master of University, and the Chancellor of the University, Ellesmere, did their best to get the king to interfere even before the election.   The other candidate was Dr. Rawlinson, a former Fellow.   When the day came, May 10, 1611, the feeling was so warm that young Richard Baylie snatched up the voting papers which had been laid on the altar and tore them in pieces.   The case was of course referred to the Visitor.   Bilson, who was then Bishop of Winchester, sent it on to the king, and James I. sat in person for three hours to hear the cause.   The excitement in College was intense.   It appeared as if the Visitor himself had become a party man.   The amount of material for the history of the dispute is copious, and is well worth publication *in extenso*; it can here be only briefly referred to.   It seems several questions arose.   Had the undergraduate Fellows a right to vote?   Was there corrupt influence?   The same sort of charges were bandied about and the same petty intrigues set on foot as, it may be gathered from Mark Pattison's memoirs, are possible even in the nineteenth century.   James showed both tact and patience, and after the investigation he confirmed Laud as President "considering that the election was no farther corrupt and partial than all elections are liable to be."   He then ordered "clearer interpretation of the statutes be made for the future."

At first it appears that his opponents in College

were "very eager and bitter" against him. Not till the audit, and the choice of new officers, did he win his way. "There so God blessed me," he wrote, "with patience and moderation in the choice of all offices, that I made all quiet in the College. And for all the narrowness of my comprehensions (he is jesting at those who called him narrow) I governed that College in peace without so much as the show of a faction, all my time, which was near upon eleven years."

His first act was to make friends with Baylie. His next it would seem was to take in hand the discipline and the material improvement of the College.

One of Laud's earlier regulations for the encouragement of study is worth noting. The register contains the following note:

"Memorandum. That whereas heretofore the hower for supper was five of the clocke, and some inconveniences were found both in regard of the publicke exercises of the College, and particularly men's howers for private studdy, by supping att that hower; and that there is noe hower particularly appointed in statute, but onlie that it should be 'Hora debita' (Statuto de mensis Præsidentis et aliorum); it was thought fitt, and soe decreed, by Mr. President and the ten Seniors, September 14, 1616, that the hower for supper should bee att six of the clocke, and that the Bachelor's disputations, which on Wednesday night were wont to bee att six of the clocke, and after supper, should bee at five of the clocke the same daye, before supper. In witness whereof the said President and ten Seniors have sett their hands."

"Moderate" though he was, Laud was a good disciplinarian. In later years, as Chancellor, he effected

a wholesome reformation in the University at large.
Now he maintained good order in the College.   Instances
of the rules enforced, though they do not belong
strictly to his time, may find place here.

Discipline in the seventeenth century was a more
serious matter than to-day.   There were no silly
attempts to burn colleges down, no diversions of fire-
works and bonfires it is true, for then the undergraduates being much younger than now prided themselves
on being men; but such breaches of decorum as
there were were looked on by the reverend seniors
with a profound disgust, and met with a solemn
punishment.   In the College register it is not uncommon to find quaint expressions of contrition such as
these.

" March 23, 1636.   ·   ·   ·

" I, John Cooke, having been ye second time convented
before ye President and Deans of ye Colledge for disturbing ye publick Prayers by laughing and other insolent
actions whereby I attempted to make others laugh, do
acknowledge my very great fault, humbly submit to the
Punishment imposed upon me of being out of Commons
for twelve days and a confinement to ye Colledge during
ye same time.

" Witness my hand, I. COOKE."

To this are added two other signatures of like
offenders :   T. Makell and Nat. Markwich.

So again, we have many instances of undergraduates
convented for " disturbing the College at a very un-
seasonable hour with rude and disorderly noises."   Or
we may take another instance, Thomas Tuer.

"April 4, 1668.

"Memorandum that I, Thomas Tuer, being convented & convicted before yᵉ Vice-President & Seniors of yᵉ breach of yᵉ Statutes *de Morum honestate* by injuriously striking Sir Waple, was for this my fault according to yᵉ Statutes on yᵗ behalf put out of Commons for 15 days.

"Thomas Tuer."*

A strict attention to discipline was necessary as the numbers of the College grew.

By the beginning of the seventeenth century it is clear that the College had already become popular. A record of the "number of Scholars and students in the University of Oxford A.D. 1612, in the Long Vacation"† shows S. John's as follows:

"Præses	.	.	.	' .	.	1
Socii	.	.	.	.	.	50
Communarii	.	.	.	.	43
Pauperes scholares			.	.	20
Famuli	.	.	.	.	14
						128

This shows that the limitation of commoners had already been abolished.

In 1617 the College was in danger of being burnt, "under the staircase in the chaplain's chamber by the Library," Laud notes in his diary for September 26: Prynne kindly added when he published the garbled extracts in his *Breviate*, "he was very likely to have been burnt by fire in S. John's College in Oxford for

---

* This Thomas Tuer was afterwards Rector of Bardwell, Suffolk.
† *Oxoniana,* ii. 247 *sqq.* from Tanner MSS.

his sins." Among the Archbishop's private devotions is the prayer which he said ever after on the anniversary.

Laud from the first seems to have been eager to enlarge the College. Two years after his election the " Cook's Buildings," to the west of the hall, were begun. The register records that leave was given to Thomas Cook, senior cook of the College, to make a cellar behind the kitchens to serve for a larder in the summer time, and over it a kitchen and over that four sets of rooms, " the rent of which four chambers he and his executors should have for twenty years and then to come to the College." Towards this the College gave three loads of lime, five loads of old stones and nine trees. The lease was dated December 29, 1613, but was surrendered in seven years. The College completed the building in 1638.

In 1616 it was ordered that battlements should be erected on the inside of the quadrangle. Among the Tanner MSS. in the Bodleian Library is:

"A general note of all the expenses layde out about Mending ye Foundation in ye sellar & making a new stayrecaste, with some new Lodgings over ye Kitchen fines (?) Battlementing ye West side of ye College in ye outer quadrangle & making eight faire stone windowes, enlarging ye Hall & Butterie, making three new buttresses against the Hall, with many other parcells of worke as appeared by the several particular bills of ye Workmen & hath beene examined & allowed by Mr. President and ye officers, ANNO DOM. 1616."

Laud's presidentship was a time of quiet work. The College grew in influence under his rule. He himself withstood, and in the end conquered, the extreme

Calvinism which was strong in Oxford in 1611. It has often been told that he was preached at from the University pulpit as a " mongrel compound of Protestant and Papist," and told to "get himself to the other heaven" if there were two. Coarse railing like this defeats its object, and Laud, by his prudence and his determination, was able to build up a great reputation for himself, and for his College. The king sent down injunctions in 1616 to the University for the restraint of rash preachers and the confining of the Divinity studies to "the Fathers and Councils, schoolmen, histories and controversies" in their bearing on Holy Scripture.

In 1616 Laud became Dean of Gloucester, a post the duties of which it was not difficult to combine with those of the headship of S. John's. In 1621 when he was elected Bishop of S. David's, James gave him licence still to retain the presidentship, but this he would on no account do, as it would be in direct violation of the statutes. He resigned on November 17, and next day was consecrated to the Welsh bishopric. He was succeeded as President by William Juxon, of whose life some further detail may well be given.

William Juxon (1582-1663), who lived to be Archbishop of Canterbury and Lord High Treasurer of England, was the son of Richard Juxon of Chichester. He was born in that town, probably in the parish of S. Peter the Great, where he was baptized October 1582. His grandfather John Juxon was a Londoner: the family had long been settled in the City and was closely connected with the Merchant Taylors' Company.* His father resided in Chichester as

* Wilson, *History of Merchant Taylors' School.*

receiver-general of the estates of the see.   He was sent to the Merchant Taylors' School in London.   On June 11, 1597, S. Barnabas Day, when the President and two Senior Fellows of S. John's, always attend at the school to elect scholars to their College for the year, he was chosen to pronounce the customary Latin oration.   On the same day in the following year, Sunday June 11, 1598, he was elected scholar of S. John's. While at Oxford he applied himself chiefly to the study of Law; "eique dubium est an jus Caesareum an Theologiam magis ornarit" says a college annalist.*   He matriculated, May 7, 1602.†   He was admitted Bachelor of Civil Law on July 5, 1603, " being about that time a student in Gray's Inn "‡ as was the fashion then for Oxford Scholars, a fashion to which Laud also conformed by placing his name on the books of Gray's Inn, November 11, 1615. Soon after this he was ordained, and on January 20, 1609 he was nominated by his college to the Vicarage of S. Giles in the City of Oxford, where he "was much frequented for his edifying way of preaching." On January 8, 1616 he resigned the living, having been presented by Mr. Benedict Hatton on June 16, 1615 to the rectory of Somerton, Oxon.   At Somerton he built at his own cost a new rectory house, in which he resided continuously, coming rarely to Oxford till Laud's resignation of the presidency of his college, on December 10, 1621, when he was unanimously elected to the vacant office, on recommendation of Laud.§   He then took the degree of D.C.L.

* Joseph Taylor, in *S. John's College MSS*.

† Juxon, William, Sussex, gen. fil. *æt*. 19, Register of the University, ed. A. Clark.   ‡ Anthony Wood, *Athenæ Oxonienses*.

§ Heylin, *Cyprianus, Anglicus*, and *Clarendon*.

In 1626 and 1627 Juxon was Vice-Chancellor of the University. In January 1626–27, having already been made Prebendary of Chichester and Chaplain in Ordinary to the king, he was appointed Dean of Worcester, on the election of Dr. Joseph Hall to the see of Exeter. In August 1627, as Vice-Chancellor, he received the king at Woodstock with a Latin speech.

From Laud's election as Chancellor of the University in 1630, Juxon was engaged in the reform of the University statutes, and he governed his College with skill and discretion : he was friendly both with Laud's bitter opponent, Dr. Rawlinson, and with his firm friend, Sir William Paddy. On July 10, 1632, he was sworn Clerk of the King's Closet, at Laud's recommendation, "that I might have one that I might trust near his Majesty if I grow weak or infirm."* For several years he had been Laud's chief correspondent at Oxford, writing to him chatty letters of University doings and prophecies of preferment, so that he might see " the good conceit we have of ourselves at Oxford."† He aided him too in the reconciliation of Chillingworth to the English Church. In March 1628, several letters passed between Laud and Juxon on the affair, and Juxon procured interviews between Sheldon (then Fellow of All Souls', and described by Juxon as " an ingenuous and discreet man ") and Chillingworth. Eventually he brought Chillingworth directly under Laud's influence, though he doubted if " all his motives be spiritual, protest he never so much."‡

Towards the end of 1632, Juxon was nominated to

* Laud's *Diary* in his works, "Library of Anglo-Catholic Theology."
† Letters printed in Laud's works, and *Calendar of State Papers.*
‡ For correspondence, see *Calendar of State Papers.*

the see of Hereford, and on January 5, 1633, he resigned
the headship of S. John's College. Before his consecration
Laud procured for him the see of London on his own
election to Canterbury, and on October 3, 1633, he was
consecrated, and from that time he became immersed in
public affairs as well political as ecclesiastical. In his
episcopal office he seems to have enforced the law, and
obeyed the injunctions of Laud, without offending the
people. Lloyd * says that he was " the delight of the
English nation, whose reverence was the only thing all
factions agreed in, by allowing that honour to the
sweetness of his manners that some denied to the sacred-
ness of his function; being by love, what another is
in pretence, the universal bishop."

In the Star Chamber and High Commission, the
records prove him to have been almost always in favour
of lenient sentences. In the case of Prynne, Burton and
Bastwick, like Laud he gave no judgment. As Bishop
of London he shared with the Primate the duty of
licensing books. He was also brought into relation
with foreign religious bodies and was charged with the
supervision of the English congregations on the
continent. A letter of June 21, 1634, to the English
merchants residing at Delft, shows him solicitous for
the observance of the rules of the Church. In the
business of the Scots Prayer Book and Canons he had
some share, the revision being committed to him with
Laud and Wren; he seems, however, to have left the
chief work to his colleagues. He was fully aware of the
difficulties that beset the scheme of reformation ; writing
to the Bishop of Ross on February 17, 1635–36, he .

* *Memoirs of Those that Suffered.*

said, " with your letter of the sixth of this month, I received your book of Canons, which, perchance, at first will make more noise than all the cannons in Edinburgh Castle." *

His zeal and activity as Bishop marked him out for further employment. Laud, during his work on the Treasury, had seen the difficulties of its management, and the need of officials of the strictest probity.

"He had observed," says Heylin, "that divers Treasurers of late years had raised themselves from very mean and private fortunes to the titles and estates of earls, which he conceived could not be without wrong to both king and subjects, and therefore he resolved to commend such a man to his Majesty for the next Lord Treasurer, who having no family to raise, no wife and children to provide for, might better manage the incomes of the Treasury to the king's advantage than they had been formerly."

He desired at the same time to serve the king and dignify the Church, as well as to secure a coadjutor in secular matters on whom he could himself thoroughly rely. Already his friend Windebanke, whom he had made Secretary, seemed turning against him, and he suspected that Cottington was anxious for the Treasurership. He had a list drawn up of all the ecclesiastics who had held that office since the Norman Conquest† and he finally induced the king to give the post to Juxon. No ecclesiastic since George Grey, Bishop of Ely, in 1450, had held the post. "I pray God bless him to carry it so," wrote Laud in his Diary, "that the Church may

* Baillie, ed. Laing. vol. i. p. 438.
† *Calendar of State Papers.*

have honour, and the king and the State service and contentment in it.   And now if the Church will not hold themselves up under God, I can do no more."   On March 6, 1635-6, Juxon received the white staff from the king's hand, and took the oath as a Privy Councillor. The appointment caused great surprise and sharpened the edge of envy and malice against the Archbishop himself.

The multifarious nature of the duties of his different posts may be seen in the Records.   He was concerned with the granting and control of monopolies, the farming of customs, the capture and trial of " Sallee Pirates," with the royal forests, the regulation of trade and ship-building, regulations for the transport of foreign goods in English bottoms, the repair of fortifications, and of the royal palaces and stables, contracts for the victualling of ships, the boom in Dover harbour, the composition for unlicensed buildings in the suburbs, the support of Christian of Denmark, the draining of the fenlands, the Great Level and Eight Hundred Fen, the appointment to all naval offices under the rank of captain, the licences for the transportation of oysters. He was appointed to report on innumerable petitions, he received arguments " proving the King's Majesty's propriety in the sea-lands and saltshores thereof," and concerning the king's " assumption of all the saltpetre of the land into his own hands to be converted into gunpowder."

He was present at Laud's reception of the king and queen at S. John's College, when the new library and rooms were thrown open.   Of this more anon.   He had hit upon the marble used for the pillars when hunting at Bletchingdon.

It has seemed desirable thus to treat the life of Juxon, because it is so little known, and because it shows the important position of the College which had him, as well as Laud, for its advocate before the king.

It must not be thought, however, that in spite of the powerful influences at work, that the "Laudian movement" was without check even in S. John's itself. In the year in which Juxon resigned the Headship, Richard Spinke, one of the Fellows, made a violent attack on the dominant party. On May 17, 1632, he read a very strong anti-Laudian "commonplace" in Chapel. He attacked the ceremonial revival and he touched the Bishop of London himself not obscurely. S. Paul, he said, "would never have given his consent that those who had once professed themselves of this calling [the ministry] should leave the word of God to serve tables— no, not council tables."* The matter was not taken lightly. The College resented the attack on its great patron, and in February 1633 Spinke was forced to read a recantation in the College Chapel and in congregation.†

While Juxon and Laud were watching over the interests of the College, the one in Oxford, the other in the world, the College had a third, and in his way, a no less notable benefactor. The Choir and the Library, representing the most characteristic features of the old foundation, "true religion and sound learning," were to owe much to a distinguished layman and physician. The earlier years of the century show that both needs were recognised.

---

* Tanner, MSS. 303, fol. 108.
† "In domo Regentium in plena congregatione."

John Lee, by his will in 1609, left £70 towards the restoration of the "College Quire," whensoever it shall be. The receipt of Sir William Paddy's benefaction gave probably the first opportunity to the College to utilise this gift.

Already, in 1619, an organ was set up "on the north side of the Chapel," and a "window taken down to set it up"—presumably where the Baylie Chapel now stands. The Library also was remembered. December 12, 1633, a "Library Keeper" was elected. His "wages," says the minute in the Register, were to be paid from the rent of the "new chambers" (presumably the cook's building). The wages were thus to continue till Sir William Paddy should augment them, as he promised to do, "with forty shillings." The Library had now been "in compleat sort replenished with books," by Sir Thomas Tresham and Sir William Paddy. Many earlier gifts of books had, of course, been made, the most noteworthy being the bequest of Henry Price in 1600, of books then valued at £134. Paddy added a magnificent collection of medical literature.

His career is one that should not be forgotten in S. John's.

William Paddy was born in London in 1554. He was entered on the register of Merchant Taylors' School January 15, 1568–69. Thence he proceeded in due course to S. John's, not, however, as a scholar with right of succession to a fellowship, but as a commoner. From Oxford, as a B.A., after the fashion of the time, he passed over to Holland to study medicine in the best school of the age. Holland was the teacher of

Europe in anatomy and physiology: Rembrandt's "Dissecting School," is, as it were, a figure of the service which the Dutch were doing for the world. Their schools were cosmopolitan: and they gave the only scientific training that the age afforded. Paddy returned to England already famous. He had taken the degree of Doctor in Medicine at Leyden. He applied to be incorporated in that degree at Oxford.

The courtesy of learning was then maintained by a great freedom in admitting graduates of one University to status at another. Paddy "supplicated," October 22, 1591, but was not actually incorporated as D.M. till July 11, 1600. Meanwhile he had been engaged in practice in London. He then became attached to the Royal College of Physicians (he became Fellow, September 25, 1591), and he received in turn all its highest honours. Of his reputation in London we hear from Anthony Wood that he was "esteemed one of the prime physicians of his time." He was highly valued by the chief men of his faculty and especially by Sir Theodore Mayerne, who was admitted to be the leading physician of the day. The culmination of his dignity was reached when he became physician to the king, and was knighted on July 9, 1603. He had probably attracted the king's notice by his verses on the death of Queen Elizabeth, in which he said of James "Solus eris Solomon." It was now no longer necessary for him to devote himself wholly to his profession, and he sat in Parliament for Thetford from 1604 to 1611. He had become a prominent public man. The College of Physicians were glad to secure his advocacy in 1614 when he vindicated the claims of their members to immunity from providing arms.   When James came to Oxford in 1605, Paddy debated two medical theses before him.   In one he attacked smoking as dangerous to health, doubtless to the king's great satisfaction.

How closely he attended the king during his health is not clear ; but James was not a man to pay heed to the advice of physicians.   At fifty-eight, the royal patient was beyond the help of the medicine of the time.   Constant attacks of gout had at last combined with a " quartan ague meeting many humours," says Clarendon, " in a fat unwieldy body."   Bishop Williams in his funeral sermon * describes the king's last hours, and dwells upon his attachment to Catholic doctrine, and his reliance upon the absolution which he earnestly desired.   Shorter, and very touching in their simplicity, are the few words which Sir William Paddy wrote in the king's prayer-book given to him after his master's death, and by him placed in the Library of S. John's College.   The book is a Common Prayer printed by Barker 1615, and bound in leather, stamped in gold with the royal arms and the letters I. R.   On the fly-leaves at the end are written the special prayers which the Archbishop and Bishop Williams said by the dying king, and after them in Sir William Paddy's hand his own account of the end, with the date, Martii 27, 1625. The account is as follows : †

" Beyng sent for to Thibaulde butt two daies before the death of my soveraigne Lord and master King James : I

* " Great Britain's Salomon, a sermon preached at the magnificent funeral of the most high and mighty King James, the late king of Great Britain, France and Ireland, &c." London 1625, pp. 68 *sqq*

† It has been printed in *Oxoniana*, vol. ii. p. 235-6.

held it my Christian dutie to prepare hym, telling hym that there was nothing left for me to doe (in y⁰ afternoone before his death y⁰ next daie att noone) butt to pray for his soule.   Whereupon y⁰ Archbishop & y⁰ Lord Keeper, byshop of Lincolne, demaunded yf His⸱ Majestie would be pleased that they shold praye wᵗʰ Hym, whereunto he cheerfullie accorded.   And after short praier these sentences were by y⁰ Bishop of Lincolne distinctlie pronounced unto hym, who with his eies (the messenger of his Hart) lyfted up unto Heaven, att the end of every sentence, gave to us all therby, a godlie Afsurance of those graces and livelie faith, wherunᵗᵒ He apprehended the merite of our Lord and onelie Saviour Christ Jesus, accordinglie as in his godlie life he had often publiquelie expressed.   Will: Paddy."

Paddy was now over seventy years old, and he retired to Oxford to spend the rest of his days in quiet.   He had always borne a singular attachment to his old College, and it is in this connection that his position as a prominent layman greatly interested in ecclesiastical affairs chiefly appears.   As early as 1606, when Laud had offended the Vice-Chancellor, Dr. Airay, by a sermon before the University in which he proclaimed the Catholic doctrine and position of the English Church, Sir William Paddy went to intercede with the Chancellor, the Earl of Dorset, on his behalf. Lord Dorset at once wrote to Dr. Airay, speaking of Sir William as his "good friend, a man religious, learned, and one whom I love and trust."   Paddy had reported that he himself had been present at the sermon for which Laud was "convented" and that he heard nothing that might give any just cause of offence—moreover that "some two or three very learned men about the Court had seen and considered of his sermon and had given approbation of the same." The Chancellor's suggestion of a reference to the Archbishop of Canterbury and the Bishop of London caused the Vice-Chancellor hastily to retreat from his opposition and to cease all proceedings against Laud.

Paddy was indeed a warm friend to Laud throughout his early struggles, as he was "a worthy benefactor to his poor College." He was not only influential at Court but also intimate with the learned men of the day. Through him Laud made the acquaintance of Sir Robert Cotton to whom he lent "an ancient volume of *Beda* from the College Library."

The Court physician was not only interested in the rising fame of the young Fellow of his old College; he never ceased to keep up his connection himself with S. John's. In the Christmas festivities of 1607 his subscription towards the entertainment was the largest given.*

When he returned to reside permanently in Oxford rooms were assigned to him in the College—a "lodging" which now stands between the two quadrangles, the inner of which Laud designed while Paddy was still alive, planning a "flying stair" to his apartment.†

While he lived he did his best to adorn the College; in 1618 he gave a "pneumatic organ of great cost;"‡ and by his gifts he began the fine collection of early

---

* Sir William Paddye, £3. *The Christmas Prince:* College MSS.
† Aug. 15, 1630, *Works,* vol. vii. pp, 196–7.
‡ See Laud's Works, iii. 136.

medical books which is one of the treasures of the Library. It was his ambition also that the choir should be a rival to those of the earlier and greater foundations, and for this purpose he bequested £2800. To this he added by a codicil £400. From this benefaction the township of Wood Bevington was purchased in 1636,* and the "skilful organist" was paid from the rents, with eight singing men and four choristers. In advanced age Paddy still occasionally attended to the duties of his profession. In June 1634, only six months before his death, he signed a certificate on the case of Chief Justice Richardson, recommending his going to Bath "towards the end of the summer" because he was in danger of palsy. A few years later Archbishop Neile recommended for the post of apothecary to S. Thomas's Hospital one Rouswell as "much used by our auncient friend Sir W. Paddy"—evidently during the last years of his life.

At length, full of years and honours, he passed away. His College made haste to commemorate him, and she still recalls his name among the chiefest of her benefactors. His picture was given to the College by his pupil and colleague, Dr. Gibbons. It represents a tall thin man with black hair and close-trimmed beard, in the red gown of a Doctor of Medicine. It still hangs in the College Library. Another portrait, now in the hall, represents the knight at full length dressed in black.

An elaborate monument was erected in the College Chapel, where his coloured bust depicts him in old age,

* Licence in Mortmain dated March 10, 1636.—*Calendar of State Papers.*

with small moustache and short straight close-clipped
beard.   The lengthy inscription, while it witnesses to
the affection and reverence of the learned society in
which he spent his last years, contrasts curiously with the
simple words on that famous monument in the great
church of the city where he had first studied the healing
art—*Salutifero Boerhavii genio sacrum.*   As an "incom-
parable soul" he was well worthy of his elaborate
memorial.*

Bishop Buckeridge died on May 23, 1631.   He left
some altar furniture for the chapel, and some money to
be spent in lands.

The bequest of Sir William Paddy supplemented by
that of Bishop Buckeridge was used to purchase land
for the endowment of the choir.

"Sir William Paddy's benefaction .	£3200
Bishop Buckeridge's „ . .	500
	£3700

This sum was paid to Ferrers Randolph for the village
or hamlet of Wood Bevington in the parish of Salford,
Warwickshire, formerly in the possession of the Abbat
and Convent of the Monastery of Kenilworth.   Adam
Torless, Laud's faithful steward and friend, acted for the
College in taking possession.

Paddy's benefaction was left under the visitation of

* The interesting article in the *Dictionary of National Biography,*
though it is full of information, contains some errors which deserve
correction here.   Paddy was never a Fellow of S. John's.   The
prayer-book in which he wrote his account of James I.'s last hours
had belonged to the king.   The College possesses three portraits of
him.

Laud ; and by his direction it was placed on a secure
footing, the regulation then drawn up (May 25,
1638) lasting till our own day.

APPENDIX

Calendar of Documents Relating to the Election of a President of S. John's College, Oxford, in 1611

Contained in MS. Tanner 338, Bodleian Library. Probably from
Laud's own Library. [The College Register supplements and
occasionally duplicates these.]

Folio

328. [The Visitor's statement of the evidence given by
     certain of the Fellows against the validity of Laud's
     election, with marginal comments, probably by the
     Lord Keeper, Egerton.]

330. "Mr. Towse his Cause as he will depose it. 22 Aug.
     1611." [Signed by him.]

331. [Statement, on the part of Juxon, Jackson and Tuer,
     concerning the conduct of Downer.]

332. [Replies to] "Ob. against Dr. Laud, Aug. 22, 1611 "
     [signed by Theoph. Tuor, Edm. Jackson, John Towse,
     Dan. Washbourne, Chr. Wrenn, Chr. Ryley and Wm.
     Rippin.]

333. "That the Fellowes not Graduatts went out of the
     Chappell voluntarilye &c. They would have givē
     Dr. Laud their voices hadd they knowen &c. Aug.
     22, 1611." [Signed by Chr. Ryley and Wm. Rippin.]

335. [Depositions by Richard Williams, Fellow of All
     Souls, endorsed :] "Mr. Tuer about a speeche of his
     to Mr. Morris & Mr. Anderton. This agrees with
     the originall takē August 24, 1611."

336–7. "The Examinations of Mr. Tuer, Mr. Juxon, &
     Mr. Towse. With other observations sent to his

Majestie bye the L: B: of Winton: in his letters, Septemb: 1 : 1611."

338. [The Visitor's letter to Laud and the Fellows, Oct. 9, 1611, giving the King's decision.]

340. "Mr. Jackson & Sr Grice about two schollers &c. Aug. 22, 1611."

342. [Extracts from the Registers of the University to prove that] "Thear wear Vndergraduatts Fellowes att the tymes of Election of D^r. Matthewe & M^r. Willis to the Presidentshipp of St. Johns.   Aug. 22, 1611."

344. [Extracts from the College Registers to the same effect.]

345. "The Visitor's letter to ye Kinge & exceptions. August 5, 1611."

346. "Julij 30, 1611.   The Coppye of D. Lauds Petition wch he himeself deliuered at Basinges."

347. "Julij 30, 1611.   The Coppye of the petition wch Mr. Tewer deliuered att Basynge," [on behalf of Juxon, Jackson, and himself.]

348. "To the Kinges Most Excellent Maiestye.   The humble petition of R^d. Andrewes D. of Divinitie Vice President of St. John's Coll : in Oxford with other the Fellowes and Schollers of the sayd Colledge. This Coppye of petition was not deliuered, but left with my L: of Litchfeeld, with hands to it."

349. [Another copy with some alterations.]

350. "Julij 20, 1611.   The L : B: of Winchester's Decisiõ that Undergraduat fellowes ar to give voice in the Election of a President of St. Johns in Oxford. This was his finall decision."

352. "Julij 11, 1611.   A Coppye of o^r Acts sent to the L. B. of Winchester bye Felix Swaddlinge Porter of the Colledge, in answeare to his Decision sent by Mr. Tilleslye.   Dated Junij 28, 1611."

354. " The proof for the offer of the three seniours to be scrutatours.   And the Vndergraduatts voluntarye goinge out of the Chappell.   Julij 10, 1611."

356. " The Coppye of his Majesties letters sent to the L. B. of Winchester for the Confirmatiō of Dr. Laud in the Presidentshipp of St. Johns.   I receaued thiss letter Septemb : 25, 1611."

358. " Maij 14. 1611.   A Coppye of the Instrument of Dr. Lauds Admission to the Presidentshipp of St. Johns."

360. " Aug. 23. 1611.   The sexton of St. Johns Colledge " [Thoˢ. Bowyer] " warned other Fellowes to be present att the seale for Dʳ. Lauds Admission " [May 11. 1611.]

362. [July 10. 1611.   Signed testimonies (4) by the Vice-President and several other Fellows as to the conduct of the parties adverse to Laud on the 10th of May, 1611.]

363. " June 9. 1611."   [Copy, without signatures, of an account by the Vndergrduates Fellowes of the proceedings in the Chappell on the 10th of May.]

364. " Instructions of the forme of electinge the President of St. John Baptists Colledge in Oxford.   And the Oath that the fellowes take.   Collected against Maij 10. 1611. Dʳ. Lauds Election daye."

365. " Mʳ. Cliff.   His letter about his Conference with D : Benfeeld "   " From Oxon this 5 of Maie 1611."   [Enclosing the next document.]

366. " Mʳ. Cliffs Conference with Dʳ. Benfeild about the youths graces."   [Attested by Thomas Loueden and Francis Hudson.]

367. " The Originall Citation.   Maij 3. 1611."   [by the Vice-President, John Sone and Martin Okin.]   [Sealed.]

368. "To the Kings most excellent Matie : 'The humble
petition of Christopher Reelye, William Harris, &
William Rippin, fellowes of St. Johns Colledge in
Oxford." [Apparently a draft, unsigned and undated.]

369–72. [Four documents relating to the subject of the
above petition, viz., Dr. Benfield's action, as Deputy
Vice-Chancellor, in staying the petitioners from
taking their degree of B.A.]

373–88. "The Estate of St. Johns Colledge in Oxford
Ann: 1611. Which was the first Auditt after
D^r. Laud came to be President."
"And howe I left it Nouĕb: 17. 1621."

In this list, though the order is not strictly chronological, the course of the dispute on the important
election which gave S. John's as president its greatest
benefactor can be clearly traced, with its results in
punishment by delay of their degrees of the most
prominent rioters.

CHAPTER VIII

THE CANTERBURY BUILDINGS AND THE TROUBLES

On Juxon's resignation, Richard Baylie B.D. was elected on January 12, 1633. He had matriculated on July 3, 1601, at the age of fifteen, and taken the B.A. July 3, 1605, M.A. June 27, 1609, B.D. July 18, 1616. He was a conspicuous instance of Laud's generosity. The bitterest of that great man's opponents in 1611, twenty years later he was his close friend and kinsman. After his violent and disorderly conduct at the election to the Presidency it was doubtful if he would not be expelled from his fellowship; but after full consideration the Visitor had decided that his offence might be forgiven.*

Laud's tact and freedom from personal aim soon won over the hasty partisan. In the earlier years of Laud's presidency he became his supporter in the discreet governance of the College, and he remained the friend of his successor Juxon. It was some time, as we have already seen, before matters were quiet in College. On June 30, 1624, we have a letter from Bishop Andrewes,

* See College MSS. (Muniments) lii. 128. Bishop Bilson's decision that Baylie was not to be expelled for tearing the voting paper.

then Visitor, sharply insisting on the observance of the statutes and the avoiding of unseemly squabbles.* But as the College came more prominently before the world, wider interests overcame the petty personal affairs which had led to internal disagreement. With Laud's appointment to Canterbury, 1633, the College seems to enter on a new life.

Every one connected with the first days of the foundation had now passed away. In 1631 the last link with the days of the Founder was broken: in that year the College annalists noted the death, in the eighty-sixth year of her age, " being more ripe in goodness than in years," of Mrs. Amy Leech, wife to Mr. William Leech, Master of Arts, and niece to Sir Thomas White. A " most worthy and reverend gentlewoman," they called her; and it is clear that she retained her interest in the College, and that a sort of Founder's interest, till the last.†   The record of the Founder was tending now to become almost a hagiology.   The College had found an eloquent "laudator temporis acti," who embalmed the fame of the great merchant in the choicest Latin of the time.   Griffin Higgs, a scholar of the College, who took the B.A. in 1611, and became à Fellow of Merton in the same year, gave the College, for the first time, a formal life of its Founder.‡   Higgs had commemorated, too, the " Christmas Prince," and without ceasing to be loyal in his attachment to S. John's he became a loyal

* College MSS. (Muniments) lii. 132.

† See College MS. 213; verses on the death of the most worthy Mrs. Amy Leech.

‡ See College MS, 52; Nativitas, Vita, Mors Honoratissimi illustrissimique viri Thomæ White militis aurati . . . authore Griffino Higgs.

son and a generous benefactor to Merton College. His connection with the Court, as a royal chaplain, and chaplain to Elizabeth, the Electress Palatine, and for so brief a space Queen of Bohemia, is another instance of the close association between Charles I. and the sons of S. John's. Of those who had been undergraduates or Fellows of the College during Laud's Oxford residence it would be interesting to see how many were afterwards attached to the Court and promoted by the Archbishop. Higgs, like Sir William Paddy, took his Doctor's degree at Leyden and was incorporated therein at Oxford.

The Presidentship of Baylie was to be marked by a special effort to extend the influence and the usefulness of the College. Laud found in him a ready assistant in his determination, made as early as November 1630, " to build at S. John's in Oxford, where I was bred up, for the good and safety of that College." Baylie had on April 3, 1626, married Laud's niece Elizabeth, the daughter of his sister (the issue of his mother's first marriage), whose husband was Dr. William Robinson, Prebendary of Westminster, and Rector of Long Whatton. Already, in 1621, Laud had nominated him Chancellor of S. David's (he resigned in 1626), and in 1626 he had resigned in his favour the rectory of Ibstock. From that date preferments, after the fashion of the time, were heaped upon him ; when he became President of S. John's he was already Archdeacon of Nottingham, and two years later he was made Dean of Salisbury.

Something has already been said of the beginnings of Laud's buildings at S. John's. The first stone was laid on July 26, 1631, of what was to be one of the most beautiful buildings in Oxford. The king gave timber from the royal forests of Shotover and Stow : the rest of the material and all other expenses came entirely from Laud.

The design was first to complete the inner quadrangle, of which the south side, the old library, had been finished in 1596. An east front, looking upon the Groves, was designed, it would appear, in accord with the work already existing. A north side contained private rooms, designed for the accommodation of rich commoners, and not, as Laud expressly stated, for the members of the foundation. The west already had a narrow line of building, partly occupied by the President's lodgings, partly by two sets of chambers, one of which, it appears, had been held by Sir William Paddy. To this Laud added new rooms, a long gallery to the President's house, and a corresponding inner room to the private chambers. Underneath this addition, and on the opposite side, under what was to be the new library, were cloisters " of a form not yet seen in Oxford, for that," as Juxon wrote, " under Jesus College Library is a misfeatured thing."

It has been the custom to assert that Inigo Jones designed the building that has long been considered one of the architectural glories of Oxford ; and this has been repeated with more or less confidence by architects and historians of the last two centuries.* But search up to the present has failed to discover the slightest evidence for the attribution.

For a characteristic expression of the effect of the work, I do not know where better to look than to the

* *E.g.*, W. J. Loftie, *Inigo Jones and Wren*, p. 33.

“ History of Architecture ” of a great Oxford writer who well knew the details of the building.*   A revival of Gothic, Mr. Freeman would call the work, rather than Renaissance.

“ The Collegiate buildings in Oxford afford, as might reasonably be expected, an excellent study of the progressive decay of Gothic architecture.   At the same time it must be allowed that this view is one which exhibits the declining architecture of England to the best advantage, and moreover the late Gothic of Oxford was rather a return to, than an actual continuance of, the older forms. Yet in this point of view it is still more interesting; a deliberate return to Gothic architecture is a fact more valuable for our purpose than a mere lifeless retention of its forms. . . . ”

So far by way of introduction—but he adds :

“ It is a most remarkable fact that the revived Gothic of Oxford, a truer and better Renaissance than that which usually monopolises the name, actually improved and developed as it went on.   Laud’s buildings at S. John’s College are indeed an exception. Even these are in general outline Gothic, but in their Gothic features much more Italian or rather nondescript detail has intruded itself than in the structures already mentioned; and, farther than this, the cloister, though supporting a Gothic upper story, consists of round arches on single columns. Yet even this is Basilican rather than Italian; it is the very arrangement against which classical pedants so bitterly cry out in the first Christian Churches. But this erection was extraneous rather than native : it was not the genuine production of the Oxford school, but an intrusion of the court architect, Inigo Jones.”

* *History of Architecture,* E. A. Freeman, p. 436.

The mingling of the classical with the tall Perpendicular domestic architecture of the time so skilfully and with such originality is certainly the remarkable feature of the work, but it is impossible, when the detail is examined, to forget certain Spanish work of the same date, or how the court-yards of great English houses, had gradually been coming to something of the same development. Mr. Reginald Blomfield has recently shown, by a comparison of the Patio Casa de la Infanta at Saragossa with the court-yard at Knowle, how differently the same feature could be treated by architects of different countries.* The quadrangle at S. John's however bears a much closer remembrance to the Spanish (though it is much less rich) than to the English work.

But to continue:

"Now is it too much to suppose," says Mr. Freeman, "that this decided revival and strong adherence to the old Northern and Christian forms is but the material reflection of that Catholic movement in the English Church which has immortalised the names of Andrewes and Laud, and a host of inferior worthies? Of course we are not to look for any direct influence; the very structure raised in Oxford by the martyred Archbishop paganises, as we have seen, more than any contemporary building in the University, and it was under his auspices that the most fatal changes were inflicted upon old S. Paul's. But under the notion which I have all along taken of the deeper meaning of architecture, there is no absurdity in supposing an unconscious influence to have emanated from a source which would have actually disclaimed it. We might even suppose, though I know not of any actual

* See an interesting paper on "Some Architects of the English Renaissance" in the *Portfolio*, 1888.

authority for the supposition, that Laud despised Gothic architecture, and yet that its revival was owing to the spirit which he kindled. The most remarkable feature of this page in the history of architecture is its being so strictly a *revival.* Its date exactly coincides with the period when there was so eminent a revival of catholic feeling and doctrine; the age of Elizabeth, in Oxford emphatically the age of Puritanism, produced no building of any consequence; the revived Gothic dates, as we have seen, from the reign of James the First."

The building generally is of Headington stone and on inspection in 1887 it was found to be generally sound, the surface only peeling. The mouldings are in Headington stone, and some of the copings of Bath stone, some of Taynton stone, from the quarries near Burford.

The decoration of the colonnades, it should be observed, was according to a defined scheme. On the west side the figures represent Religion, Charity, Hope, Faith, Temperance, Fortitude, Justice, and Truth, and the spaces are filled with appropriate detail. On the east side are Astronomy, Architecture, Music, Poetry, Mathematics, Philosophy, Rhetoric, Literature. Thus the one side represents " true Religion " the other " sound Learning."

The " Canterbury Quadrangle " took five years in building. It was finished in 1636; and the total cost, it would appear, was £3208 4*s.* 3*d.** " If their gratitude were mute," the College had written to their benefactor,

---

* *Cf. Calendar of State Papers* for details of the progress. The completion is notified by Baylie to Laud, April 26, 1636. *Cf. William Laud,* by W. H. Hutton, p. 110.

" the very stones of their college would like the statue of Memnon commemorated by Tacitus, give forth music to his glory." The new buildings were given the distinction of a royal inauguration. Laud had shown his loyalty in the decoration of the east and west of his quadrangle with life-size bronze statues of the king and queen, by Herbert le Sueur, the most famous sculptor of the day * at the cost of £400, and a gilded bust of Charles also decorated the Library. The sculptor had most probably already been employed to give the College a representation of its great benefactor. Two busts, both probably by Le Sueur and both dated 1633, are in the possession of the College, one in the library and one in the President's lodgings.

For the year 1636 Laud (Chancellor of the University since 1630) appointed Baylie Vice-Chancellor, and thus all the official dignity of Oxford was centred in S. John's. It was arranged that the king as usual should stay at Christ Church but that he should be entertained by contributions from all the colleges. Plays were still deemed to be the fittest amusement for him, and it was arranged that they should be given at Christ Church, but Laud added, " for the play which I intend shall be at S. John's, I will neither put the University nor the College to any charge, but take it wholly upon myself. And in regard of the great trouble and inconvenience I shall thereby put upon that house as also in regard it shall set out one of the plays by itself, I think there is great reason in it, and do therefore expect it, that no

---

* See *Calendar of State Papers*, May 2, 1633, and May 8, 1634, where Le Sueur's receipt is given. I cannot understand why they have been so persistently attributed to Fanelli.

contribution should be required from S. John's towards the plays at Christ Church."

On Monday April 29 the king and queen with the Elector Palatine and his brother Prince Rupert entered Oxford from Woodstock. They were met by a distinguished train of citizens and University officials, five Masters of Arts holding offices, then the Proctors, then the Doctors, followed by the Bishops of Winchester (Curle), Oxford (Bancroft), Norwich(Wren), and London (Juxon), the last now Lord Treasurer. Last of all before the Sovereigns rode Laud as Chancellor with the bedells before him. As they passed S. John's Mr. Thomas Atkinson, Fellow of the College, made a brief speech, which was " very much approved of by his Majesty afterwards to me," says Laud. So on to Christ Church.

Next at Convocation the two Palatine princes were admitted Masters of Arts and their names were " by his Majesty's leave entered in S. John's College to do that house that honour for my sake."* After the Convocation the king joined the queen in her coach " and they went away to S. John's to dinner, the princes and nobles attending them." The rest had best be told in Laud's own words.

" When they were come to S. John's, they first viewed the new building, and that done, I attended them up the library stairs ; where so soon as they began to ascend, the music began, and they had a fine short song fitted for them as they ascended the stairs. In the library they

* What is the ground for supposing Prince Rupert to have been a member of Magdalen College? It would be a gracious act of that College to present its portrait of him to the College of which he was a member.

were welcomed to the college with a short speech made
by [Abraham Wright] one of the fellows."

This was the " short speech," afterwards published as

A COPY OF VERSES

*Spoke to King Charles by way of entertainment
when he was pleas'd to grace S. John's
Colledge with his visit.   1636.*

Were they not Angells sang, did not mine eares
Drink in a sacred Anthem from yon sphears?
Was I not blest with Charles and Maries name,
Names wherein dwells all musick? tis the same.
Hark, I myself now but speak Charles and Mary,
And 'tis a poem, nay 'tis a library.

All haile to your dread Majesties, whose power
Adds lustre to our feast, and to our Bower :
And what place fitter for so Royall guests
Then this, where every book presents a feast.
Here's Virgils well-drest venison, here's the wine
Made Horace sing so sweetly ; here you dine
With the rich Cleopatra's warelike love ;
Nay you may feast and frolick here with Jove.
Next view that bower, which is as yet all green
But when you'r there, the red and white are seen.
A bower, which had (tis true) been beautified
With catechising Arras on each side ;
But we the Baptists sons did much desire
To have it like the dwelling of our sire
A grove or desart.   See (dread Liege) youle guesse
Even our whole Colledge in a wildernesse.
Your eyes and eares being fed, tast of that feast,
Which hath its pomp and glory from its guest.*

* Wright, *Parnassus Biceps*, pp. 121-2.

Laud continues:

"And dinner being ready, they passed from the old into the new library, built by myself, where the king, the queen, and the prince elector dined at one table, which stood cross at the upper end. And prince Rupert with all the lords and ladies present, which were very many, dined at a long table in the same room. All other several tables, to the number of thirteen besides these two, were disposed in several chambers of the college, and had several men appointed to attend them; and I thank God I had that happiness, that all things were in very good order, and that no man went out at the gates, courtier or other, but content; which was a happiness quite beyond expectation."

The dinner was quaintly served. A diarist of the times says that "the baked meats were so contrived by the cook that there was first the forms of archbishops, then bishops, doctors, &c., seen in order, wherein the king and courtiers took much content."

Thus did the local wit recall the scene:

EPULAE OXONIENSES

*Or a jocular relation of a banquet presented to the
best of kings, by the best of prelates, in the
year 1636 in the mathematick library
at St. John Baptists Colledge.*

THE SONG.

I.

It was (my staff upon 't) in Thirty Six,
Before the notes were wrote on great Don Quix
That this huge feast was made by that high priest

From a Photo by the]   [Oxford Camera Club

CANTERBURY QUADRANGLE

Who did caress the Royalist of guests
Oves and Boves, yes and Aves too
Pifces, and what the whole Creation knew.

II.

For every creature there was richly dreſt
As numerous as was great Nevils feaſt
Here we crave leave only to make you smile
(For in the Terme we must be grave a while)
At the exhibit of a banquet brought
Where all our gown men were in marchpane wrought.

III.

The ladies watered 'bout the mouth to see
And tast so sweet an Univerſitie.
In mighty chargers of most formal past
A convocation on the board was plac't:
In Capp and Hood and Narrow-ſleeved gown
Juſt as you ſee them now about the Town.

IV.

With this conceited difference alone.
The Scholars now do walk but then did run.
There might you see in honour of his place,
Mr Vice-Chancellor with every mace,
The greater Staffs in thumping marchpane made,
In smaller, the ſmall stick of the ſmall blade.

V.

And after these, as if my brethrens call
Had fetch't them up (Sol, Hal, & Stout Wil: Ball)
In humble postures of a bowing leg
Appear'd the Doctors, Masters, Reg. non Reg.
Then in a maſs, a ſort of various Capps
(But could not hum, for sealed were their Chaps).

VI.

Crouded the Senate, as if they'd mind to heare
Some fpeech, or fall upon themfelves the cheare.
It put their majefties unto the laugh
To fee the Bedels refigne up every staff,
And were eat up, not as it us'd to be
Returned by his gracious majeftie.

VII.

I think that Jeffry waiting on the Queen
Devoured at one Champ the Verger clean.
But then (O rude !) as at a Proctors choice
In run the Mafters, juft like little boyes,
So did the Ladies, and their servants fall
Upon the Marchpane fhew, Doctors and all.

VIII.

The noble men like to Clarifsimos,
Grandees of Venice, did adorne thefe shews
In velvet round Caps fome, and fome in square,
(A spectacle most excellent and rare)
But their good Ladyfhips moft courteoufly
Simperd and eat the soft nobilitie.

IX.

Never was Oxford in fuch woful cafe
Vnless when Pembroke did expound the place :
Here lay a doctors scarlet, there a Hood
Trod under foot, which others fnatched for food
Capp, Gowns and all formalities were rent
As if the fhew had been ith' schools at Lent.

CHORUS.

If in the Trojan horfe inclofed were
Men of the Helmet, Target, Sword and Speare,

If by Ingenious Pencil ere was cut
The Learned Homers Illiads in a nut,
Why in a Bisk or Marchpane Oleo
Might not a Convocation be a fhew
Where for to please the beauteous ladies bellies,
Mafters were fet in paft, Scholers in jellies.*

After dinner came the play.   Laud says :

"When dinner was ended, I attended the king and the queen together with the nobles into several withdrawing chambers, where they entertained themselves for the space of an hour.   And in the meantime I caused the windows of the hall to be shut, the candles lighted, and all things made ready for the play to begin.   When these things were fitted, I gave notice to the king and the queen, and attended them into the hall whither I had the happiness to bring them by a way prepared from the president's lodging to the hall without any the least disturbance; and had the hall kept as fresh and cool, that there was not any one person when the king and queen came into it.   The princes, nobles, and ladies entered the same way with the king, and then presently another door was opened below to fill the hall with the better sort of company, which being done, the play was begun and acted.   The plot was very good, and the action.   It was merry and without offence, and so gave a great deal of content.   In the middle of the play, I ordered a short banquet for the king, the queen, and the lords.   And the college was at that time so well furnished, as that they did not borrow any one actor from any college in town. The play ended, the king and the queen went to Christ

* Then follow two pages.   On one, first verse set to music ; on the other, chorus set to music.   The piece was by Edmund Gayton, superior Bedel of Arts, 1638.   He apparently lived in S. John's; see p. 153.

Church, retired and supped privately, and about eight o'clock went into the hall to see another play, which was upon a piece of a Persian story. It was very well penned and acted, and the strangeness of the Persian habits gave great content; so that all men came forth from it very well satisfied. And the queen liked it so well, that she afterwards sent to me to have the apparel sent to Hampton Court, that she might see her own players act it over again, and see whether they could do it as well as it was done in the university. I caused the university to send both the clothes and the perspectives of the stage; and the play was acted at Hampton Court in November following. And by all men's confession the players came short of the university actors. Then I humbly desired of the king and the queen, that neither the play nor clothes nor stage might come into the hands and use of the common players abroad, which was graciously granted. But to return to Oxford. This play being ended, all men betook themselves to their rest, and upon Wednesday morning, August 31, about eight of the clock, myself with the vice-chancellor and the doctors attended the coming forth of the king and queen; and when they came, did our duties to them. They were graciously pleased to give the university a great deal of thanks; and I for myself and in the name of the university, gave their majesties all possible thanks for their great and gracious patience and acceptance of our poor and mean entertainment: so the king and the queen went away very well pleased together.

"That Wednesday night I entertained at S. John's, in that same room where the king dined the day before, at the long table which was for the lords, all the heads of colleges and halls in the town, and all the other doctors, both the proctors, and some few friends more which I had employed in this time of service; which gave the university a great deal of content, being that which had never been done by any chancellor before. I sat with them at table, we were merry, and very glad that all things had so passed to the great satisfaction of the king, and the honour of that place."

So the great day in the life of S. John's passed, and the College settled down again into its quiet working order, yet not before Abraham Wright had commemorated the new building in such verses as he could, somewhat too readily, command.

UPON THE NEW QUADRANGLE OF S. JOHN'S COLLEDGE
IN OXFORD.

*Built by the most Rev. Father in God the
Lord Archbishop of Canterbury.*

'Tis done; and now where's he that cryed it down
For the long tedious businesse of the town,
Let him but see it thus, and heel contend
How we could such a Quadrat so soon end,
Nay think 'twas time little enough to frame
The exact modell only of the same.
'Tis finish'd then; and so, there's not the eye
Can blame it, that's best skilld in symmetry:
You'd think each stone were rais'd by Orpheus' art.
There's such sweet harmony in every part.
Thus they are one; yet if you please to pry
But farther in the quaint variety
Of the choise workmen, there will seem to be
A disagreeing uniformity.
Here Angels, stars, there virtues arts are seen,
And in whom all these meet the king and queen,
Next view the smooth-faced columns, and each one

Looks liks a pile of well-joined pumice stone
Nor wonder, for as smooth, as clear they are
As is your mistresse glasse, or what shines there.
So that you'd think at first sight at a blush
The massy solid earth Diaphanous.
But these are common, would you see that thing
In which our king delights, which in our king?
Look up, and then with reverence cast your eye
Upon our Maryes comely majesty:
'Tis she, and yet had you herself ere seen
You'd swear but for the Crown 'twere not the Queen:
Nor ist the workman's fault; for what can be
I would faine know like to a Deity?
Unlesse her Charles; yet hath his statue proved
So like himselfe you'd think it spoke and mov'd
But that you plainely see tis brasse, nay were
The guard but near, they'd cry "the king, be bare."
Rare forme, and as rare matter; that can give
Our Charles after his reigne ages to live.
Not like your graver citizens, wise cost,
Who think they have king enough on a sign-post:
Where he may stand (for all I see) unknown,
But for the loving superscription,
No; here he reigns in state, to every eye
So like himselfe in compleat Majesty.
That men shall cry, viewing his limbs and face
All fresh three ages hence, long live his grace.
Blest be that subject then, which did foresee
The kings (though he's as God) mortality;
And through a Princely care hath found the way
To reinthrone his dust and crown his clay;
That so what strange events soere may fall
Through peace or war antimonarchical;
Though these three kingdoms should become one flame

And that consume us with our king and his name;
Yet here our gracious Charles whenever lent
To his much honourd Marble, and there spent
To a dust's atome, being then scarce a thing,
May still reigne on, and long survive a king.*

Laud adds, in the History of his Chancellorship, a few words as to his own state and the cost of the entertainment; but he never filled in the exact sum in his MS.

"My retinue (being of all my own, when I went to this entertainment) were between forty and fifty horse; though I came privately into Oxford, in regard to the nearness of the king and queen, then at Woodstock. There was great store of provision in all kinds sent me towards this entertainment; and yet (for I bare all the charge of that play which was at S. John's, and suffered not that poor College to be at a penny loss or charge in any thing) besides all these sendings in the entertainment cost me. . . ." †

The total expense of the entertainment to Laud was £2666.‡ Adam Torless, his steward, who acted also from time to time for the College, remained behind in Oxford to collect the accounts and pay the bills.

The next quarter after this may well be taken as an example of the expenses of the College at this period.

* Wright, *Parnassus Biceps*, pp. 122–4.
† These passages have been quoted from Laud's *Works*, vol. v pp. 152–155.
‡ Account in *Calendar of State Papers* (Domestic), 1636–7, p. 477.

Expences between Michāmas & yᴱ Auditt 1637.

(That is to say, the last month of 1636.)

Imprimis to Mr. Champneys for keping yᵉ Courts . . .	iijˡ	
Item to him for writing yᵉ Court roules	xiijˢ	iiijᵈ
Item to him for entertainmᵗ of yᵉ parish of Northmoore at Easter	xlˢ	
Item to Stanton Harcourt out of yᵉ parsonage of Northmoore at Easter	xiijˢ	iiijᵈ
Item to yᵉ poore of Northmoore at Xtmas & Easter . . .	xlˢ	
Item to Mr. Champneys for a respite of homage . .	iijˢ	iiijᵈ
Item to him for his fee therein .	iijˢ	iiijᵈ
Item to him for Oxford highwaies	iiijˢ	ijᵈ
Item to him for maimed souldiers & Marshalsey	ijˢ	viijᵈ
Item for Ship money . . .	xxxiiijˢ	
Item for a Robbery done in the Hundird	iiijˢ	
Item for reparacions about the Chauncell &c. . . .	viijˢ	vjᵈ
Item for writting yᵉ Præsidᵗˢ yeare booke	xxˢ	
Item to ye Præsidᵗˢ man for extra-ordinary writing . . .	xxˢ	
Item for necessaries yᵉ whole yeare	ixˢ	
Item to Sr. Miller for writing yᵉ yeere booke	xxˢ	

Item	£	s.	d.
The procuracions of the Bpp. of Oxon due this last Trienniall & thacquittance		iij^s	viij^d
The Synodalls at Easter 1637 .		ij^s	
Item to goodwife Jones for the Chappell at 4^d ye weeke for 14 weekes		iiij^s	viij^d
Item to ye sexton for 2 Cōmunions		v^s	
Item to Felix Swadling for his Bayliffe wyk for ye whole yeere		xl^s	
Item for his Bayliffe wycke of St. Giles's		vj^s	viij^d
Item for keeping ye wood at Stokebasset		ij^s	vj^d
Item for Candles for ye whole yeere	xxij^li	x^s	vj^d
Item for searching for dishes .			viij^d
Item for Salt for ye whole yeere .		lix^s	
Item to Mr. Dale's man for bringing provision to ye Auditt .		ij^s	vj^d
Item for digging and laing gravell in ye new Quadrangle . .		vj^s	vj^d
Item for 2 brasse candlestickes in ye Chappell		v^s	
Item for scouring of dishes . .		j^s	ix^d
Item to Mr. Dennis for greene-cloth more then it could bee sold for, by reason it was much injured by the use ye Colledge made of it	v^li	vij^s	vj^d
Item for mending of plate . .		xxviij^s	
Item for hooping ye Covers in ye seller		j^s	

Item p^d to ye Vicepresid. & deane of Divinity for horsehire to Fyfeild		xviij^s	
Item to Jackson for the pitt in the old quadrangle . . .	x^{ll}		
Item to ye workemen for digging ye pitt and gravell . . .		xxiiij^s	ij^d
Item to Mr. Wilde for Thaches chamber.		xxiiij^s	viij^d
Item for Mr. Gaytons chamber 1 qrtr.		xij^s	vj^d
Item for 2 Baskets for ye Buttry		iij^s	
Item to Felix for expences at ye Courts	vj^{ll}	x^s	
Item for Procuracons to ye Archdeacon for North Moore & for ye acquittance . . .		ix^s	
Item for servants fees for waiting at ye Auditt		l^s	
Item for making cleane ye Lodging		v^s	
Item for 24 trees for ye old grove		v^s	vj^d
Item for ye Organists allowance out of ye Overplus of Cōmons for ye whole yeere . . .	iiij^{ll}	, ij^s	iiij^d
Item overcharge in Casuall receipts ; Mr. Champneys money rent the whole yeere *forgotten*	vj^{ll}	xiij^s	iiij^d
Item to Mr. Charles for ye cariage of 60 loades of turfe and other stuff into ye College		xx^s	
Item allowed to Fælix Swadling for his extraordinarie paines in gathering of Rents and some losses susteined thereby· 50^s 8^d .		l^s	iij^d

Item to Mr. Inkersol for a Serm : }
   preached at St. Maries . . }   xx^s

    xcix   j^s iiij^d

IMPOSITIONS BETWEEN MICHM̄AS & THE AUDITT 1637.

Imprimis pro Tonsore pro 7 }
   hebdom.   .   .   .   . } i^{li} xvij^s viiij^d
Item imp. hebd. 4^a pro Arbusto   xxxij^s
Item 5ta pro   apud Kidlington   xvj^s viiij^d
Item 8^a pro Caminis .   .   .   xj^s iij^d

    4^{li} 17^s 7^d

          Summa pag. ciii^{li} xviij^s xj^d
            Exh. p. Ric: Baylie P^{s}sid.

The rents for the chambers near the Library begin to be received from Christmas Day 1636, and are usually £3 7s. 6d., distributed among the various tenants, five Masters, a bachelor, and an undergraduate. A separate account is kept of the receipts " ex ædificiis Cantuariensibus," and out of this were paid the Library keeper 15s. a quarter, 10s. to the porter, 2s. 6d. for sweeping the gutter, and 3s. 4d. for sweeping the Library.

The College was now high in public estimation, and it held this position until the drain upon its finances at the eve of the Civil War again reduced it to the poverty which Laud lamented. During the next four years, 1636-1640, the Archbishop continued to make generous benefactions.

The new Library was at first, by Laud's direction fitted up as a " mathematical library." Bookshelves were set up " with shutters made before the shelves to keep both books and instruments in better safety."

Noting this in 1638, Laud sent an astrolabe and the works of S. Gregory the Great in folio with a collation of the MSS.*   Later letters show him constantly adding to the collection, and consulted by the College in every alteration which they proposed in the arrangements.† A characteristic letter may here be quoted, which illustrates the common expressions of his generosity—the enriching of the Library, and the present of advowsons.

" After my hearty commendations,

"These are in a great deal of haste, by reason of Term business, and therefore will be short.   I pray acquaint the Fellows that I have paid you the Thousand Pounds given you by Mr. Benson, and taken your own acquittance for the receipt, and I heartily wish that all these things given by their Benefactors may be turned to the best, first for them, and then by them.   I have likewise sent you down, to be placed in my Mathematic Library, six maps made up after the newest and best fashion for use ; and I hope that the Fellows will make good use of them.   With these I have likewise sent you nine manuscripts, some Arabic, some Greek, for the better furnishing of that Library ; they being all Mathematical.   There is a book, also, set out in two great volumes, in folio, concerning the Liberties of the Gallican Church ; this book hath been checked at, if not called in ; but is most to be preserved in the Libraries of Reformed in Churches.   One more there is of the entertainment of the Queen Mother in the Low Countries, which will become that place very well, though the use of it be not great.   With these books I send you the per-

* Letter in College MSS. printed in Laud's *Works*, vii. 434-5.
† *Cf.* letter dated Sept. 17, 1641, written from the Tower; printed in *Works*, vii. 611.

petual inheritance and donation of a Benefice called East Codford, worth near £300 per annum, and [which] stands very finely in Wiltshire. And do hereby pray and require you and your successors, so often as this parsonage shall become void, to dispose of it according to the conditions and limitations expressed in the Deed, and to register these my letters and the Deed itself, and then put the Deed into the Tower. And if Sir Giles Mompesson,* who gives this Rectory, have any evidences which belong solely to the same, you shall have them looked up and sent. So wishing you all health and happiness, I leave you all to God's blessed protection and rest,

"Your very loving friend,

"W. Cant.

"*Postscript:*

"I have likewise sent you, Ward de Re militari, and Junius de Picturâ Veterum and Periplus of Scylax, with Isaac Vossius his notes upon it.

"Lambeth, *June* 28, 1639.

"To my very loving friends yᵉ Psidᵗ.
        and Schollers of S. John Bapᵗ.
        Coll. in Oxon, these."†

Laud had already given, or procured, several benefices for the endowment of the College. In 1635, he arranged for the transfer of the patronage of Gatten, Surrey, but this seems never to have been carried out. In the next year he gave the Rectory of Bardwell, Suffolk (directing a preference in the nomination to be

---

* This is of course the monopolist who was impeached, the *Sir Giles Overreach* of Massinger's play, who now we may hope would "purge and live cleanly."

† Laud's *Works*, vol. vii. pp. 582-583.

given to a Reading Fellow*), and that of South Warnborough, in Hampshire (for the additional endowment of the Presidentship†), and in 1638, Hanborough, Oxon, both on the gift " for my sake," of Mr. William Sandys. In 1637, Viscountess Campden, whose mother, Lady May, had endowed a Divinity Lectureship, which Laud had held, in S. John's, where several of the family were " bred," gave the rectory of Great Stoughton, Huntingdonshire.

A reasonable endowment indeed was the grant of an advowson to the College. In the days when Oxford was a practical School of Divinity, it was natural that the Fellows should pass from their theological studies, while they were still young, to the discharge of the sacred work of a parish priest. A quaint letter, undated and unsigned, among the College archives is worth quoting, as an illustration of the nature of these benefactions. Bloxwich has now nearly seven thousand inhabitants. For some years, until 1891, the College ceased to exercise its right to appoint.‡ In that year the Bishop of Lichfield declined to receive the clerk nominated by the parishioners until application was made to the College, which, by resolution of a special meeting, agreed to waive its right for this occasion only.

The following is the letter offering the presentation:

* This benefice is now held by the Rev. F. E. Warren, B.D., Canon of Ely, a late Reading Fellow of the College, eminent in the study which Laud did so much to foster.

† This was altered in this century in accordance with a proviso in Laud's letter on the subject.—*Works*, vii. 307.

‡ See *College Register*. College meeting dated July 22, 1891.

" Reverend Sir :

" Mr. William Parker who was a worthy benefactor to us gave twenty pounds yearly for ever by his will [to be paid by the Merchant Taylours in London] to a minister to serve the cure in Bloxwich Chappell in Staffordshire where he was born, the qualification of such minister must be that he be a single man unmarried and must teach freely in the Chappell or Parsons house there, the men-children to read English both printed and written hand and is to be obedient to the Queen's laws, and to be allowed by the Bishop of Litchfield and Coventry, and must be taken from your Colledge ; and to be one sent thither from Merchant Taylours School in London and for want of the so qualify'd the inhabitants of Great Bloxwich are to make choice of a fitt man ; both for learning and good life, always provided that he live a single man unmarried as aforesayd, for longer than he so doth he is not by the will to have the benefit of ye £20 per annum.   And though the place seem to be but a place of £20 per annum, yet there is a pretty chappell house in good repair, and a convenient chappell yard, and some other land, the preaching of 4 Sermons appointed by a Benefactour all which will not be less than £7 per annum more y^t the £20 in case that the gentleman that comes (so qualified) will take pains and preach in the afternoon the inhabitants will incourage him by a subscription, and besides if he teach boys in Latin or to write he will be paid for that, so that it will be in his power to make the place a pretty beginning for a young man and he comes into this place without any charge of institution or induction."

One later instance of a similar benefaction may be noticed here.   Charles Woodroffe, D.C.L. (whose picture now hangs in hall ; he matriculated 1688, took the

B.C.L. degree 1696, D.C.L. 1704, became Canon of Winchester 1704, and died 1706), bequeathed the Manor of Winterslow, with the advowson, to the College, the income of the land to be applied to the purchase of more advowsons.

Up till the date of his imprisonment, and even afterwards, less regularly, Laud corresponded with the College. He wrote often to Dr. Baylie condoling with him on his ague, employing Mr. George Gisbey, one of the Fellows, on the translation of his book, against Fisher the Jesuit, into Latin. With Juxon, when he was Lord Treasurer, the great Archbishop could still find time to look into little details of College business, even down to the kitchen book.* And from time to time he sent down young men to be entered at S. John's, such as Sir Henry Sedley, whom he despatched with his tutor in 1639, with a "hearty prayer" that you "take such charge both for chambers or anything else that you conceive fitting, that his mother may see he is entertained there with more than ordinary respect."

From the date of Laud's imprisonment, it may be said that the College began to fall. A note of the annual revenues of the Colleges, drawn up apparently about this time, gives the value of the Headship as £80 per annum (this fell to £60 during the wars), the number of Fellows (which of course includes Scholars) as 50,† of clerks, exhibitioners and choristers as 14, of

* See Laud's *Works*, vii. 553.

† This remained the number till the creation of another scholarship from the estate of William Lambe by statute 35 & 36 Victoria c. cliv. The last Commission has of course "changé tout cela."

commoners as 30 (a considerable falling off), and of annual revenue as £1500.

In 1642, the College first began to suffer from the king's necessities. S. John's was probably the first college to receive and to answer to the king's request. The Baskervilles' MS. account* says that

" when King Charles I. first had his residence in Oxford in the time of our civil wars, the king wanting cash to pay his soldiers, he was necessitated to send for the College plate to coin money, and accordingly had it delivered to him. But S. John's Colledge people being loath to loose the memory of their benefactors gave the king a sum of money to the value of it, and so it stayed with them some time, but the king's urgent occasion for money still pressing him forward, he sent to demand it a second time and had it; upon which the king ordered the rebus of Richard Baylie the then President of S. John's 1644, to be put on the money coined with the plate. Mr. Rod did help me to half a crown of this money which had the rebus of Rich. Baylie on both sides; viz., under the king a horse-back on one side, and under this motto : REL. PRO. LE. ANG. LIB. PAR. The Protestant religion, the laws of England and the privilege of parliament."

The College records do not bear out this account. We have the following letter inserted in the *Register*, vol. iii. p. 343.

" CHARLES R.

" Trusty & Welbeloved Wee greete you well. Wee are soe well satysfyed wth your readynesse & Affection to Our

* Wood, *Life and Times*, ed. A. Clark, vol. i. p. 94 note

Seruice, that Wee cannot doubt but you will take all occasions to expresse the same.   And as Wee are ready to sell or engage any of Our Land soe wee have melted down our Plate for the payment of Our Army raysed for Our defence and the preser acion of the kingdome.   And having received seuverall quantityes of Plate from divers of our louing Subts Wee have removed our Mint hither to our Citty of Oxford for the coyning thereof.   And Wee doe hereby desire you that you will send unto Vs all such plate of what kind soever wch belongs to your Colledge, promising you to see the same iustly repayd unto you after the rate of 5^s the ounce for white and 5^s 6^d for guilt Plate as soon as God shall enable Vs, for Assure yourselves Wee shall neuer let Persons of whom Wee haue so great a Care to suffer for their Affection unto Vs but shall take speciall order for the repayment of what you have already lent to Vs according to Our promise, And alsoe of this you now lend in Plate, well knowing it to bee the Goods of your Colledge, that you ought not to alien, tho noe man will doubt but in such a case you may lawfully lend to assist your King in such visible necessity.   And Wee haue entrusted Our trusty and Welbeloved Sir William Parkhurst, Knt, and Thomas Bushell Esq, officer of Our Mint or either of them to receive the said plate from you, who, upon weighing thereof shall give you a Receipt under their or one of their hands for the same.   And Wee assure Ourselves of your very great willingness to gratify Vs therein since besides the more publique Considerations you cannot but know how much yourselves are concerned in Our sufferings.   And Wee shall always remember this particular Seruice to your Aduantage.   Given at our Court at Oxford this 6th day of January 1642.

"To our trusty and welbeloved the President and Fellows of St Johns Colledge in Our University of Oxon."

The Register of the College records the unanimous agreement of the President and Fellows to comply with the king's request, and the receipt of Sir William Parkhurst, and of Mr. Bushell, Warden of the Mint, for 176 lbs. 2 oz. 10 dwt. of 'white plate' and 48 lbs. 7 oz. 10 dwt. of 'gilt plate.' The following is the entry in the Register :

"In answer to his Mty's letters it was consented & unanimously agreed by ye Pres. & fellows of ye College that ye plate of ye College should be delivered unto his Majesty's use & withal an humble petition that his Majesty w^d be pleased to assign a considerable part of the plate to be coined for the use of the College. It being apparent unto them that unless his Majesty do graciously yield unto this their humble petition the College is plainly unable to answer ye debts contracted for the new building, sustain the necessary burden of ye House & provide Commons for ye Students."

A receipt for £300 from the Mint is added.

Earlier entries in the College books explain whence some of the plate had come. It is believed that all was given up to the king except the altar plate and possibly some in the President's house.

"In Mr. Hucheson's Presidency, William Asshebrooke, sometime Butler of the said College, hath given thereunto, to be bestowed in a dossen of silver spoons, vili. xiiis. iiiid., which was performed accordingly ; the weight 24 oz."

And again :

"George Danbatte, of Elbing in Poland, Commoner at the Bachelors' table, gave to the Colledg, as a gratuytee, one beker of sylver, with his name engraved thereupon, about the value of xls., 1595."

"In 1606, Richard Bellingham, in consideration that he was admitted to sit at the Masters' table, gave to the Colledge for a gratuitye a white silver pott with 2 eares, haveinge engraven on the one side thereof his oune armes and name, and on the other side the founder's armes, wayeinge 14 oz. 3 quarters."

Later on there is

"A noate of Colledge plate, usually kept in the Tower, and left there, signed by William Laud, President, Nicholas Cliff, Vice-President, Michael Boyle, Bursar :—A basin, salt-cellar, goblet, three cups, two tankards, beaker, and dozen of Apostle spoons."

On p. 68 are entered

"Parcells of plate lately sold."

The last plate entries are in 1614.*

A second letter is also inserted in the College register, but there is no record of the answer returned, probably because the request was not made to the College as a corporate body, but to individual members of it.

"Charles R.

"Trusty and Welbeloved Wee greet you well. Wee doe wth great Unwillignes renew Our desires of trouble & charge to any persons from whom Wee haue rec^d such ample testimonyes of their duty and affeccion as we confess to haue rec^d from you. But Wee are confident you doe enough understand your owne wellbeing to be so much Comprehended in Ours that you will upon all occasions extend the utmost of your abilityes to assist Us, And therefore Wee haue thought fitt to impart a busines to you, wherein all well-affected persons about Vs, haue

* See Hist. Commiss. 4th rep. p. 465.

expressed great redines and allacrity to serue Vs, in undertaking severally to pay soe many of Our foot Soldiers at four shillings the weeke (for one moneth) as they think fitt, in wch wthout any great burthen to themselves they aduance Our Service in a very considerable degree. Wee doe hereby recomend the consideracion to you not doubting but you will so farr express yourselves this way, that Wee shall not be disappointed of Our Expectacoñ. Wee doe assure you in the word of a King that this charge shall lye on you but one moneth beyond wch you shall not need to feare it shall be comended to you. And Our pleasure is that you retorne the names of the severall members of your Colledge who shall subscribe wth their subscripcoñs (for Wee expect this supply from particulers not from the publique stock, wch Wee belieue to be exhausted already for Our ayde) to Our Chauncello^r of Our Excheq^r within two dayes after the receipt of this Our, lre, that he may present the same to Vs, & soe Wee maye be informed of the particulars who in this Our Extremity are soe sensible of Vs. And soe Wee bid you heartily farewelle. Given at Our Court at Oxford this 27th day of June 1643.

"To Our trusty and welbeloued the President and Ffellowes of S John's Colledge."

So Oxford prepared for the Civil War, and when it came S. John's took its full share in it.

Before the danger had come home to the College, Laud went bravely to his death. In his will there was no place with which he had been connected that was forgotten, but nearest to his heart lay his College. The two references to it are full of personal feeling.

"Item, I give to S. John Baptist's College, in Oxford,

where I was bred, all my chapel plate, gilt or parcel-gilt; all my chapel furniture; all such books as I have in my study at the time of my death, which they have not in their library; and 500*l.* in money, to be laid out upon land. And I will, that the rent of it shall be equally divided to every Fellow and Scholar alike, upon the 7th day of October, every fourth year. Something else I have done for them already, according to my ability: and God's everlasting blessing be upon that place and that society for ever."

Something indeed he had done, which can never be forgotten while the College stands; and its sons in piety towards their second Founder may trust that his last prayer for them will ever come up for a remembrance.

And Laud wished his bones to lie among his friends.

" And for my burial, though I stand not much upon the place, yet if it conveniently may be, I desire to be buried in the Chapel of S. John Baptist College, in Oxford, under the Altar or communion table there. And should I be so unhappy as to die a prisoner; yet my earnest desire is, I may not be buried in the Tower. But wheresoever my burial shall be, I will have it private, that it may not waste any of the poor means which I leave behind me to better uses."

His last wishes were not fulfilled. Little, if anything, of what he bequeathed reached the College, and it was not till sixteen years after his death that he was laid beside Sir Thomas White in the chapel they had both loved so well.

During the wars special permission was given to the

scholars from Merchant Taylors' to study at Cambridge, since they could not go to Oxford, and the Committee of Lords and Commons for Sequestration from time to time made order for the payment of sums from the College estates to scholars who were prevented from residence in the University, " being the King's head-quarters."*

S. John's bore no special part in the war. No doubt during the earlier days when the city became the refuge of the Court, the ladies with their gallants walked in the groves and then came to the choral evensong. No doubt the sermon breathed the fiery indignation of the loyal College against Puritans and Roundheads. S. John's sent its sons to the trenches, and when the siege began in earnest a cannon shot, which is still preserved, lodged in the gateway tower. Here we have only to tell of the ejection of the President and Fellows, and of how they fared.

Two letters interesting in connection with the history of the University during the period of the Rebellion are inserted in the College register. The first, dated November 3, 1646, is an order from " the Committee of the House of Commons touching the breach of the articles," ordering that tenants shall pay their dues to the College " according to the articles of the treaty for the surrender " of the city, " notwithstanding any restraint or order of any Committee of Parliament to the contrary." The second, which is dated January 20, 1647 (*i.e.*, 1648), is an order to the commission for the reformation of the University of Oxford for the removal of Dr. Baylie from the Presidency of the College as

* *Calendar of State Papers* (Domestic), Addenda, 1625-49, p. 696.

" being adjudged guilty of high contempt by denial of
authority of Parliament." The Vice-President is required
to publish this order to the College.

This order was issued by the Parliamentary Commission which began its work in September 1647. The
best account of its execution is to be found in Walker's
" Sufferings of the Clergy." * Baylie, it appears, had
been already obliged to leave Oxford. Walker's
account is full of the delightful humour with which the
cavaliers met, and recorded their misfortunes.

"When the Visitation came on in the Latter End of
1647, he made a Stand in Defence of the Rights and
Liberties of his College, was on that Account summoned
before the Reforming Committee at London, and by them
Voted out of his Presidentship in December the same
Year. March 17ᵗʰ following he was by the same Committee, Threatned to be taken into Custody, for not
Paying Obedience to such Orders as the Parliament and
themselves had issu'd out relating to this College. However, nothing of this could drive the Old Gentleman from
his Hold; until the Chancellour in Person, at the Head
of a Party of Dragoons (commonly known in those Times
by the Name of Visitors) and these again supported by
another Party of the Garrison-Soldiers, came to this
College in their Grand Round, Apr. 13, 1648 : At which
time he found Dr. Bayly in the Quadrangle, coming out
to Receive him at the Gate. When the Earl was come
into the College with his Train, they went directly to the
Hall; and taking Dr. Bayly with them, there Required
of him to Submit Himself and his College to the Visitors ;
and that he shall be obliged immediately to quit his
Presidentship, on the very first Notice from them in

scriptis. But the good Old Gentleman told the Chancellour, that he could not Submit to the Former, without manifest Perjury; and that the Latter would be in a manner to cut his own Throat: Adding, that he believ'd the Answer which he had in Writing deliver'd in to the Visitors, relating to that Matter, had never been laid before the Parliament; for that he had therein shewn, from Eight several Places of his College-Statutes, that they could not, under Pain of Perjury and Expulsion, submit to any Visitor, than what the Statutes had themselves appointed; And that he had also requested the Visitors, that they would use their good Offices with the Parliament, that the Case might be Try'd in any Court of England; or any other Course might be taken to Examine their Cause, than this of a Visitation. But what he had then said, or what he now offered, was all in vain; saving that it put the Visitors to such miserable Shifts for Pretences in Answer to Plain Facts, and the undoubted Rights which were alledg'd, that it Exposed them to the Laughter (and probably the Indignation and Contempt too) of all that were present (themselves excepted). However, they go directly from the Hall to the Lodgings, to put the Successor, Dr. ——, in Possession of them. There they meet the Doctor's Lady, who had brought her Children (then very small) with her, in hopes to move Compassion, if any thing could pierce their Stony Hearts; but alas! to little purpose: For Sir Nath. Brent goes immediately to her, and tells her, She must prepare to leave the Lodgings, and they would allow her a Fortnight's time to Remove her Goods. To whom the poor afflict'd Lady reply'd, that she could not do it in a Month; because her Children were Sick of the Ague. Upon which they were so Merciful as to allow her a Fortnight longer; but withal declare —— President, and Possess'd of the Lodgings. And here I can't forbear to add, a pleasant Passage which happen'd on this melancholy Occasion. The Old Doctor, in the Heat of Discourse, under these Unheard of and Barefac'd Oppressions, had said By my Faith; At which the Godly Sir William Cobbe cry'd out in Astonishment, Blasphemy! O horrible Blasphemy! Whereupon the Old Gentleman desir'd to know what was the matter? what was it he had said? Why, saith Cobbe, he hath Sworn by his Faith, when Faith is not his own. Say you so, Sir William, reply'd the Doctor? But, with your good Leave, I do not know what is my own, if Faith be not, and I doubt, Sir William, you will come but Lamely off, when you are to be Saved, if you depend upon another's Faith. No, said Cobbe, Faith is not your own, it is the Gift of God. Alas, Sir William, returned the Old Gentleman, How much a Wise Man may be mistaken! For that very Reason it is my own: For what gives a man a Fuller, and more unquestionable Right to any thing, than a Free Gift?

" Such was the Exquisite Hyprocrisie of those Times and Saints; who, tho' they came to commit the most Outrageous Robbery and Oppression imaginable, yet were their Consciences so very Tender, that they could not without Astonishment, hear a Man swear by his Faith: And so perfectly Holy and Righteous were they, that they had their Very Ears (and every thing else, except their Hearts) sanctify'd. But to proceed with the account of Dr. Bayly, who was not actually Dispossess'd at this time neither; but continuing in his Lodgings some Weeks longer than the Visitors had allow'd him, the Patience of the Person whom the Committee had appointed to succeed him, was quite worn out: and at length he comes to the College, breaks open the Lodgings, and takes Possession of them by downright force June 2, 1648. Nor must one circumstance of his sufferings, which renders them Barbarous in a very peculiar manner, be omitted; which was, That one of the Greatest Persons concern'd in them, as well in point of Quality, as Malice afterwards (with Pleasure and Delight) boasted that he Had turned out by force, Dr. Bayly, his Wife, and Six pretty Children from St. John's."

The history of the relations of the Visitor with the College after Baylie's expulsion can be more briefly, and less humorously, told.*

In April, Taylor and Wray, the butlers, were summoned before the Visitors and made submission, having not appeared on a former summons. On May 8, the Vice-President (Nathaniel Croocher) and the Fellows gave their answers. Most of them referred to the general reply previously given which had declared that the College could only obey the Visitor appointed by its Statutes. Some of the Fellows, such as Henry Osbaston (who gave the Second Folio Shakespeare in 1637), gave argumentative answers, trying to keep on the windy side of the law: others gave a simple refusal. Most said they feared perjury, "deliberate and complicated," said one, "quæ in æternum absit a mente Christianâ." The Visitors were not satisfied with depriving the Fellows of their College emoluments; they must also turn them out of their ecclesiastical benefices. In June, Edmund Tillesley was "suspended from exercising any ecclesiastical function at North-More."

Another College incumbent was also turned out. John Goad, B.D., was Vicar of S. Giles's "in the suburbs of Oxford, where he continued to perform his

* See Burrows, *Register of the Visitors* (Camden Society).

duty notwithstanding the siege, to the hazard of his life from the enemies' cannon, who used to fire upon the church in the time of service." He managed to retain the Vicarage of Yarnton, which he afterwards held, and at the Restoration he became Master of Tonbridge School, and later, Head Master of Merchant Taylors'. Under James II. he became a Papist and he died in 1689, "a very learned and pious man."

College annalists have naturally not regarded the Commission with favour. Joseph Taylor, who drew up an account of the College history after the Restoration— "a lame fellow," Antony Wood calls him, and his account "short and trite"—says that the Visitors lacked "nothing save religion, virtue and learning," and that the oath they demanded was "as ridiculous as it was detestable. The President they now appointed was "non tantum fanaticus sed et furiosus." This was Francis Cheynell, Fellow of Merton and already Margaret Professor of Divinity. Himself one of the Visitors on June 24, he was appointed by the Visitors to the Presidentship. The lodgings were broken into and Cheynell was put in possession, and the butler was made to promise obedience. Three days later George Gisbey, who was no doubt well known to the Visitors for his employment by Laud, and Dr. Edwards, the Bursar, were apprehended and lodged in safe custody by the Provost Marshal of the Oxford garrison. Francis Webb, one of the Fellows who had submitted, "a person very scandalous as by the generality accounted," says Wood, was placed in charge of the College in Cheynell's absence. On August 10, a new convention of seniors favourable to the Parliament was appointed, and at the end of the year new Bursars were chosen by the same authority.

In July 1649, the Visitors made order that Sir William Paddy's benefaction should be employed in increasing the President's salary, with reservation of gaudies and a sum for poor scholars: since the choir for which it was intended was "to such uses in the service of God which are now taken away and not likely to be set up again."* The value of the headship was stated about this time to be £60 a year.

Cheynell held the headship only two years. He resigned on September 12, 1650, being unwilling to take the "Engagement" and also having to make choice between the rectory of Petworth and the College.

The first signature of Cheynell as President occurs in the Register on January 3, 1648. On September 6, 1650, is inserted the order of the committee for the reformation of the University that, since he has by their order made choice between his benefice and the Presidency of the College, Thankful Owen be made President in his stead. No S. John's man has taken pains to preserve his not undistinguished memory. His baiting of Chillingworth on his deathbed, because, Dr. Gardiner quaintly says, "dimly in the distant future," he "descried behind the bed of the dying man the shadowy forms of Voltaire and the Commune of Paris," is embalmed in the prose of our modern master of seventeenth-century history. In this case the learned author may be thought by some to let loose his vigorous imagination: and indeed it may be

* An arrangement was made with the tenant of Wood Bevington for a reduced rent during "the heat and violence of the civil war."

remembered that Chillingworth's "fantasy which he called his religion," as his opponent politely phrased it, had received the sanction of that name most obvious to Cheynell's part, William Laud.

Cheynell was an Oxford man by birth : the name still lingers in the city. Perhaps he was no better liked for that. He was succeeded by Thankful or "Gracious" Owen, Fellow of Lincoln.

He was a noted preacher, prominent among *

"the representatives of the Independent party, which had now come into power. On September 6, 1650, at the Committee for the Reformation of the Universities he was appointed President of S. John's College. The intended 'ten seniors' of the College consented. His first signature as President occurs on December 18. His management of the College property was far from satisfactory : during his tenure of office much of the College estates was assigned on leases of lives to his friends and relations. On June 15, 1652, a new Committee was appointed by Parliament, of which Owen was a member. He was constant in his attendance. He was a member also of the new body of Visitors appointed by Cromwell on September 2, 1654.

"As one of the most important of the Independént party in Oxford, and as having been actively concerned in all the most obnoxious proceedings of the Parliamentary authorities in the changes in University discipline, direction and patronage, it was clear that Owen would not be permitted to retain his post after the Restoration. He was ejected by the Commissioners in 1660. His last signature in the College Register is July 19, 1660, and is

---

* From this point I quote from an article contributed by me to the *Dictionary of National Biography.*

attached to a receipt to Mr. John Powell, Fellow of Merton College, for the benefaction of Mr. Griffin Higgs to be applied to loyal lectures. He lived privately in London, and did not conform. He died in 1681.

" When Dr. John Owen gave notice of his funeral he said 'that he had not left his fellow behind him for learning, religion, and good humour.'

" ' He was a man ' (says *Calamy*, vol. i. 181) ' of genteel learning and an excellent temper; admired for an uncommon fluency and easiness in his composures and for the peculiar purity of his Latin style.' "

Owen seems to have been better liked, and more kindly remembered in S. John's than his predecessor: but than the majority of the new Fellows, says the College annalist, " there could be nothing more ignorant or more abject."

CHAPTER IX

THE RESTORATION

THE Restoration was welcomed nowhere with more
delight than in S. John's. Before we tell of the return
of the President and Fellows it may be well to say a
word of the experiences during the deprivation of one
who had been, and one who was to be, President.

The experiences of Juxon in the years that passed
between the king's death and his own may well be told
here.

After his deprivation for the next ten years he
resided at Little Compton, Gloucestershire, a manor
which he had purchased some time before. Whitelocke, who it will be remembered was himself a S. John's
man, speaks of his hunting, and of his pack as exceed-
ing " all other hounds in England for the pleasure and
orderly hunting of them." Tradition says that he read
the church services every Sunday at the neighbouring
Chastleton House. He assisted many of the deprived
clergy. In 1657 he gave four Oriental MSS. to the
Bodleian Library. Beyond this we have no record of
his life for ten years. At the Restoration the universal
love and respect pointed to him as the only possible
Primate. On September 13, 1660, he was elected, and
on the 20th the election was confirmed in Henry VII.'s

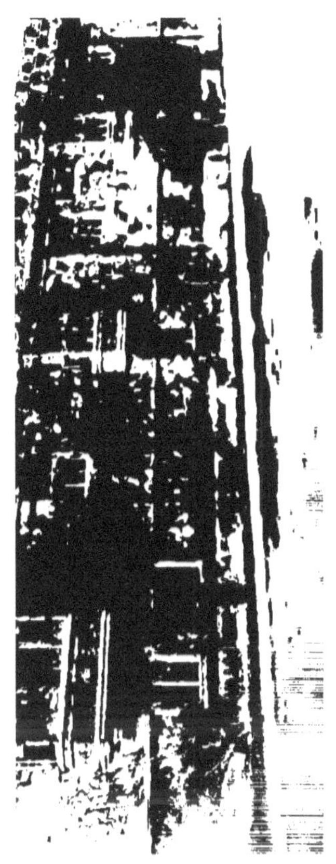

Chapel amid a great concourse of clergy and laity, and every sign of rejoicing.

He died on June 4, 1663. A strong, self-contained yet sympathetic man, laborious, loyal, unflinching in his pursuit of duty, bearing great troubles and sharp anxieties lightly because strengthened by the steady inspiration of a spirit within, a man who thought never of himself but of the work set before him and of those for whom he laboured, and thus one whom all men trusted and loved—this is the portrait which the records of his time have left us of William Juxon.

By his will, dated September 20, 1662, he left to S. John's College £7000 for the purchase of lands "for the increase of the yearly stipends of the Fellows and scholars of that College."

More varied was the career of Peter Mews. He was born at Purse Candle near the Dorset Sherborne, March 25, 1619, and was the nephew of Dr. Winniffe, Dean of S. Paul's, who sent him to Merchant Taylors. He was elected to S. John's the year after Charles I.'s visit : he took B.A. 1641 and M.A. 1642.

In 1642 he enlisted in the force raised by the University, serving in the King's Guards throughout the war, and obtaining the rank of Captain. "Ardenti bello civili Regiis in castris stipendia meruerat honesti nominis miles impiger."* "He received several times near thirty wounds, and was taken prisoner at Naseby."† In 1648 he retired to Holland and was constantly at work during the Commonwealth as an agent of the Royalists, being chiefly employed by

---

* Godwin, *De Praesulibus Angliae*, ed. Richardson, p. 244.
† Nicholas Papers, vol. ii. p. 19.

his intimate friend, Secretary Nicholas. He was an adept at disguise, and went through some very curious adventures.* In August 1653, he sought the Philosophy Readership at Breda, and Nicholas asked the Princess of Orange to use her influence to gain him the post.† Hyde said the place needed a man " that hath not bene a truant from his bokes ; " and it does not seem that he obtained it. His Churchmanship made him disliked by the " Presbyterian gang," but he was nevertheless with Middleton in his Scots expedition of 1653–4, acting as his secretary. It was then probably that he narrowly escaped hanging by the rebels, and perhaps then also that he won that scar on his cheek, ever after covered by a black patch, which is shown in his portrait in the College hall. His information of the state of Scotland was of great importance to the Royal cause. Like another good man he " served in Flanders."

" ‡ The date of his ordination is uncertain, but he is said to have been collated Archdeacon of Huntingdon, November 19, 1649, though he was not installed until after the Restoration.§ He was also presented but not instituted to the Rectory of Lambourn, Essex, during the Commonwealth.‖ On the Restoration he returned to England and petitioned the King for money to pay his debts contracted in the royal service and to furnish him with books to prosecute his studies at the University.¶ He took the degree

* Nicholas Papers, vol. ii. p. 236.

† *Ibid.* p. 19.

‡ From this point I quote from my article in the *Dictionary of National Biography.*

§ Cassan, *Lives of the Bishops of Winchester,* vol. ii. p. 188 *sqq.*

‖ Granger, *Biographical Dictionary,* vol. iii. p. 237.

¶ *Calendar of State Papers,* Sept. 1660.

of D.C.L., December 6, 1660.* Preferments were rapidly
heaped upon him, and he was re-admitted to his fellowship
at S. John's College on the special recommendation of the
King.† On October 30, 1662, he was installed Canon of
Windsor, and shortly afterwards Canon of S. David's. He
resigned the Archdeaconry of Huntingdon in 1665, and on
August 30 was made Archdeacon of Berks. During these
years Mews was a constant correspondent of Williamson,
who then edited the *London Gazette*."

Mews was long afterwards described by Hearne as
"an old honest cavalier." No doubt it is the title he
would have liked best.

The same name could well have been borne by
Baylie, who returned in August 1660 to quiet possession of the Presidency. He gave his daughter in
marriage to Peter Mews, who was to be his successor,
and he settled down quietly in the College as if nothing
had happened. In November the surplice was resumed
in chapel, and the organ was again played "together
with the singing of prayers," says Wood, "after the
most antient way," and the "resort of people" was
"infinitely great."

Next year the new Chancellor Clarendon was received in State and dined in the College hall, Baylie
being Vice-Chancellor. He was greeted at his entrance
to the College by William Levinz, one of the Fellows.
Thence he went to the President's lodgings where he
was "ushered up into the dining-room there," which
was no doubt the long gallery built by Laud.

"The cloth and napkins were laid," Wood adds,

* Wood, *Athenæ Oxonienses, Fasti* ii. 809.
† *Calendar of State Papers*, Dec. 29, 1661.

"with great variety of works in them, and clouds of flowers upon them, soe done by Mr. Thomas Banks, Dr. Woodward's man of New College, for which he received (as I have heard) five pounds for his paines." This was on September 9, 1661.

The winter brought the great storm which blew down several trees in the grove, three chimneys above the library which "beat into the library with great loss," and half the battlements over the east cloister, erected only twenty-six years before. The benefactions which now fell in must have been a welcome help, needed even for such a loss. Tenants had taken advantage of the "bad times" to delay their rents, and letters among the College muniments show the stern orders that went out to the laggards.

At first it is clear that the Fellows had but scanty means of subsistence, and they were released from the obligations of residence in order to serve the church. A letter to Dr. Barwick, Dean of S. Paul's, from Thomas Turner, dated August 18, 1662, shows this.

"There are 2 or 3 of ye Fellowes of S. Jo in Oxford yt preacht at S. Paul's. . . . I have heard them much commended and in ptar by Dr. Baylye the Psdent there. If you want some men, I suppose that any of them will be ready to offer themselves to doe the Church service."*

Juxon's bequest came opportunely, and not long after was the loyal gift of Tobias Rustat, Yeoman of the Robes to King Charles, and Under Housekeeper to the Honour of Hampton Court.

By deed dated December 14, 1665, he gave £1000 to

* Tanner MS. 48, fol. 26.

purchase lands worth £50 a year, the income to be thus distributed :

" to thirteen of the Fellows or Scholars that are most indigent, £3 apiece for an encouragement in their studies, he or they having no ecclesiastical promotion or office in the College that year, or any Greek, Rhetoric, or Mathematical lectures therein ; to the Dean of Divinity and the Dean of Civil Law forty shillings apiece, for which the latter is to read a lecture in the College on the 23rd of October, on which day the rebels were so bold to give pitch battle at Edgehill against K. Charles I. The other is to read a lecture on the 30th of Jan. on which day the same King was beheaded (to the amazement of all the world) by some of his subjects. To the Deans of Arts, each of them £3. To the three Moderators each of them £3. To one, whether Fellow or Scholar, that speaks a speech before supper on the 30th of January, declaring the barbarous cruelty of that unparalleled parricide, 10s. To another that setteth forth in an oration on the 29th of May, the glory and happiness of that day, 10s.*

This benefaction continued to be enjoyed on its original terms till the unhappy era of University Commissions.

Within three years of the Restoration the College gave burial to the bodies of its two greatest sons. Juxon was given a solemn public funeral by the University. His body lay in state in the Divinity School, and an oration was delivered by South, then Public Orator. On July 9, 1663, a solemn procession went by way of the High Street and Carfax to the great gate of S. John's—eighty-two poor men in black

* Gutch, Wood's *History of the Colleges*, p. 542.

gowns and hoods with tippets, then sixty servants in long cloaks, and others of higher rank in hoods—last of all the President of S. John's before the coffin. This was surrounded by flags with eight Doctors in mourning and hoods. Before walked Elias Ashmole, Windsor herald, with the crozier, and another herald carrying the mitre on a cushion. Behind was the Bishop of Oxford, his train borne by a boy in mourning, the Archbishop's kindred, and lastly the University Vice-Chancellor, Doctors, Proctors and Masters " in their formalities."

Wood's description may well be given from this point.*

" When they came from·Carfax into S. John's quadrangle they found there these things thus provided for, viz., a part of the quadrangle containing 30 of my strides in square, rayled in with mourning over it; in the middle a desk for him that made a speech with an escocheon over it; from the rayle to the chapel were boords set up to keep off the people. Over the chapel doore was a mourning cloth with 4 escocheons thereon : and the chapel itself was thus ordered, all the place within the communion rayle was loyned (with the bottome of it) with mourning and half way up to the top, another place also as large as that without it rayled in and all covered as the other with mourning in which place the corps were to lye on tressells . after it was come into the chapel and in which the chief mourners and heralds were to set ; all the chapel was hung round with bays (a stripe) and thereon escocheons as also all the seats, &c.

But to returne—after they had entered the gate the quire assisted by Xt Ch quire met them in their surplices, and Dr. Bayly going before and all the fellows behind

* *Life and Times*, ed. Clark, vol. i. pp. 482-3.

them and soe going half round the quadrangle they began
to enter the rayle. But there standing they began an
anthem which lasted to the doore. Then all went in, soe
many that were suffered. And when all men and things
were setted in their places they began another anthem.
Then Mr. Richard Levinz, fellow there, in mournings
made a speech on a desk fastened to the rayle of the communion table which should have bin delivered in the
quadrangle but hindered by rain. After that, another
[anthem] was sung ; then several prayers by Dr. Bayly ;
then other things. Which being done, and Dr. Bayly com-
ming up to the grave to read, Mr. Richard Berry, chaplain
of Xt Ch sang a vers anthem. After which was don, Dr.
Bayly read some prayers; then the corps was taken off
from the tressels (which because not well imbalmed was
put in three coffins) and by the supporters thereof with the
heralds and others was layd in a little vault at the upper
end of the chapel in the middle and walled round very
completely. On his coffin which was loyned round with
bays, was inscription on a copper plate ; the words of the
inscription :

*" Depositum Reverendiss. in Xto patris Guliel. Juxon.
Archiep. Cantuariensis qui moriebatur iv Jan MDCLXIII.*

" After he was buried Mr. Owen, one of the heralds,
proclaimed him buried, naming his name and all his titles,
with a conclusion of ' God save the King.' After that
was done, they departed in order and one of the heralds
led the Bishop of Oxon by the hand out of the chapel.
The mourning and the escotcheons remained in the
chapel."

The burial of Juxon was followed within a few days
by the translation of Laud. The ceremonies were in
marked contrast. Juxon was interred with all the pomp

that seemed to befit the reception by a great University of the body of the first subject in the realm. But Laud had asked that his funeral should be private, and his wishes were regarded. The leaden coffin was removed on July 23 from Allhallows Barking. The next night some sixteen or twenty of the Fellows rode out to Wheatley to meet it. At ten at night they entered Oxford, passed by S. Mary's Church and Cat Street to the backdoor of the grove, whence the coffin was carried into the Chapel. Mr. George Gisbey, then Vice-President, and one of the last of the Fellows to be personally connected with the Archbishop, spoke a speech, and then "they laid him, inclosed in a wooden coffin, in a little vault at the upper end of the chancel between the Founder's and Archbishop Juxon's."

No monument has ever been made by the College to its greatest benefactor. It has been felt that his own splendid work, one of the architectural glories of Oxford, is the only memorial he would have wished, and that it will not suffer any rival. But one touching survival there is of the day of his burial in the College he loved. His faithful secretary, William Dell, placed in the chapel a copy of the plate which was fixed on the coffin, and it remains behind the sedilia on the south wall.

These and the like works of piety were the first care of the College after the Restoration. It was probably about this time that the curious portrait of Charles I. with the penitential psalms written in a minute hand in the lines of the hair and face, was presented by some now forgotten loyalist. The picture was regarded as a great curiosity, and indeed has remained one of the " sights " for which visitors most often inquire.   Charles II. himself,* it is said, at his visit in 1663 asked the College to give it him, and could not be refused.   But when he thanked the Society for its loyal reception of him, and asked what he should do for them in return, they requested

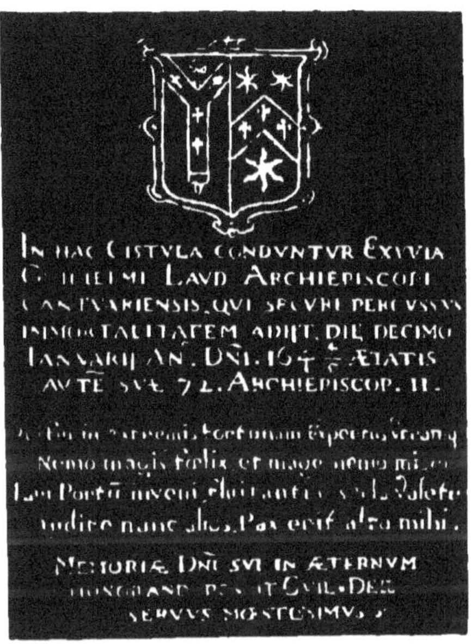

DELL'S BRASS IN MEMORY OF LAUD

that he would restore to them the martyr's picture. The story, true or not, expresses the reverence with which the picture was regarded.   It was described a few years later by Jeremiah Wells, one of the Fellows, in a poem printed in a volume now so rare that, for rarity and quaintness alike the lines may well be inserted here.

* The story is told in *Terræ filius.*

ON THE PICTURE OF KING CHARLES THE FIRST, IN
ST. JOHN'S COLLEDGE LIBRARY OXON, WRITTEN
IN THE PSALMS.

With double reverence we approach to look
On what's at once a picture and a book :
Nor think it Superftition to adore
A king made now more facred then before :
Here no fond artift at our fight lets in
The fly debauchery of painted fin ; .
Provoking real luft by feigned art,
As if his pencil were a Cupid's dart ;
Nor no diffembling painter's flattering glaffe
Turns grofs deformity to beauteous grace,
And mending, doubly counterfets a face :
The object here's Majeftick and Divine,
Divinity does Majesty enfhrine,
Each adds to th'other's luftre : fuch a thing
Befits the image of a Saint and King.
Each lineament o' th' face contains a prayer,
Phylact'ries fill the place of common hair :
Which circling their belov'd Defender fpread
Like a true glory round his Royall Head.
His mouth with precepts fill'd befpeaks our ear,
Summons that sence too, bids us see and hear,
Both are Divine : Bleft Mofes thus did fee
At once the Tables and the Deity :
Thus faith by seeing comes : religion thus
Enamours, when to th' Sences obvious :
This fight would worke a miracle on the rout :
Make them at once both loyall and devout.
  No maffy crown loads his diviner brow,
This would debafe, cannot adorne him now ;
'Tis farre too grofs 'mong spirits to have place,

A greater majefty fhines in his face.
Thus after Death eterniz'd, he out-vies
The New Rome's Saints, and the Old's deities.
While pilgrims from the world around fhal come,
Not to adore thy birth-place, or thy tomb,
No sacred relique, or remain of thine,
Thy statue, or thy picture, hearfe, or shrine :
But the bright luftre of thy heav'nly brow,
Thy felf thus plac'd in glory here below.
But well has art, lest our weak fight should fail,
Cover'd our Mofes with a double veil.
Firft then i' th' middle of some brighteft day
Oppose thy fight to the Sun's fierceft ray,
Outface him in his zenith : if this light
Do not deftroy, but purify thy fight,
Then mayft thou draw the outer veil, and pry
Into this image of Divinity :
But not the next : fome myft'ry fure there was
That we muft yet but see thee in a glafs.
Had Mofes seen thy radiant majeftie,
That Prophet had refign'd his veil to thee :
Nor had he needed it, wert thou in fight,
His twinkling splendour had held in its light :
His veil had hid his pious fhame, and Hee
Had doubly been obfcured, by that and thee :
His dazling luftre, though ador'd before,
Had only ferved to fhew that Thou hadft more ;
And well thou might'ft, for that Divinity
He only gaz'd upon, is lodg'd in thee.
Thy count'nance does with innate luftre fhine,
Whofe every feature's like thy felfe, Divine.
The lines and thee fo like in ev'ry thing,
That while we fee the Pfalms we read the King
Inabled thus Thy felf, Thy felf to infpire,

To be at once the sacrifice and fire.
Glorious without, thy bodie's every part
Is fafhion'd, as thy soul, after God's heart
Those parcels of religion we adore
In others, are compleated here and more.
That imprefse of the Deity in the mind
Of others ftampt, we in thy body find.
Thy frame fo like Divine in ev'ry part,
That thou doft not refemble it, but art.
The Artift has defin'd, not drawn thee here,
Nor is't a picture, but a character.
The emblems of thy mind ; Pofteritie
May hence learn what thou wert, and they fhould be:
Thy own example : fafely mayft thou goe,
Thy self the paffenger and conduct too.
Know but thy self, all other things are known ;
All science here is self reflexion.
   The Presbyterian maxim holds not here,
That calls locks impious if below the ear :
When every fatall clip lops off a prayer,
And he's accurf'd that dare but cut thy hair
The mad Phanatick, feeing thefe thy rayes,
Struck with the light, falls on his face, and prayes,
And blind with luftre that did round him fhine,
Acknowledges the vifion is divine
And wafhing off his hypocritick paint,
He reconciles the subject and the saint.
Those madder zealots, that as foon as come
From the Arabian Impoftors tomb,
Put out their eyes the Image to retain,
Counting all future objects are but vain,
Would here be fav'd the labour, and fhould find
True miracles strike their beholders blind :
Nor would they reft, till come where they might be

Bleſt with the laſting ſight of Heav'n and thee.
And now, bleſt spirit, while thy glorious ghoſt
Remains above, may we thy mantle boaſt.
Still like Apollo 'mong our Muſes ſit,
Improving both our piety and wit.
Still with us as our Guardian Angel ſtay:
(Thou art full as glorious and as bright as they.)
To our new Troy thou the Palladium be,
May we ourſelves loſe when we forfeit thee.
From thee protection may we find, and light,
Safe in thy guard, & with thy luſtre bright:
May our continued piety load thy eares
With pilgrim's vows, & with our daily prayers:
And may'ſt thou oft 'mong us deſcend, and ſee
What's far too holy to be ought but thee.
Reſolve our scruple, ſince none other can,
Our too much piety makes us profane;
While, ſeeing thy luſtre ſo divinely clear,
We ſcarce believe thou art in Heaven, but Here.*

It was in September 1663, that Charles II. and
Catherine of Braganza, with James of York and his
wife, who was the Chancellor's daughter, visited the
University. The Duke and Duchess of York came to
evening chapel at S. John's on Sunday the 27th, and
were met by the Fellows at the gate with a speech by a
young gentleman commoner, Richard Aldworth. Two
days later the royal party came in state to visit the
College. They were met at the gate by the President
and Fellows, and John Speed, M.A., Fellow, "spake a
speech."

* J. Wells, *Poems upon Divers Occasions*, 1667. The College had
till this year no copy of this rare book, but has now by the kindness
of Mr. C. H. Firth been able to obtain one.

They saw the Chapel, with " two bishops' herses,"
and then the library where Thomas Laurence, a gentleman commoner, addressed them in the following lines :

AN ADDRESS*
TO y^{eir} MAJESTIES

*In ye Librarie at S^t. John's Coll: Oxon:
by a Gentleman of ye house:*

Your Station twixt y^{ese} Globes doth prompt our pen
To fancy Princes plac'd twixt Gods & Men.
Here Men, y ^r Angells plye y^{eir} different Spheres,
Our house of Comōns, & y^r house of Peeres.
May y^r last Progress here, reach Nestors sūme ;
Ere y^t Supreme Starr-Chamber call y^u home.
Whilst Angells propagate, & you display
A little Charles his Waine, & Milky-way :
These Asterismes are only wanting yett,
To make White-Hall a Heaven, & Heaven compleate.
   Perfection, Maddam from y^r Selfe must grow :
   Kings are im̄ortall, but Queenes make y^m so :

AN ADDRESS†
TO HER HIGHNESS y^e
DUTCHESSE OF YORKE

*In ye Librarie Att S^t. John's Coll Oxon
By a Gentleman of y^t house:*

If duty without complement might stand,
And they whoe cann but kneele, might kiss ye hand
Wee'd rally all our forces to expresse
Your noblest welcome in a plain Addresse

* Tanner MS. 306, fol. 365.
† *Ibid.* fol. 366.

Mars wee'd assigne ye Guarde, but y^t wee are
Assur'd y^r Dukes a greater God of Warr.
The Graces to attend you wee'd call forth
But y^t y^{eir} All's compris'd in your owne worth
And Venus with her Cupid too, should come,
But y^t y^n have a sweeter Prince att home.
Thus Poets dream, and Muses fancy less,
Then w^t ye Fates iudge y^u worthy to possess.
  Our Pegasus wth Duty wing'd wee show,
  Other may higher fly, none stoop soe low.

Pleased with his reception, Charles, probably about this time, offered Baylie a bishopric, which he declined, and regarded some at least of the Fellows of S. John's ever after with special favour. Dr. Delaune, afterwards President, was long attached to the Court. "He was looked upon as a very gentle, well-bred man, as indeed he is. After some time he left the Court and went into Orders, upon which King Charles said: 'We have lost one of the finest gentlemen in England.'" *

The College for a long time remained the resort of rich men. The account of the expenses of Sir John Williams, Bart., kept by his uncle, is preserved.† He was taken to Oxford by his uncle in September 1660. Twenty pounds was left in his tutor's hands to account for on his behalf. His uncle continued to dole out money to him in sums of twenty pounds during his residence. Special expenses also were allowed for. Among these occurs "October 4, 1661. For six paire of long fine white gloves for you to give ye President's lady. 00. 10. 00." The account goes on till October 1664,

* Hearne MSS. xxix. 136.
† MS. Bodl. 14,943.

when £3485 had been received by the uncle as trustee, and £2029 12*s*. 4*d*. disbursed. He then, doubtless, on Sir John's coming of age paid the balance.

On July 27, 1667, Dr. Baylie died at Salisbury. His presidency had witnessed great alterations in the College chapel. Dr. William Haywood, formerly Fellow, gave £100 in 1663 that the altar and the steps leading to it should be paved with black and white marble. In 1662 Baylie himself built the beautiful little chapel on the north side of the altar, with its exquisite roof of fan tracery. The work he had begun was completed, it would appear, as a memorial to himself. The old floor was replaced by black and white marble, a new screen was put up, and the chapel was wainscoted. Towards the expense, John Goad, now Master of Merchant Taylors', gave £500, and the Baylie family largely contributed. Baylie himself was buried next to Juxon. His son Richard Baylie, a London merchant, was buried in the new chapel in 1676. The chapel was consecrated on March 13, two days before Baylie was buried, by the Bishop of Oxford. The College MSS. contain an account of the reception of the bishop and of the ceremonial.*

The Baylie Chapel has a large tomb with the recumbent figure of the President Baylie in cassock, gown and skull cap, and long inscriptions commemorating himself and his son.

Within a few days of the late President's death the College received the royal commands, from Arlington, and from the Visitor.

---

* MS. I.47. Account of the consecration of the *Cemeterium in Sacello*.

" Trusty & well beloved we greet you well. Being given to understand that the place of President of your Colledge is now become voide by the death of Dr Bayly, the late President & remembering ye exemplary zeal and affection wth w^hch our Trusty & well beloved Dr. Peter Mews hath all along deserved from us and of our late royall father of ever glorious memorie having wth an inseparable duty followed the fortune of our affairs at home and abroade during the late times of Rebellion, we have thought fit, hereby very effectually to recommend him to you to succeed in ye place of our President as one who by his orthodox learning & sober life, of which your fellows have had in y^t College many years experience, as every way fitted for y^t trust. And therefore we cannot but again enjoin it to you as a mark of y^r duty & good affection to us cheerfully to comply wth this our recommendation in his favour. And so wee bid you farewell Given at our Court at Whitehall the 29th day of July 1667 in ye 19th year of our reign By his m^tie's command

" ARLINGTON."

" MR. VICE-PRESIDENT,

" You will together herewith receive a letter from his Maj^ty in behalf of Dr Mews (his chaplaine in ordinary & one that hath formerly & of late very well deserved of him) to recommend him to you & ye fellows of ye Coll. to be chosen President in his father in law's place as being every way capable of it & fit for it In which regard I as Visitor of ye College & in compliance with his Maties will & pleasure doe as earnestly & as effectually as I can recommend Dr Mews to you & ye rest of ye fellows to be made choyce of for ye President. And if there be anything in ye Statutes forbidding you to choose any one if absent or obliging you to make the election before Dr Mews (who is now at Breda by yᵉ King's leave and upon yᵉ Kings special service) can return I do hereby (as yʳ visitor) dispense with yᵉ Statute in yᵗ particular; & require you not to proceed in an election of any other until Dʳ Mews return or until you hear further from yʳ visitor & very loving friend George Winton.

"Whitehall, Julii 29. 1667."

The College replied in a letter from Francis White, Vice-President, that the College had always been "loyal to its prince and obedient to its Visitor," and that while Dr. Baylie was a person so eminent that his memory could not soon be forgotten in Oxford, or in other places, yet Dr. Mews is well worthy to succeed. Somewhat quaintly it is added that several others in the College are also well worthy; nevertheless the College will obey the King and the Visitor.

Mews was elected on August 5, 1667, and held office till October 3, 1673, when he resigned on his appointment to the See of Bath and Wells. He was absent at Breda, as one of the royal envoys, negotiating peace with the Dutch, when the election took place. He returned next month and was admitted, according to the ancient form, by the Dean and Canons of Christ Church.* As President, and afterwards as Visitor (he was Bishop of Winchester from 1684 to his death in 1706), he was able to do much for the College, and it appears that he was not always strict in enforcing obedience to the letter of the statutes. An "old honest cavalier," he made a good Bishop, and a sound constitutional adviser of the crown. He had not forgotten his

---

* Joseph Taylor's MS. History of the College.

military training in his old age, and it is said that his horses helped to draw the royal cannon to Sedgemoor, and that he directed their operation from an eminence.

It was under Mews's presidentship that Anthony Wood saw and noted the College muniments. He speaks warmly of the President's kindness and antiquarian interest, and from this time he notes many facts of interest, and more gossip, relating to the College. In 1670, when Mews was Vice-Chancellor, the Prince of Orange was received by the University. He dined at S. John's and saw the Library, and "upon his looking on King Charles's statue in the inner quadrangle, one Marsh, a little gentleman commoner, made a speech to him."

S. John's has always been considered to have the healthiest site in Oxford, and it is interesting to note that in the winter of 1672, the "malignant fever" which killed many in Oxford, passed by the College altogether.

In 1675, the College right to nominate Edward Waple M.A. to the Proctorship was contested by the Halls, to whom the election fell in cause of default. He had not been M.A. four years of "quatuor terminos et quatuor vacationes": but the point was decided in the College favour.* To Waple we must return later.

In the same year, when Tromp visited Oxford " much gazed at by the boys, who perchance wondered to find him, whom they found so famous in Gazets, to be at last but a drunkeing greazy Dutchman," Humphrey

* See letters of Humphrey Prideaux, Camden Society, p. 38.

Prideaux wrote that John Speed, M.D. of S. John's, " stayed in town on purpose to drink with him." The contest was a severe one: Dr. Speed had with him about five or six " as able men as himself": in the end they were fain to carry Tromp to his lodgings. It is a curious picture of University life; but it is hardly fair to tell the tale as if it were typical of S. John's. More fitly might it point to the boldness and endurance of the medical profession.

The records of these years contain many references to breach of the Founder's statutes, which were now become very irksome. For instance, the stress laid by the original statutes on residence—the order being that no Fellow was to be absent from College above eight weeks unless through sickness, the College business, or that of the king or a bishop, was enforced, though with difficulty, till comparatively recent times. No one, not even a Doctor of Divinity, could be away from the College without permission, and this could only be obtained, with very rare exceptions, for the cause of a bishop's or the king's business. Even Dr. Smith, Master of Merchant Taylors' School, who died in 1738, was obliged to have the formal leave of the College to attend to his duties in London. The case of the famous Dr. Sherard* was a notable one. He was long a traveller in the East, searching for manuscripts. He was chaplain at Smyrna, and ministered to the great English colony there for many years. At last it is said that he had to lose his fellowship when he had exhausted the " business " of all the bishops on the bench. The registers contain many references to such requests. In 1692, Mr. Francis Lee

* See below, p. 188.

is granted leave of absence on a letter from Henry
Viscount Sydney, who, as a Minister of the Crown, may
have had some royal privileges. Peter Mews, when
Bishop of Winchester, asked leave of absence, on behalf
of George Conyers, for six months, " who (as I am
satisfied) is obliged to be absent upon an extraordinary
occasion." In 1688, leave was given to Mr. Pinhorn,*
" a preaching cause, upon the account of his preaching
in oppido notabili, he performing all conditions
required of him in the statutes for that purpose."

In 1679, it was, that John Snell, the founder of the
exhibitions which have brought so many clever Scots to
Oxford, joined the President of S. John's to the Master
of Balliol in the government of his trust. In 1681,
Wood notes in a list of how " every College in the
University of Oxon is to be rated in all taxes," that S.
John's stands equal to Merton, at £400 a year, having
after it only Christ Church, Magdalen, New College,
All Souls and Corpus.

To continue Wood's Annals, it may be noted that,
in 1683, when James, Duke of York, brought his second
wife and his daughter Anne to Oxford, they entered
S. John's through the groves, and were met at the
entry to the inner quadrangle by the Fellows and .
greeted with a speech by William Delaune.

" Which being done, John Stawell, a young nobleman,
son to Ralph Lord Stawell, a late created baron, spoke a
couple of English verses made by Ambrose Bonwick, B.D.
and Fellow, his tutor. Afterwards they went into the
Library and viewed the rarities there. Thence into the

* I doubt if I have read the name correctly, for I have failed to
dentify the person.

Chapel, and viewed the hangings at the altar (but no organ played, which was an oversight); and then to the college gate."

At the time of Monmouth's rebellion, S. John's showed its loyalty by forming a company of foot; and when Peter Mews, as Visitor of Magdalen, came to restore the Fellows, he stayed at S. John's with the President. His successor, as President, was William Levinz, D.M. (matriculated 1641, submitted, after a time, to the Parliamentary visitation, and took his medical degree in 1666), elected on October 10, 1673. He was Regius Professor of Greek from 1665 till his death, March 3, 1698, and from 1679, Canon of Wells.

For the rest, the last quarter of the seventeenth century was uneventful in College. It still kept up, as strongly as ever, its London connection, and the Reading connection that had been strengthened by Laud.

College records and the manuscripts of the Reading corporation show the constant association between college and town, in the election of scholars, and later on through Laud's charities. Of the maidens whose marriage portion the archbishop bequeathed, it is stated that several of the earlier candidates were of kin to the benefactor. The visitation of the charities still continues. In 1728 the President of S. John's applied for £4

"to defray coach hire from Oxford for the visitation. Refused, there being no warrant or precedent. But at length, the Visitors being strange to the methods adopted, and not having travelled with their own horses, £3 are allowed on this occasion, but not for the future." *

* MSS. of Reading Corporation, 205, Hist. MSS. Commission.

This connection still survives, but unhappily the College parted with its ecclesiastical patronage in Reading to the See of Oxford, under the influence of Bishop Wilberforce's persuasive eloquence.

With London the constant supply of scholars from Merchant Taylors' and the supply of masters to the school from the College continued; and the College remained closely associated with great legal and mercantile families. One of the most notable of the families associated for generations with S. John's was that of Whitelocke. Sir James Whitelocke, afterwards a justice of the Common Pleas, was elected scholar in 1558. It is of him that Wood tells the tale that "he had the Latin tongue so perfect that, sitting judge of Assize at Oxon when some foreigners, persons of quality, purposely came into the court to see the manner of proceedings in matters of justice, he briefly repeated the heads of his charge to the grand jury in good and elegant Latin, and thereby informed the strangers and scholars there present of the ability of the judges and the course of proceeding in matter of law and justice."

His son Bulstrode matriculated at S. John's on December 8, 1620. He never forgot his old college when he rose to eminence under the Commonwealth, and his old association has no doubt helped to preserve for us some of the happiest of the reminiscences of Juxon which we owe to his memoirs. William Gibbons (1649-1728) kept up the connection of the College with medicine. He took his B.A. degree in 1672 and his D.M. in 1683. His fame is said to lie in his having introduced mahogany into fashion. He certainly was warmly admired in his own college, and he did his best to preserve the remem-

brance of a distinguished physician of an earlier generation by presenting a portrait (probably a copy) of Sir
William Paddy, which now hangs in the library.   His
own portrait in the gown of a doctor of medicine hangs
in the hall.

Other eminent members of the College were the founder
of the Sherardian Professorship of Botany in the
University and Edward Waple, Archdeacon of Taunton
and Vicar of S. Sepulchre's, London. The latter, whose
picture is among those of the benefactors in the College
hall, died in 1712 and was buried in the ante chapel.
He was a high churchman and Tory of the school S.
John's in the seventeenth century did so much to support.
His sermons, published after his death, went into a second
edition, and show him, as their commemorative preface
well says, " a person who had studied human nature and
was well acquainted with the springs thereof." He gave
and bequeathed to the College £500 for the purchase of
an advowson, and £700 for the purchase of land for the
endowment of a " Preaching Lecture for the advantage
of young students in Divinity," Fellows thereof, and a
catechetical Lecture "after the method and manner of
the Catechetical Lecture which is settled in Balliol
College."*

Dr. William Sherard, one of the earliest and greatest
of English botanists, did not in his wanderings forget
the College which had retained him so long among its
Fellows.   He was born in 1659 and died in 1728.   The
repeated licences to travel, granted on the request of
bishops, enabled him to study at Paris and at Leyden,
to visit Geneva, Rome and Naples, and eventually the

* See below, pp. 258–260.

East. It was not until April 21, 1703, when he had become Consul for the Turkey Company at Smyrna, that his fellowship was declared vacant. He lived at Smyrna till 1717, and when he died, besides leaving money to found a Botany professorship, he bequeathed most of his books to his old college. Botany had always been his first interest, from the time when in 1700 he wrote from Badminton, where' he was for a short time tutor to the young Duke of Beaufort, that it was his " chief divertion." But his interest in archæology was second only to his love of botany. He visited the Seven Churches in 1705, and travelled over nearly all Asia Minor in 1709, collecting a mass of inscription. He told Sir Hans Sloane he had spent out about £300 in medals " but last summer (1708) when I was at my country house about six hundred of them were stolen." " The drudge," he called himself, " of all the gardens in Europe."

The battel-books of the last years of the century show Gibbons and Sherard in possession of their Fellowships. The former was Vice-President in 1687, and in the same year Sherard was, as usual, absent. The receipts show from what sources the Fellowships were now paid. It is clear that a resident Fellow did not find that his receipts balanced his expenses.

1687

DR. GIBBONS, MR. VICEPRSDÑT.

	ll	s.	d.
Allowances . .	06	03	04
Rowney* . .	02	16	00
Overplus† . .	01	12	06
Office . .	05.	00	00
Geldings . .	01	02	02
Wood fee . .	01	16	08
Sir Wm. Paddys exhibition out of Wood Bevington Acct. }	05	00	00
As Coll. Physitian out of yᵉ same	05	00	00
	28	10	08
	40	16	04
	28	10	08
	12	05	8 due to Coll.

	ll	s.	d.	
Batt. Termº jᵐᵒ .	09	09	06	pd.
2ᵈᵒ .	07	10	09	
3ᵗⁱᵒ .	11	03	02	
4ᵗᵒ .	12	05	11	
Wood carriage .	00	07	00	
	40	16	04	

* This was the share of the income from the manor, grange, &c., of Rowney, or Roundhay, Bedfordshire, bought by the College from Mr. Brett Norton in 1663.

† This was the allowance beyond Sir Thomas White's original meagre commons.

Mr. Sherard.

	li	s.	d.
Allowances . .	03	16	08
Benson . .	01	00	00
Rowney . .	02	16	00
Comõns & allowances ter^{no} j^{mo} 2do	04	00	02
3^{tio} & 4to	04	03	05
	15	16	03
	06	19	03
	08	17	0 due to him

	li	s.	d.	
Batt. pro toto Anno	00	10	09	Received Eight Pounds
Wood car. . .	00	08	06	17^{s} for ye use of Mr.
Com̄. Roome . .	06	00	00	Sherrard per 10^{tr} ye 7,
				1687. J. Smith.
	06	19	03	

An examination of the battels of the college servants
(the Janitor, Tonsor, Sadler, and Painter), side by side
with those of the Fellows shows that S. John's still
kept but a modest establishment. It had links with
the great world, yet as a corporation it lived as poor
scholars should. But it was among the famous
colleges of the University, and visitors in their
memories of Oxford never forget to record their
sight of the relics and curiosities of the College
of Laud. Evelyn noted the new Library "and the
2 skeletons which are finely cleansed and set together." These it may be noted, with what was called
the ' Museum Pointerianum '* were for some time in this

* See *Oxoniensis Academia* 1749, by John Pointer.

century in the rooms under the new Library dignified by the name of the " Otranto passage." They have now disappeared, and the 'Museum' with them. Evelyn saw also the " store of mathematical instruments chiefly given by the late Archbishop Laud," and they too have left not a wrack behind.

About 1695, Mistress Celia Fiennes, sister of the third Lord Saye and Sele, visited Oxford. Thus she writes of S. John's:

" Here I met wth some of my relations who accompanyed me about to see some of the Colledges I had not seen before. St. John's Colledge which is large and has a ffine Garden at one Entrance of it with large Iron-gates carved and gilt; its built round two Courts : the Library is two walks, one out of the other the inner one has severall Anatomy's in cases and some other Curiosity of Shells, stone bristol Diamonds, skins of ffish and beasts.

" Here they have the Great Curiosity much spoken off King Charles the ffirsts Picture; ye whole Lines of fface band and garment to the Shoulders and armes and garter is all written hand and containes the whole Comon prayer, itts very small the character, but where a straight line is you May read a word or two.

" There is a ffine grove of trees and walks all walled round." *

This ' fine grove ' had already come to be one of the College glories.

* *Diary of Celia Fiennes,* pp. 26–7.

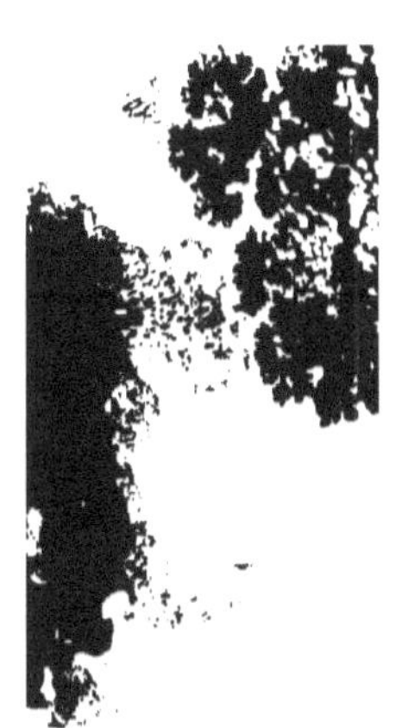

CHAPTER X

THE EIGHTEENTH CENTURY

WITH the reign of Anne the College settled down into the humdrum life which the University came to prefer.

Dr. Delaune, of whose gentlemanly manners Charles II. had spoken so politely, was elected President on the death of Dr. Levinz. He was born April 14, 1659, and as a child of the Restoration he remained to the end, like Mews, an " old honest Cavalier." The election was March 12, 1698, and Delaune lived till May 23, 1728. During these thirty years the College was notoriously Jacobite.

S. John's in the eighteenth century has suffered from the *chronique scandaleuse* of a personage who had every reason to speak ill of his College. Nicholas Amhurst was admitted on June 20, 1716, having been elected a Scholar on S. Barnabas's Day. The note ' per triennium probationis ' did not prove to be a mere form in his case. He went to Oxford he says " when the seeds of the late *unnatural Rebellion* were not yet extinguished; and continued there till June 1719, during which time he was a witness of that disloyal and treasonable disposition, of those corruptions, follies and vices, which " he denounced in the two bitter little octavos that made him famous. *Terrae Filius* he called his paper, which came out in fifty numbers in 1721. It was the name of the licensed jester at the Encaenia, and with all its buffoonery and rudeness it had been borne by many worthy as well as witty sons of S. John's, by Christopher Wren among them.* But since the person had been suppressed, Amhurst took the name and more than the licence ; and what was declared to be a revelation of the vices and disloyalty of the University was in reality a pouring out of his own spleen against the College which had expelled him for his bad conduct. His resentment against Dr. Delaune (President 1697–1728) is grotesque in its fury. "Father William," as he calls him, is a gambler, fond of low company, and, worst of all, a Jacobite. Of his sermons in the College Chapel there is a lively record ; he thundered forth (or was it Mr. Wharton ?) the words "*Restoreth* all things," we are told, so that no one should doubt the restoration that he looked for, while another preacher significantly announced as his text "James the Third and the Eighth." Nor is that all, for other preachers must needs attack the Whig theologian Hoadly. Thus it was, according to Amhurst's report :

"On the 30th of Jan. last, the Reverend Dr. Brimstone, in a latin oration, spoken in our chapel, against rebellion (for which a certain sum is settled upon us for ever), abused the bishop of Bangor, in the most barefaced and insolent manner by name, calling him not only Bangorensis, but Hoadleius iste malus logicus, pejor politicus,

* William Levinz, too, afterwards President, was *Terrae filius* (with Thomas Careless of Balliol) in 1651, " to speech it in the act celebrated in 1651, being the first act that was kept after the Presbyterians had taken possession of the University."

pessimus theologus : a bad logician, a worse statesman, and the worst of all divines.

"Such is the respect which some people (who call themselves the soundest members of the Church of England) entertain of Episcopacy; which is esteemed one of the most essential doctrines of the Church of England." *

To hear this is bad enough; yet all this is as nothing when compared to the sufferings of the honest man among such vile thinkers. "The tyranny of a School is nothing to the tyranny of a College." There are parts which smart less "than a bullied conscience. What was Busby in comparison to De—l—ne ?" Facetious too he is upon the Library and its treasures, upon the stables, built because the President had an expectation of marrying a rich widow, but unused, and bitter upon the benefactions which "I leave it to the consideration of every member of that College, whether they are all still distributed in the manner directed by the respective benefactors." It is not ill fooling, some of it; but it is no honest record of S. John's in the days of Dr. Delaune.

Delaune is Amhurst's great butt. No passage of the *Terrae Filius* has been more often quoted than this—

"One of these academical pickleherrings scurrilously affronted the learned president of S. John's College (in defiance of the statute *de contumeliis compescendis*) by shaking a box and dice in the theatre, and calling out to him by name, as he came in, in this manner, *Jacta est alea*, doctor, Seven's the main, in allusion to a scandalous report handed about by the doctor's enemies, that he was

* *Terrae filius,* i. p. 178.

guilty of that infamous practice, and had lost great sums of other people's money at dice; which story all, who have the honour to be acquainted with that profound divine, know to be a most groundless and impudent defamation." *

What we know of Dr. Delaune from other sources shows him to have been by no means worthy of Amhurst's malignity. He held many important offices, and with credit. He was incorporated at the sister University in 1714 as D.D., certainly a token that he had more than a mere Oxford notoriety. From 1715 to his death he was Margaret Professor of Divinity, the election to which post is a proof of wide popularity among the clergy, and he was appointed by William III. to a canonry of Winchester in 1701, a sign that he was not irreconcileably Jacobite.

Social interests no doubt he had—King James I., and one at least of his own successors at S. John's, would have considered some of them failings—but he was a pleasant man enough, fond of his pipe and of good company. A letter from Dr. Dobson to Dr. Charlett, April 15, 1714, speaks of him in a social gathering: " Your friends drank your health here last night in a competent number . . . The President of S. John's was moderate, and finished his last pipe before 10 "; and certainly there is nothing to support the picture of a society plunged in fuddled Jacobitism which Amhurst's sarcasms endeavour to suggest.

Hearne's chief intimate in S. John's seems to have been Mr. Philip Ayres:

* *Terrae filius*, vol. i. p. 3.

"an antient gentleman . . . who lodges as a commoner (on purpose to direct a young gentleman commoner then newly entered) [who] having been a great Traveller has pickt up several curiosities, as Books, Coins, etc., one of which I saw last night at the coffee house, viz., a Roll neatly written in Arabick which seems to be the Alcoran. He gives a very good account of the places where he has been especially as to the state of Learning, and is of a communicative temper."

Of the character of his acquaintance Hearne does not seem to have been very sure, and indeed he was doubtful if he was a clergyman. But later inquiry proved him to be interested in the reunion of Christendom and to have written, thirty-five years ago (this is in 1707), on the subject. On King Charles's Day, 1708, Ayres preached before the House of Commons a sermon "which would have made the ears of the Whigs glow had they heard it." Jacobites no doubt they were at S. John's. It is said that Dr. Holmes, President 1728–48, was the only Fellow for a long time who was a Hanoverian and was the first Hanoverian Head.

When there were riots at Oxford in 1716 on the Prince of Wales's birthday, though nothing was charged against S. John's, it is clear that the suspicion that Jacobitism was rampant there was in the minds of the soldiery. There was a "great disturbance in the town by the soldiers," drinking the healths of the Hanoverian house, and Mr. Vice-Chancellor (the Master of Balliol) went out. When he "came amongst the elms against S. John's College" a pistol was discharged. It "was shot out of one of the windows of S. John's College," deposed Faustin Magger of Colonel Leathes's company in the Royal Regiment of Foot of Ireland: but the matter went little beyond suspicion, for the University managed to assume the position of accuser, and the soldiers were put on their defence. The House of Lords declared that the riots originated from the neglect of the University to celebrate the Prince's birthday. Who was the young man of S. John's who celebrated it with a pistol shot?*

But all this harmless merriment, this boyish dissatisfaction with the red-faced Hanoverians, the toasting the king (but never the Church) over the water, which lingered it is said till quite recent years, and is even now revived by phantastics, argues no more than that the young men, and the old ones too who remembered the Stewarts, were something sentimental—that they still loved poetry and painting like their predecessors, but unlike their Brunswick sovereign.†   It certainly

* The several Papers which were laid before the House of Lords, published by order of the House, 1717, contain details.

† I am glad to have been able to remove one reproach from the College by pointing out that Rawlinson, MS. c. 936, fol. 93, did not refer to a member of the College as had been stated in the printed catalogue of the Rawlinson MS.   The sheet is headed:

"Received by the Penny Post this day Sept. 19, 1733, the following lines:

> "This small Urn contains ye Ashes
> Of an high-minded little Man.
>
> Fellow of S. John's not Master
> As his rash ambition promised him he should be.

"Sept. 9, 1654."

It accuses him of ignorance of theology and unsuccessful amours, of a dainty palate, cups, and indolence, and of being won over to the "usurper" by a fat benefice.   Mr. Macray has now identified the object of this rather feeble wit as Dr. S. Drake of S. John's College, Cambridge, who had published a satirical epitaph on Rawlinson.

does not show that the sneers of Amhurst are worth remembering, though it accounts for the fact that Dr. Rawlinson kept note not without a certain satisfaction of the discreditable character of his later years. Thus he wrote:

"Nicholas Amhurst died at his Booksellers M^r. Franklyn's Country House at Twickenham in Middlesex on 27 April and was in the most private manner buried there 1 May 1742. The cause of his death was his immoderate drinking of Geneva, which he took to, on the death of a Mistress, with whom he lived alone 20 years, and who died the Xmas before him, and since which time he never was concerned in the Craftsman. His friends, as much as possible, encouraged him, to whom he owed large sums, which they never did, or thought of troubling him for: M^r. Pulteney promised to forgive his own, pay others' debts, and make him easy, but all perswasions were to a deaf Ear. One of his friends in Bucks, one Mr Basil passed a severe sarcasm on him for his drinking, which was that he was lyable to be taken up by the Custom or Excise Officers, not having a permit for carrying with him a vessell of spirituous liquors." *

From her slanderer it is not a far step to one of the College's greatest benefactors. "Patronus, benefactor inter munificentissimos," are the phrases that gratitude employed in later years of the eminent man who left so much of his property to his "alma mater." In the Baylie Chapel is the simple urn of black marble which contains his heart, and under it is the inscription:

"Ubi Thesaurus ibi Cor

Ric. Rawlinson, LL.D. et A.S.S.

Olim hujus Collegii superioris ordinis commensalis."

* Rawlinson MS. J. fol. 19.

The arms are familiar in many parts of the College "Gules, two Barrs gemelles between three Escallops Argent." He was buried, by his own direction, in S. Giles's Church.

The life of Richard Rawlinson is soon told. He came of an old London family. His father Sir Thomas (1647–1708) had been Lord Mayor. His ancestor, John Rawlinson (1576–1631), the rival candidate for the headship when Laud was chosen, had been a confidential correspondent of Laud and Juxon, was long a Fellow of S. John's and later on Principal of S. Edmund Hall. Thomas Rawlinson, an elder brother of Richard, was matriculated from S. John's College, February 25, 1699, but left Oxford two years later and devoted himself entirely to amassing books and manuscripts. "The leviathan of book-collectors," he inspired his brother with his enthusiasm. Richard was born on January 3, 1690. He became a commoner of S. John's, March 9, 1708, and a year later a gentleman commoner. After long travels abroad he settled in London where he collected books, manuscripts, coins and all sorts of "curios." He was created D.C.L. at Oxford on June 19, 1719. Believing that Henry VIII. had no power to deprive the University of the right to confer the doctorate "utriusque juris," he always described himself as LL.D. He was an indefatigable antiquary, who visited every parish in Oxfordshire for the purpose of collecting materials for a history of the county, and a colossal collector of all that interested the archæologist or the historian. He left over 5700 manuscripts; and his printed books, in 9405 lots, took over sixty days to sell.

But Rawlinson was famous as a non-juror no less than as an antiquary. He was ordained deacon September 21, and priest September 23, 1716, by Bishop Jeremy Collier, and consecrated bishop, March 25, 1728, by Bishops Gandy, Doughty, and Blackbourne. As a non-juror he kept in the background, showed no violence, and when Collier and others restored the "usages" of Edward VI.'s first prayer-book remained with the "non-usagers," who differed in little but loyalty from the Church of England. He did not openly avow his episcopal office, though he joined in the consecration of Bishop George Smith, 1728, and as far as the College and the outer world were concerned he lived much as a layman. He issued privately the records of non-juring consecrations, and never abandoned his principles though he did not advertise them. But he was known everywhere as a staunch Jacobite.

His singular attachment to S. John's, from which he was so long separated, was no doubt largely caused by the belief that in his old College his political views were still shared by a majority of the Fellows.

The College possesses an imperfect letter-book of his, 1735–1742, which shows the trouble he had with his servants at Wasperton Hill, and at Waltham Abbey. He seems to have been an indulgent landlord but a tart correspondent.

A copy in the Library of *L'Anfiteatro Flavio discritto e delineato dal Cavaliere Carlo Fontana*, 1725, contains an inscription of Rawlinson's, "D.D. Ric: Rawlinson LL.D. et S.R.S. aliquando socio-commensalis, Animo semper Joannensis." Another of his gifts was his anonymous *Records of the new Consecrations since the*

Revolution in 1688, which he expressly ordered should never be taken out of the Library. His MS. collections relating to S. John's are mostly in the Bodleian. They contain the most minute information as to the College at different dates. Nothing seems to have been too small for him; lists of College estates, history of benefices, records of scholars, commoners, servants, copies of battel sheets, all was fish that came to his net.

It is clear that in spite of his principles he retained the most cordial relations with the Hanoverian Head to the end. Among his MSS. are many letters from Holmes, signed always "your most affectionate humble servant."

The conjunction of these two names leads us further; Rawlinson suggests the non-jurors, and Holmes brings us back again into the more domestic life of the College.

Besides the generous bishop another name among the non-jurors is of special interest in S. John's. George Hickes was of us, but for too short a time. Thankful Owen, it seems, dismissed him because "he would not take notes of the sermons nor attend the meetings of the young scholars for spiritual exercises." Magdalen and Lincoln were kinder, and Hickes lived to be Vicar of S. Ebbe's in Oxford, Rector of Allhallows Barking, and Dean of Worcester, and to "go out" for his king when there came the offering of oaths.

The association of Hickes and his friends with Rawlinson belongs rather to general history. We ourselves turn to the materials which the College register, and the antiquary's diligent collection, afford for the internal history of the foundation. The most important event in S. John's during George I.'s reign was probably the appeal of one of the Fellows who had been expelled for contumacy: and here again the interest shifts back to the incorrigible Amhurst. Hearne thus describes the incident:

"Dec. 21, 1721. On Saturday last (Dec. 16) M^r. Thomas Tooly M.A. & fellow of St. John's Coll. was expelled that house. It seems he had abused the President & Fellows, & some say assisted one *Amhurst* (lately expelled the same college) in writing his Paper called the Terræ Filius (of wch many have been published, but I think it does not come out now) & other scandalous Papers. M^r. Tooly begg'd Pardon and asked Forgivness, but they would not grant it, unless he would register himself. So that it seems (as I understand the matter at present) he is expelled because he would not enter his crime, & his acknowledgment, with his own hand in the college Register. He took Horse immediately and 'tis supposed went to the Visitor, the Bp. of Winchester. He is a good scholar, & hath been a hard student, & among other things hath put out Tully de Officiis, printed at the Theater in 8vo."

And three months later he adds:

"March 8, 172½. M^r. Tooley of S. John's coll. being lately expelled that coll. (of which he was M.A., and fellow) immediately applyed to the Visitor, the Bp. of Winchester, Dr. Trimnell, who summoned the President and the ten senior fellows to appear at Chelsey which accordingly they did and it appearing that Toley had mos t scandalously abused the President, &c. and the Statute being express against him, the Visitor hath confirmed the expulsion." *

* I quote from Bodl. MS. Top. Oxon. e. 54.

The College muniment room keeps Trimnell's letter of review and decision.

Amhurst's and Tooly's were not the only expulsions. The witty Abel Evans, who was chaplain, was ejected because in a speech in hall he 'reflected on' Delaune and others.* Sarah Duchess of Marlborough took up his cause; and, though he was a "loose ranting gentleman he was mightily caressed," and eventually reinstated. He won enough fame as an epigrammatist,—the well known epigram on Vanbrugh was his,—to be put into the Dunciad in good enough company.

> "To seize his papers, Curll, was next thy care
> His papers, light, fly diverse, tost in air ;
> Songs, sonnets, epigrams, the winds uplift,
> And whisk'd 'em back to Evans, Young and Swift."

He published 'the Apparition' in 1710, and 'Vertumnus' in 1713. In 1725 he was nominated to the College living of Cheam, which it was said had been held by no less than six bishops.

He will be remembered in S. John's, as some later Bursars might perhaps be, by the following epigram,

> Indulgent nature on each kind bestows
> A secret instinct to discern its foes ;
> The goose, a silly bird, avoids the fox ;
> Lambs fly from wolves, and sailors steer from rocks ;
> Evans the gallows as his fate foresees,
> And bears the like antipathy to trees.

It is clear that there were often troubles at this time, no doubt often for political reasons, about elections.

Among Rawlinson's MSS. are minute memoranda about the method of election.

* See Hearne's Diary, ed. Doble, vol. i. p. 314.

There were many oaths taken to elect honestly, and much intrigue nevertheless, and the way to a scholarship was strewn with pitfalls. Even when they were admitted the troubles of the scholars were by no means over. There was often trouble about the " overplus commons " —the grant made above the Founder's scanty allowance —and among Seniors about the wood cut during the year, which Peter Mews had given the Seniors leave to divide among themselves.

Another note from Rawlinson's MSS. throws light on the nature of some of the complaints. I do not know who was the writer; but he hints at much juggling in the matter of overplus commons, as well as cooking of accounts.

These charges and squabbles were not unnatural where the government of the College was in the hands of so small a body, and where the emoluments of the junior Fellows were so small.

In 1737 the College—or rather the Convention— sought permission to divide the fines. This was against the statutes, and the Visitor (Hoadly was then Bishop of Winchester) refused. After Hoadly's death some arrangements were made by which the Seniors succeeded in obtaining what they wanted. They divided one third of the fines, the rest going to " Domus."

Holmes, who supplemented his income from the College by the Regius Professorship of Modern History, several benefices and eventually the Deanery of Exeter, was a good ruler and a generous benefactor. One part of his bequest added to the College buildings. The executors were instructed to save up some of the rents due to him till " it amounts to the sum of £2000, which is to be employed in a convenient building for the Fellows." The site of the Old Dolphin inn, which is shown as still standing in Loggan's plate, was used before the end of the century for the erection of four sets of rooms which since that date have been generally in the occupation of Fellows. Laud had especially desired that members of the Foundation should not occupy the rooms he had built.

That such benefactions were needed is shown by not a few cases of large debts, and even sequestration of fellowships. The following account, from among the books collected by Rawlinson, gives one of these cases.

Sr. Jackson (20 Senr.) ¾ yr.

Batt. Qr.	£	s.	d.	Allowance.	£	s.	d.
1st.	0	6	0		7	17	9
2nd.	0	6	6		1	18	9
3rd.	0	0	6				
4th.	1	1	0	Due to him .	5	19	0
Wood cut.	0	4	9				
	1	18	9				

" Jan. 18, 1733. I have received the sum of five pounds and nineteen shillings of the Rev. Mr. Saunders, Fellow of S. John's College, being due to Moore on his sequestration of Mr. Jackson's fellowship, recd. I say for the use of the said —— Moore by me

H. BEAVER."

The terminal battels of the Fellows at this time, judging from the books of 1744 and 1750, seem to have rarely exceeded £8, while some who were constantly in residence did not much exceed a quarter of that sum.

The terminal charge to graduate members of the College out of residence, judging from the cases of the Earl of Lichfield and Lord Carteret, seems to have been only 1s. 3d. The total amount of all the commoners' battels for a term would be about £160.

A sheet slipped into the 1583–1584 bursary book, and having an account for March 1769, shows the simple fare and small expenses of those living in the College at that date. At "Fry^d Din^r" Dr. Henbourn, Dr. Thorp and Mr. Cure had veal and bacon at 1s. 8d., and roots and butter 4d. On Saturday they had Harslet* and apple sauce, which cost 2s. 8d. ; on Monday a lamb's head, spinach and butter for 2s. 10d. It was vacation and only three undergraduates, Speed, Farraine and Hall, seem to have been "up." They dined well on Sunday on "roast veal, butter, &c.," for 3s., a shilling each, which would not be counted cheap in these days. Mr. Clare paid for his dinner on Tuesday—

	£	s.	d.
"Pleace & Lobster Sauce . .	0	4	0
Neck Mutton, &c. . . .	0	2	6
Brokerry & Potetoes, &c. . .	0	1	2
	0	7	8 "

while others were faring more simply together for 3s. 4d. In Common Room on Wednesday there met the Vice-President, Dr. Nichols, Dr. Chalmers, Dr. Thorp, Mr. Clare, Mr. Warneford, Mr. Dennis, Mr. Luntley and Mr. Cure, and the dinner for them all only came to

* Probably my readers are too elegant to have met with this dish, so I give them Dr. Johnson's definition, "the heart, liver and lights of a hog, with the windpipe and part of the throat to it."

12*s*. 9*d*., though it consisted of " beef stakes pye, three boiled fowl, oyster sauce, bacon, roots and butter." The same night two undergraduates gave supper in their rooms, the one two fowls and oysters, 5*s*. 6*d*., and two lobsters 2*s*., the other, cold veal 1*s*., cold ham 1*s*. 6*d*., pick. salmon 2*s*. 4*d*., oyl 3*d*.

Whether or no high thinking accompanied this comparatively plain living, it is difficult to say. The College did not rank many persons of distinction among its Fellows in the later years of the eighteenth century. Charles Wheatley was an industrious divine, whose book on the Thirty-nine Articles was long used in Oxford and outside. Eminent men, such as Dr. Dillenius, with whom Linnæus came to stay in Oxford, were attached to the College. But the Presidents who succeeded Holmes* were not men of special eminence, and the College certainly lost some of its influence in the University. William Derham D.D. was President from Dr. Holmes's death (elected April 14, 1748) to his own on July 16, 1757. He was an indefatigable worker, and made an almost perfect calendar of the College archives. His successor, William Walker D.C.L., held office only from July 26 to November 30, 1757, when he resigned, preferring to retain the Principalship of New Inn Hall. Thomas Fry D.D., his successor, was a Bristol scholar. He ruled till his death, 1772, and was buried at Clifton. Samuel Dennis, who took the degree of D.D. after his election, was President

---

* An interesting account of a journey of Dr. Holmes to Scotland in 1737, from the note-book of his butler, George Quartermaine, was printed in the *Antiquary*, July 1897. This Quartermaine came of a family long connected with the College. In 1694, A. Quartermaine was Porter (as an inscription in the lodge records).

from December 2, 1772 to his death, March 4, 1795. With the election of his successor, Michael Marlow, a new era began.

Long before this the College had made its peace with the reigning dynasty. Diana Lady Lichfield, whose husband had been Chancellor of the University and was a S. John's man, left in 1779 a large picture of George III. to the College. The king and queen themselves visited Oxford, accepted the President's hospitality, and sent their pictures, which now hang in the lodgings.

In Dr. Fry's Presidentship the College " restored " the chapel, adding much classical ornament. A list of subscribers preserved in the Library shows the costly nature of the proceeding. Of its results it is impossible now to judge, the chapel having undergone still more serious treatment in the present century. The hall was enlarged and ceiled during the same period.

The chapel in the eighteenth century was constantly used for what would, earlier or later, have been considered strictly parochial services. The register of the chapel still preserved, and of which Dr. Holmes gave Rawlinson a copy, records one baptism—that of Brian Jackson, scholar of the College, October 29, 1722, " by me, William Holmes, Fellow of S. John's College." Among the burials are those of Waple 1712, Tadlow 1716, Delaune 1728, Holmes 1748. The list of marriages is a long one. It extends from 1695 to Lord Hardwick's Marriage Act. Over two hundred couples were married in the half-century, many from North-More, Fyfield, and Hanborough, but others with no apparent connection with the College.

A record of the life of one college in the eighteenth century is very like that of another. There are lawyers, travellers, scholars, among the Fellows, but the interests of the majority are clerical, and there is every variety in the way in which they are expressed. Good men like Waple in their benefactions expressed the desire of their lives that benefices should be given only to such of the Fellows " as they should verily believe in their consciences to be duly qualified for so weighty an office and work as the cure of souls." But others, no doubt, felt with the wit of the " Oxford Sausage,"

> " These fellowships are pretty Things;
> We live indeed like petty kings :
> But who can bear to waste his whole Age,
> Amid the dulness of a College.
> Debarr'd the common joys of life,
> And that prime Bliss, a loving Wife ?
> O ! what's a Table richly spread
> Without a woman at its Head !
> Would some snug Benefice but fall
> Ye Feasts, ye dinners, farewell all !
> To offices I'd bid adieu
> Of Dean, Vice-Praes.—of Bursar too ;
> Come Joys that rural Quiet yields,
> Come Tithe, and House, and Fruitful Fields."

CHAPTER XI

THE NINETEENTH CENTURY

A PLEASANT vagueness best covers the dates of our last historical chapter. No harsh distinction shall separate the early Victorians from those who welcomed the Allied Sovereigns. The age of the Regency may give us some illustrations of college worthies, and we may place our other stories where we please.

Somewhere in this dim past there was no College tutor, and it was felt to be a great mistake when the President (who nominates) revived the office.

Dr. Marlow, President 1795–1828, was a dignified and important figure and a Canon of Canterbury. His wife was admired for her civil hospitality at a time when ladies in Oxford were rare. Her parties had a distinction which is never common in University towns. Mrs. Siddons, it is remembered, would read a play of Shakespeare for Mrs. Marlow's friends.*

To this period let me attribute some stories which show that the Fellows of S. John's have at times been put to strange shifts. A learned doctor, who had long fled from duns, relied upon the almost supernatural

---

* I remember the late Sir Charles Anderson, who was in her day an undergraduate of Oriel, telling me he was once invited to S. John's to hear the great actress, and had never ceased to regret he did not go.

sagacity of the College porter.   Often had this prudent man discovered and checked the entrance of a bailiff. Once, it is said, he allowed such a worthy to sit in the lodge upon the trunks of a Fellow who was anxious to depart without an interview with his unwelcome visitor. The security seemed perfect ; but the Fellow was smuggled out another way ; and then, said the porter, " Why do you tarry here ?   He whom you seek is now far on the high way to London, or Birmingham, or Timbuctoo."   There is some mention of a railway in the story, but this would bring the tale too near to our own day for any of us to believe it.   To the same undated past, perhaps to the same person, belongs a tale of a bailiff who eluded all janitorial vigilance and presented himself in the rooms of his victim, who lived on the ground floor of the front quad.   " Ah," said the hearty old gentleman, " you have caught me at last, and I am doubly yours, for my severe rheumatism prevents even an attempt at an escape.   Your skill deserves recognition.   You shall share with me the last bottle of College port which I shall taste for many a day.   This trap-door leads to my cellar.   I am too crippled to descend myself, but on the top bin at your left hand you will find a bottle well worth your tasting.   Bring it up, I beg of you, with care."   The bailiff descended into the bowels of the earth, the trap was shut on him, and it was some days before his faint cries aroused the attention of a " scout."   It is added (no doubt by a later hand), that the cellar was empty.   The learned doctor had not remained to see the results of the subterannean expedition.   He was a doctor, I am bound to add, of law, not divinity.

Stories of this kind cling to all colleges. All have had their eccentrics, and few have forgotten them. Another tale records a defence of tandem-driving, which drew forth from a famous Bishop of Oxford a witty comparison of the difference between placing the hands side by side, and stretching one in front of the other, the nose taking the position of the dog-cart behind the tandem horses. Another, which concerns the same prelate and a Fellow of S. John's, makes the latter (who spoke his thoughts aloud) delight the Common Room by declaring that the Bishop had burst into a peal of laughter when he had declared his willingness, nay, his delight, in offering an evening service at S. Giles's, if it would benefit any member of his beloved flock ; " but ₁I said *to myself*," added the divine, " I'll be hanged if I do."

These stories must belong to the primitive ages. The austerity of modern Oxford cannot contemplate the personages without horror. It is true that they probably quoted the classics as freely as do the Doctors of Divinity in the novels of Thomas Love Peacock, but their conversation after dinner, it cannot be doubted, was regrettably silent as to the details of their pupils' studies or their wives' tea-parties. A dim past indeed it must be, for it is said that there were then some sets of rooms in the College (which shall not be identified by me) that received among the impolite the designation of " Fuddlers' Hall." No doubt a commentator will enable us to substitute the reading " Muddlers'," for we have a fine contempt for the studies of the past, while we should never deny its sobriety.

The College remained a small one till of recent years,

and it was always economical. At the end of the last century it was said that a commoner might maintain himself "very respectably for £120"; * and it would be true to-day. Simplicity of living endured at least till the days when ladies introduced "Society" into Oxford.

In the middle of the century a well-known man of letters and bibliographer, the head of a house too in the University, was generally to be met at the College gaudies. He would tell a tale of his youth, to account for his attachment to these frugal banquets. When he still held a fellowship in the College, he was in debt to an Oxford lawyer, also associated with the College, to the extent of fifteen hundred pounds. He was determined that he would pay off the debt. His fellowship, his post as sub-librarian of the Bodleian, and his literary works enabled him to do this in three years, but only by the exercise of the most ascetic economy. He lived, he would say, during these years, solely on his commons and allowances, which he supplemented by an occasional red herring. When there came a College gaudy only did he allow himself to dine to his satisfaction, and he liked to preserve the pleasant memory to the end of his life. Many of the Fellows of those days lived a simple life enough. Of one it is said that his milk and roll would be left outside his "oak" of a morning, too often to be devoured by his neighbour's jackdaw; and he was unable to replace the homely fare.

On occasion, however, the Society showed a dignified hospitality. On June 12, 1834, the College entertained the Duke of Wellington, on his installation as Chan-

* Dibdin's *Reminiscences of a Literary Life*, p. 80 note.

cellor of the University. To meet him there were present the Duke of Cumberland, Lord Eldon (especially welcome at S. John's because "he never ratted") then High Steward of the University, and "other noble visitors who accompanied His Grace, and a select party of the Chancellor's particular friends." The account which Dr. Ingram, who was then President of Trinity College, gives, may be worth preserving.

"There were four tables arranged in the following manner: at the upper end was the high table, standing as usual from north to south; the President sitting in the middle, with the Chancellor and the Duke of Cumberland, on his right hand, the vice-chancellor and the high steward on his left. The three other tables extended nearly the whole length of the hall from east to west; the gallery over the entrance being tastefully decorated with flowers and evergreens and filled with ladies of rank."

The betting book preserved in the Common-room shows the keen interest taken by the College in the politics of the day.

The College, during the last hundred years, has had but three Presidents: Dr. Marlow 1795–1828, Dr. Wynter 1828–1871, Dr. Bellamy from that year.

The election of Dr. Marlow was a popular one. "He was a gentleman and a scholar, uniting great diffidence with undoubted attainments." One who was then an undergraduate tells that:

"in due course the whole College was regaled with a sumptuous dinner by the newly elected President, who came to our several common rooms for drinking wine, to pledge us, and to receive in return the heartiest attestations of our esteem and respect for him—the masters by themselves, the bachelors by themselves, and scholars and commoners each in their particular banqueting room. I remember one forward freshman shouting aloud on this occasion as the new President retreated :

> Nunc est bibendum ; nunc pede libero
> Pulsanda tellus.

The stars of midnight twinkled upon our orgies; but this was a day never to come again."

The writer of this reminiscence may well have further mention here.

A picture on the walls of the Library, as well as several rare books on its shelves, preserves the memory of a son of S. John's who, in this century, surpassed the fame of Rawlinson as a bibliographer. Thomas Frognall Dibdin (1776–1847), ignorant as he certainly was in some respects, rendered great services to the libraries and collectors of the future. He took his degree from S. John's in March 1801, and he always retained an attachment to the place of his studies, perhaps because they were not pursued to the extent of making him a close or accurate scholar. In his later life he gave large paper copies of his most famous books, the " Typographical Antiquities," the " Bibliographical Decameron," the "Introduction to the Classics," and the " Ædes Althorpianae," to his "beloved College." He was a prolific writer and a keen student of the history of books; "how alive," as he says of Bishop Dampier of Ely, "to all the subtleties of typographical distinctions and varieties." He revelled in catalogues and in book sales, " matchless copies," and the luxuries of the bookseller's table. The " Bibliographical Decameron "—three beautiful volumes printed for the author by W. Bulmer & Co., 1817—gives the reader the notion of a writer who might have come from the clerical gallery of Thomas Love Peacock. His portrait is by some late imitator of Laurence, perhaps Jackson— a kindly humourous face, not without a touch of keenness.

Dibdin's affection for the College so constantly asserted is said to have been, in Douglas Jerrold's phrase, an "unremitting" kindness. He had more interest in books than in battels. But he is a man whom the College may well be glad to have done something to train. Of the training he does not speak warmly. "College exercises," he says, "were trite, dull, and uninstructive. The University partook of this distressing somnolency. There seemed to be no spur to emulation and to excellence." We have changed all that now, and to some it would seem that we have goads as well as spurs. Men such as Dibdin learnt much from a life which would seem idle to-day. Rushworth, Burton, Gibbon are no slight works to study, and few to-day disturb the "Body of the Byzantine Historians."

The teaching, it may be, was as slight then as it is to-day excessive. "All the lectures," says Dibdin, "had only the air of schoolboy proceedings ; nothing lofty, stirring, or instructive was propounded to us. There were no College prizes, and lecture and chapel were all that we seemed to be called upon to attend to." But his conclusion saves all: "After lecture the day was over ; and, oh ! what days were these ! "

The passage in which he recounts the happiest hours of his College life is worth quoting, in spite of its style.

"Boating, hunting, shooting, fishing—these formed in times of yore, the chief amusement of the Oxford Scholar. They form them now, and will ever form them; being good, and true, and lawful amusements in their several ways, when partaken of in moderation. But who shall describe the inward glow of delight with which that same scholar first sees the furniture of his rooms as his own—and his rooms, a sort of castle, impervious, if he pleases, to the intruding foot! Everything about him begets a spirit of independence. He reads—he writes—he reposes—he carouses, as that spirit induces. All that he puts his hands upon, is his own. The fragrant bohea, the sparkling port; the friends few or many, which encircle him; while the occupation of the past, and the schemes for the coming day, furnish themes which ultimately soothe and animate the enthusiastic coterie. The anticipations of the morrow keep the forehead as smooth and the heart as warm as when the day of sport and of pastime has closed. There can be no let or hindrance. A lecture, which occupies a class only one hour, is as an intellectual plaything. It is over, and half the college is abroad; some few to wend their solitary steps 'where the harebells and violets blow'; and to return upon the bosom of Isis beneath the trembling radiance of the moon, after having visited the ruins of Godstow, or entered the sacred antiquity of Iffley.

"But I am dealing in generals, when to be instructive I ought perhaps to particularise."

And here he ceases to be entertaining.

Dibdin's picture of the teaching was no doubt not true for long. It appears from the "Life of H. W. Burrows"* that in 1832 a freshman scholar would attend eight lectures a week, and that the more serious

* By Miss Wordsworth, p. 23.

students kept up the Hebrew which they had begun to learn at Merchant Taylors'. But, at any rate before the Victorian era, the students were not over-lectured. Manners change and wines, and though the " sparkling port " may have lost its charm, and the lectures increased their terrors, the College has not ceased to train scholars because it has fallen under the sway of perpetual examinations, and thrown open its doors to students of the gas and the match, of what Americans call " the human cadaver," of the private lives of Shelley and Burns, and of the comparative philology of the South Tartar dialects.

If we were to search for the source of that natural piety which has bound the generations of modern S. John's each to each we should find it, it is most probable, in a continuous chain of literary interest. It is certain, at any rate, that the names which the College history in the nineteenth century brings most readily to mind are of literary men. Peers and administrators, bishops and lawyers, there have been in a modest proportion, but it is to men of letters that we most naturally turn. A few names taken almost at random from a period of sixty or seventy years may be briefly recalled.

Among those who in the middle of the century connected the College with the outside world John Leycester Adolphus (1795–1862) should not be forgotten. He was a Merchant Taylors' scholar in 1811, and won the Newdigate in 1814. His demonstration that Scott was the author of *Waverley* first brought him into notice (*Letters to Richard Heber, Esq.*, 1821). No one who knows Lockhart is likely to forget the records of the visits of Adolphus to Abbotsford, of Scott's charming kindness and tact, or of Adolphus's clever and agreeable personality. If S. John's is in some degree associated, as I believe it is, with Shakespeare, it is pleasant to add such an association as this with Scott. Lockhart says of the identification: "It was reserved for the enthusiastic industry and admirable ingenuity of this juvenile academic to set the question at rest by an accumulation of critical evidence which no sophistry could evade, and yet produced in a style of such high-bred delicacy, that it was impossible for the hitherto veiled prophet to take the slightest offence with the hand that had for ever abolished his disguise."* He adds: "Hereafter I am persuaded his volume will be revived for its own sake." It would be an agreeable task to any S. John's man to revive it. Adolphus's own notes are some of the happiest contributions to the "Life"; no one will forget the "truly exquisite" description of Scott's laugh, or of that rainy afternoon when they sat together in the study, "the stillness of the room unbroken, except by the light rattle of the rain against the window and the dashing trot of Sir Walter's pen over his paper."

The life of Adolphus links the days of Scott with our own. In his last years he held the office of Steward in the College. The gap between him and another prominent, though less interesting, literary figure is slight.

Charles Appleton (1841–1879) was a Reading scholar, and afterwards Fellow. As philosophy lecturer of S. John's "the metaphysics of Hegel, considered from a theological (and almost an Anglican) standpoint, was the special branch of learning to which he

* *Life of Scott*, vol. v. p. 104.

devoted himself." *   He may be longer remembered as
the founder of the *Academy* in 1869, whose distinguishing feature was the signing of reviews by the authors.
In College he was best known as a reformer with ever
new projects. S. John's has never lacked subversive
schemes, originating often in the most unlikely quarters;
but happily they have rarely succeeded in convincing a
body of conservative and sceptical opinion.

In such a College it is natural that literary interests
should have been largely directed towards theology,
and the three other names which naturally rise to
the mind in this connection have left literary work
which is largely, though far from exclusively, theological.

Henry Longueville Mansel (1820–1871) was a S.
John's man of the old type, a Merchant Taylor Scholar
and Fellow. His connection with the College began
even before he went to the school, for he was as a
small boy taught by the Rector of the College living
of East Farndon where Dr. Wynter first saw him. At
Merchant Taylors' the memories of his school-days are
associated with those of many other names honoured
in S. John's, with the present President, with Archdeacon Hessey (himself long a tutor of the College and
then Head Master of the school) and Leopold Bernays,
eminent as a translator. It is impossible for one who
has not known him to attempt to compress Mansel's
extraordinary power, knowledge, wit, generosity of
character, into a paragraph. Every record of him
emphasises his brilliancy, his extraordinary memory,
his astonishing industry and his "humbleness of

* *Dict. Nat. Biogr.* ii. 49.

mind."* Dean Burgon's sketch of him is thought inadequate by those who knew him, but indeed it is impossible to observe the immense impression his powers made upon contemporaries without feeling that no sketch can reproduce it. Of the value of his philosophy and his theology this is not the place to speak. It belongs rather to this book to say simply that memory of his goodness, his industry, and his wit is still fresh in the College of which he was ever the devoted son. A scholarship preserves his name, and many of his books are in the College Library. A bust in the hall of the Lodgings shows those who never saw him something of what he was. His work as tutor, as Waynflete Professor of Moral and Metaphysical Philosophy, as Professor of Ecclesiastical History, and as Dean of St. Paul's, still bears fruit.

But the best picture that I can give of him—and it sets his work too in special association with the College—is that drawn by the late Lord Carnarvon in his introduction to the Lectures on the Gnostic Heresies (1875).

" My first acquaintance with Dean Mansel," he wrote, " was made twenty years ago at the University—when he had everything to give, and I had everything to receive. As I think of him, his likeness seems to rise before me. In one of those picturesque and old-world Colleges—in rooms which, if I remember rightly, on one side looked upon the collegiate quadrangle with its sober and meditative architecture, and on the other caught the play of light and shade cast by trees almost as venerable, on the

* This is brought out by the Rev. E. T. Turner, for so many years Registrar of the University, who first met him in the rooms of E. A. Freeman in 1842. See Burgon's *Twelve Good Men*, ii. 177.

garden grass; in one of those rooms, whose walls were built up to the ceiling with books, which, nevertheless, overflowed on the floor, and were piled in masses of disorderly order upon chairs and tables—might have been seen sitting day after day the late Dean, then my private Tutor, and the most successful teacher of his time in the University. Young men are no bad judges of the capabilities of a teacher; and those who sought the highest honours of the University in the Class schools thought themselves fortunate to secure instruction such as he gave —transparently lucid, accurate, and without stint, flowing on through the whole morning continuously, making the most complicated questions clear.

"But if, as chanced sometimes with me, they returned later as guests in the winter evening to the cheery and old-fashioned hospitality of the Common Room, they might have seen the same man, the centre of conversation, full of anecdote and humour and wit, applying the resources of a prodigious memory and keen intellect to the genial intercourse of society.

"The life of old Oxford has nearly passed away. New ideas are now accepted: old traditions almost cease to have a part in the existence of the place; the very studies have greatly changed, and—whether for good or evil— except for the grey walls which seem to upbraid the altered conditions of thought around them, Oxford bids fair to represent modern Liberalism, rather than the 'Church and State' doctrines of the early part of the century. But of that earlier creed, which was one characteristic of the University, Dean Mansel was an eminent type. Looked up to and trusted by his friends, he was viewed by his opponents as worthy of their highest antagonism; and whilst he reflected the qualities which the lovers of an older system have delighted to honour, he freely expressed opinions which modern Reformers select for their strongest condemnation.

"Such he was when I first knew him twenty years ago —in the zenith of his teaching reputation, though on the point of withdrawing himself from it to a career even more worthy of his great abilities. . . . It was then that I formed an acquaintance which ripened into deep and sincere friendship: which grew closer and more varied as life went on; over which no shadow of variation ever passed; and which was abruptly snapped at the very time when it had become most highly prized."

Those who do not remember Mansel may have had the happiness of knowing another exceptionally brilliant Fellow of the College, whose power and wit will never be forgotten by those who came within their range. Aubrey Moore, though he was not many years a Fellow, held a College living during his absence from Oxford and on his return was constantly in College. His services to religion and the Church are too great and too recent to need emphasis.

The powerful aid which Moore gave, philosophically and historically, to the defenders of the Catholic position of the English Church recalls the memory to the first of the great periods of contest which Oxford, during this century, has witnessed. Mark Pattison described the College, in the last years of his life as being, like Christ Church, "corroded with ecclesiasticism." It is of little consequence that the epigram is not justified by facts; it may serve, however, to direct attention to the undoubted truth that the College was intimately concerned in the long troubles which followed the Tractarian movement.

Religious teaching, on the principles of what has come to be regarded as the old High Church party, before the days of Newman, had never ceased in S. John's and this followed on the systematic course of Divinity which has always been a feature of the work of the school on which the College chiefly relied.

There is an interesting passage in Miss Wordsworth's " Life of H. W. Burrows,"* which shows how the Church teaching at S. John's was prepared for by the careful and orthodox instruction of Mr. Bellamy at Merchant Taylors' (1832).

Thus many were disposed, readily, to listen to Newman's Sermons and the Tracts for the Times; and it is among the most vivid memories of several survivors of those days, that they listened among the crowds at S. Mary's or looked after Newman as he walked rapidly through the streets in his high-braced trousers, low shoes and white stockings.

Briefly, S. John's was brought into connection with the Tractarian movement chiefly through three men. Henry Bristow Wilson, B.D., then Fellow and Senior Tutor, was one of the four Tutors who addressed the famous letter to the Editor of the *Tracts*, on March 8, 1841, which began the injudicious and ignorant attempt to suppress the movement. Mr. Wilson's Bampton Lectures (1851) on " The Communion of Saints," gave open expression to the principles on which he acted in opposition to the Tractarians. His "Latitudinarianism" was further developed in the essay which he contributed to " Essays and Reviews," 1860.   Of his general attitude in controversy, no better description can be found than

* p. 16.

that given ·by Dean Stanley, who sympathised with his position. "Wilson," he wrote, "has committed the unpardonable rashness of throwing out statements, without a grain of proof, which can have no other object than to terrify and irritate, and which have no connection with the main argument of his essay."*   A subsequent prosecution and its failure are not unfamiliar incidents in theological disputes which have their rise in Oxford.

Of less notoriety, but probably of more influence, was H. A. Woodgate, who was strongly in favour of the Tractarians, a friend of Pusey, and was, says Dean Church, " a centre of influence in Oxford and in the country." †

The third name is that of the President of the College from 1828 to 1871. Philip Wynter, born in 1793, matriculated in 1811 as a Merchant Taylors' Scholar, and took second class honours in classics in the Waterloo year.   He was elected President in 1828, and he was Vice-Chancellor 1840–1844, critical years for the Oxford movement. The "Christian Remembrancer," 1844, spoke of him as " a sort of High Churchman."   It is however, clear enough, from his account of the whole proceedings, from which many quotations appear in Dr. Pusey's " Life," that he had little sympathy with the Tractarians and no very thorough knowledge of theology. Few now will be disposed to dispute Dean Church's judgment that the suspension of Dr. Pusey, and the long business that preceded and followed though " it was the mistake of upright and conscientious men . . .

* *Life of Dean Stanley*, ii. 34.
† *Oxford Movement*, p. 293.

was wrong, stupid, unjust, pernicious."*   Of Dr. Wynter,
as a Tutor and President, I do not think I can do better
than quote the words of one who was long Dr. Pusey's
assistant teacher in Hebrew, and whose own ability, wit
and kindliness will long be remembered in College.†

" I have been unable to meet with any particulars as to
the reputation of Dr. Wynter as Tutor of the College.
Of course there are few living within reach who can speak
of events that happened so many years ago.   All that I
have been able to discover is, that he was very popular
with his pupils.   And certainly if I may appeal to the
University Class List, and take the success of this College
in the Schools as any evidence of the work which was
done by him as Tutor and in the early years of his Presidency, he must have been a very successful Tutor, and a
very vigilant President.   He possessed one faculty to an
extraordinary degree, which must have been of inappreci-
able value to him as Tutor, and afterwards as President,
and that was his marvellous power of judging human
character.   If the rapidity with which he formed his
opinions was astonishing, the accuracy of them when
formed was only more so.   He possessed, among many
others, another faculty of great value to a man in his
position.   It was a gift, and one of God's gifts which a
man can only receive and not acquire, however much he
may strive to do so—which was a keen appreciation of
Art, and a delicate critical taste for Literature.   Of his
natural gifts he availed himself throughout his life, and
cultivated them till within a day or two of his death."

Dr. Wynter was succeeded by one whose lifelong

* *Oxford Movement*, p. 293.
† Henry Deane, B.D., Fellow (1856–92) in A sermon printed for
private circulation, 1871, pp. 9–10.

association with the College and with the school from which the majority of its most distinguished members have been drawn, fitted him, as no member of the College was fitted, to preside over the Society. As undergraduate, Fellow, tutor, precentor, and still more as President, he has rendered services to the College as great as have ever been rendered to it by the greatest of its sons. This much it may be allowed to say : the historian of the College hereafter will say much more.

The last fifty years in the life of S. John's have seen an almost complete change in its constitution. The original foundation was practically a close one for Merchant Taylors' School, and the schools of Coventry, Bristol, Reading, and Tonbridge. The University Commission which reported in 1858 recommended that all Fellowships should be thrown open, and the Ordinance of 1861, based upon this, provided, instead of the fifty Fellowships of the original foundation, for eighteen Fellowships, and thirty-three scholarships. Under this constitution, which was not to endure long, the College was able to add to its members several most distinguished students of other Colleges. The Fellowships under the Ordinance were for life, but were to be vacated by marriage.

The reasons given for the changes of the first Commission were : " (1) that tuition would be more efficient with open Fellowships; (2) that the College would get less good candidates for its open Fellowships if the majority of them were close; (3) that it is undesirable that a college should be permanently governed by a society of which the majority must be chosen from so confined a circle as it necessarily must be if the Fellowships remain close." These reasons, it must have been clear to persons of observation, were such as would inevitably lead to further changes; and twenty years did not pass before the constitution of the Colleges was again placed "in the melting-pot."

From 1877 to 1879 the University of Oxford Commission was investigating the affairs of the Colleges and considering every sort of scheme for the alteration of the University. S. John's was not much in sympathy with the aims which were supposed to animate the majority of the Commissioners. It remained sympathetic to the Church, and opposed to educational revolutions. It is true that some of the most startling changes proposed were advocated before the Commission by one of the Fellows of S. John's, Dr. Appleton; but, on the other hand, the College was represented on the Commission itself by the ablest and most clear-headed of its members, whose acute questions to the witnesses showed that his conservative principles in no way impaired his desire to secure a liberal education at the University, open to poor as well as rich.

Materials exist from which, if it should ever be thought desirable, a history of the attempts of the College to meet the requirements of the Commissioners, and at the same time to preserve many of the distinctive features of the foundation, could be drawn up. But the draft scheme passed by the College in December 1877 did not meet with the approval of the Commission, particularly in its resolutions that the person elected President should " be in Priest's Orders, or if not in Priest's Orders, shall be admitted to the same within four months from the day of his election to the office of President," and that the Fellowships should be divided into two classes, clerical and lay, of which the latter should always form two-thirds of the whole number.

Independently of questions affecting general policy, there were at this time many questions of financial importance. These were treated separately, and by changes made in the system of the College accounts, and many other alterations, silent as well as formal, the recognised trust funds of the College were reduced to eight. A scheme for throwing the Trust Funds held by the College into one common fund was drawn up by the Bursar in 1861. It was not carried into effect, but on appeal to the Privy Council certain funds, being those by which the members of the Foundation were paid, were amalgamated.

The eight funds now left were : the Wood Bevington trust for the maintenance of Choral service in the College chapel, the Bliss Trust for the Librarian, the Lambe, Whitfield and Smith Trusts ; the Winterslow trust (for the increase of the endowment of small livings), and the new foundations, which happily the Commissions could not destroy, of Mr. Fereday and Dr. Casberd. The latter in 1843 left money to the College from which four Scholarships have been founded, each of the value of £80 per annum, and also certain exhibitions. Candidates must be undergraduates not on any foundation, of at least one year's standing in the College. The former, Dudley Fereday, Esquire, of Ettingshall Park, Staffordshire, founded four Fellowships tenable for fourteen years. They are open with certain limitations and under certain conditions in respect of literary proficiency, first to the kindred of the Founder, secondly to natives of Staffordshire.   The foundation took effect in 1854. The Founder himself appointed the first two Fellows, Frederick Smith* and Alexander Staveley Hill. †   The Founder's restriction of the fellowships to members of the Church of England has been, as is usual with such restrictions, abolished.

We may now pass to the Constitution under which the College now exists.

The Commission on June 16, 1881, made new statutes for the College.   By these the office of President was thrown open to all persons, whether in holy orders or not, and whether connected with the College in any way or not; the Fellows only being instructed to " choose a person who shall be of at least thirty years of age, and who, in their judgment, shall be most fit for the government of the College as a place of religion, learning, education and research."

There are to be not less than fourteen nor more than eighteen fellowships, open without any restriction, save that there must be one Fellow in holy orders of the Church of England residing and giving religious instruction to the undergraduate members of the College. Seven of the fellowships may be official (attached to the offices of Tutor, Lecturer, or Principal Bursar), the rest without any restriction or duties.   An official Fellow if not married when elected vacates his fellowship by marriage, " if such marriage shall take place within seven years from the day of his election " (this the Visitor has interpreted to mean "election to such

* Now Frederick Smith Shenstone, of Sutton Hall, Surrey.

† The Rt. Hon. A. S. Hill, M.P. for Staffordshire (Kingswinford), Deputy High Steward of the University and Judge-Advocate of the Fleet.

official fellowship "). Two further *ex officio* Fellowships may be held by the Laudian Professor of Arabic* and the Professor of Civil Engineering. †

There are also not less than twenty-eight scholarships (now thirty-two), fifteen appropriated to Merchant Taylors', two to Coventry, two to Bristol, two to Reading, and one (this does not come into operation until the vacation of a fellowship on the old foundation) to Tonbridge. Four Senior Scholarships confined to former pupils of Merchant Taylors' School were also founded by the Statutes.

It can perhaps hardly be said that these Statutes have yet come fully into operation. The College has still happily no less than five Fellows of the Old Foundation surviving. Two of the life Fellows elected under the Ordinance also remain, so that there is still a majority on the governing body who hold their places independently of the present Statutes. The College preserves many of its old customs. It has no married Fellows: thus in S. John's, as it can scarcely be elsewhere in modern Oxford, " the College life is most closely centred within the College walls."

In 1877 it was calculated that the average number of undergraduates in residence was one hundred and seventeen. There are now one hundred and sixty-four undergraduates on the books, of whom perhaps fifteen may be out of residence.

Among all its changes the College has, owing chiefly to the wise rule of the last twenty-seven years, kept in

* The present distinguished Professor is unable to accept a Fellowship without surrendering that which he holds at New College.

† This is not yet founded.

harmony with its past. Within the last few years a succession of three senior tutors, all men of strongly marked characteristics and widely divergent opinions, has tended to strengthen its vitality and expand its interests. Its close association with Merchant Taylors' still happily continues, and has recently been marked by the election of the Head Master, William Baker, D.D., Prebendary of S. Paul's, formerly Fellow and Senior Tutor of the College to an Honorary Fellowship. At the same time a similar recognition of former connection was made in the election of Herbert Armitage James, D.D., Head Master of Rugby School, also a former Fellow and Tutor. The Church which has taken from S. John's in past days four archbishops in Matthew, Laud, Juxon, and Sir William Dawes, has now a fifth in William West Jones, Archbishop of Cape Town and Metropolitan of South Africa, and bishops in Reginald Stephen Copleston, Bishop of Colombo (whose brilliant early essays in letters in *The Oxford Spectator* are still fresh in Oxford memories, and to whom we owe also the most complete English study of Buddhism), and Alfred Willis, Bishop of Honolulu.

Among present members of the College, besides a goodly array of eminent ecclesiastics, Law is represented by the Right Hon. Sir James Parker Deane, and by Montague Crackanthorpe; Literature by Henry Duff Traill; those rulers of the modern world, the special correspondents, by Charles Austin; and what is not represented by Charles Lempriere?

The recruits whom the new statutes have given us may be trusted to preserve the memories of the old foundation. They have come from many different schools and Colleges, yet still the oldest association has been most worthily maintained, by none more conspicuously than by one whose loss the College has had recently to deplore, Charles Stennett Adamson, whose four first classes were followed by tutorial work of a singularly sympathetic and helpful kind. In spite of its changes the College has preserved, strong and distinct, its unity with the past: and that this may ever remain is one of the strongest wishes of one of its most grateful and loyal sons.

CHAPTER XII

THE COLLEGE TO-DAY. LIBRARY AND GROVES: CHAPEL AND HALL

THE description of the College as it stands to-day may best enable us to remember what we have preserved from the past, and how we use it now.

It is tempting to linger over the history of the Library, but adequate space cannot be allotted in so short a history as this.

In the present century its appearance has probably not very greatly changed. New cases have been added to the inner Library. It is to be feared that book-cases as old as Laud's time, and with his arms on them, disappeared in the process; one is now in the President's lodgings. A large case has been added to hold the ancient vestments; and Laud's cap and stick, a pastoral staff, and some of the rarer books are shown under glass. The portrait of Charles I. of which much has already been said hangs on the wall. By it is another contemporary portrait of the king in plaster, given by an attached member of the College, the late Rev. J. C. Jackson. The other pictures are Archbishop Laud, Sir William Paddy, the Rev. T. F. Dibdin, two little ovals of Charles I. and Henrietta

Maria, and "some very curious paintings on copper supposed to be by Carlo Dolce"* of which the less said the better.

The books have been treated, it would appear, with no uniform courtesy by librarians. The eighteenth-century regulations are well worth preserving. It were well if they were reinforced, though the taking of oaths is in these liberal times out of fashion.

The rules, it might appear, were more effective for the preservation than the perusal of books. Certainly it was the opinion of some of the Librarians that it was their duty above all things to "keep" the books. "Have you read all the books there are now in the Library, sir?" said a Librarian within living memory to a junior Fellow. There is a tale too that when, in the dark ages, the offices of Steward of Common-room and Librarian were held by the same person, the accounts were not kept so strictly separate as was desirable in the interests of literature. But the Library was always attentively if not always wisely watched. A catalogue in manuscript, interleaved with the old Bodleian catalogue, was drawn up "about 1750, apparently by Dr. Holmes.† This catalogue was perfect in its way, and was supplemented by MS. notes in many of the books referring to authorship, &c., and derived from sources now no longer accessible." In the middle of the present century confusion was introduced into the arrangement of the New Library. The Old was happily left untouched.

* *The Oxford University and City Guide*, 1817.

† I here quote, and in some later passages, from an extremely interesting report on the Library by the Rev. A. T. S. Goodrick, Fellow 1879-90; Librarian 1883-1890.

In the year 1871, and for some following years, a Library Committee made confusion worse confounded. In 1883 a Librarian of great knowledge and enthusiasm was appointed, and he soon worked a wondrous reformation. His successors have endeavoured to follow in his steps, and the work of entirely cataloguing and arranging the Library on established principles approaches completion.

When a catalogue of the entire Library " which contains many rare works not in the possession of the Bodleian or other Oxford Libraries " is ready, it is to be hoped that it may be printed, and that the Library, already, during the last six years, much used by scholars, may be made open under necessary restrictions at least to members of the University at large.

All that can be said here of the treasures of the Library must be brief. They fall chiefly into four classes. First there are the books and manuscripts given by the Founder and his friends, and during the early days of the College. The books in this class are, chiefly, valuable early editions of the classics and works on the controversy between England and Rome; William Roper's own copy of the great folio, printed by Rastell, of the works of his father-in-law Sir Thomas More is among them. The second class includes the magnificent gifts of Laud and of Sir William Paddy, the latter chiefly old medical books, many of extreme rarity and bibliographical value. Several gifts at the beginning of the eighteenth century, notably those of Nathaniel Crynes, Coventry scholar and Fellow, and Esquire Bedel of Arts and Physics, who died in 1745, and of Dr. Rawlinson, help to distinguish another class.

And during the last thirty years extensive purchases have been made. Probably from the point of view of the special student or the bibliographer the Library is most rich in liturgical and medical works. It is famous for its copies of pre-Reformation and Reformation books of devotion, public and private.

In detail it is difficult to particularise where a brief account must needs be inadequate. Looked at from their connection with college history rather than with bibliography, one or two facts may be noted about the manuscripts. There can be little doubt that many of the manuscripts were presented by the Founder, and came from the spoiled monasteries. From the same source came some of those presented by John Stonor. There are MSS. from the house of S. Mary, Reading, S. Cuthbert, Durham, S. Thomas the Martyr at Lesnes (the house founded by Richard de Lucy), and S. Edmund at Bury.

Of later donors the following is a list, with the number of MSS. presented:—John Atkinson, Commoner of S. John's (1); William Barlow of S. John's, afterwards Ch. Ch. (1); Edward Bernard, Fellow of S. John's (4); John Buckeridge, President (3); Richard Butler, Archdeacon of Northampton (19); Thomas Carill, M.A. Exeter College (1); Christopher Coles, Commoner of S. John's (3); Gabriel Colinge, chaplain of S. John's (1); Henry Cromwell, Fellow of S. John's (1); "Davenet œnopolus Oxon." (Shakespeare's friend, the father of Sir William Davenant)* (1); William Derham, Fellow of S. John's and afterwards President (1); Robert Dow, Merchant Taylor, London (1); Sir Henry

* See above, pp. 93–95.

Ellis, Fellow of S. John's (1); Matthew Gwynne, M.D., Fellow of S. John's (1); Humphrey Haggat, Commoner of S. John's (1); John Hawlye, Principal of Gloucester Hall (1); Richard Jardfield, scholar of S. John's (1); Thomas Lord Knyvet of Escrick (1); John Lambe, Registrar of Peterborough (1); Richard Latewar, Fellow of S. John's (3); Archbishop Laud (10); Nicholas Linnebye, Fellow of S. John's (2); Charles Margas (1); John Marsham, Fellow of S. John's (1); William Morice, Fellow of S. John's (1); Martin Okins, Fellow of S. John's (2); Sir William Paddy, Commoner of S. John's (18); John Pointer, Rector of Slapton, Northants (1); Stephen Pott, bookseller, London (1); Henry Price, Fellow of S. John's (1); William Sherborn, Fellow of S. John's (1); John Smith, Fellow of S. John's (1); John Stonor, of North Stoke, Oxon (10); Richard Tileslyle, Fellow of S. John's (4); Robert Travers, Commoner of S. John's (1); Matthias Turner, Commoner of S. John's (1); Thomas Turner (1); Thomas Walker, Fellow of S. John's (3); Henry Warner, Fellow of S. John's (1); Charles Wheatley, Fellow of S. John's (5); John White, the Founder's brother (16); Hugh Wicksteed, Merchant Taylor, London (1).

The names, it will be seen, cover several centuries, and the manuscripts are of the most diverse nature. Laud's gifts are chiefly Oriental, the results of his agents' ransacking in the East; and some had come to him from Sir Kenelm Digby. Sir William Paddy, in manuscripts as in books, had made a large collection bearing upon medicine and the natural sciences. Buckeridge, besides presenting several MSS. himself, was the agent in procuring the generous gift of

Dr. Richard Butler, Archdeacon of Northampton. Humphrey Haggat, a Commoner of the College in 1620, was fortunate enough to obtain, and loyal enough to present, the manuscript of Wiclif's translation of the Old Testament and Apocrypha, which has been asserted to be in Wiclif's own hand.   Charles Wheatley, a theologian of some note early in the eighteenth century, besides MSS. of his own writings, gave the copy of Hobbes's *Behemoth*, supposed to be in the author's own hand.

Of printed books, the Caxtons, Pynsons, and other early English issues are the most noteworthy.

The College possesses more of the work of Caxton* than any public library in England, except the British Museum, the Bodleian and the Public Library at Cambridge.†

It has one of the two known copies of the " Parvus et Magnus Chato," third edition, which Blades dates conjecturally 1481. It is perfect. Bound with it are the " Curia Sapientiae" (1481 ?) also perfect; the " Eneydos" (1490) imperfect; and the " Pilgrimage of the Soul" (1483), imperfect. It has a copy of the second edition of the " Game and Play of the Chess " (1481 ?), very slightly imperfect. It has the " Chronicles of Ireland," first edition, June 10, 1480, and bound with it the " Description of Britain," August 18, 1480, both slightly imperfect. It has the " Polycronicon," with thirty-four leaves missing; the " Four Sermons" (1483 ?), a perfect copy ; " Troylus and Creside " (1484 ?), also perfect ; and the only perfect copy in existence of

---

* See Blades's *Caxton*, vol. ii.

† Excluding the fragments belonging (Blades, ii. 284) to King Edw. VI.'s Grammar School, St. Alban's.

" Chaucer's Canterbury Tales," second edition (1484 ?). The last has had the cuts painted, most likely by some childish hand.

Another rare book is one of great interest in the history of English comedy, John Heywood's " Play of the Weather." Is it fanciful to trace in the survival in S. John's of this almost, if not quite, unique copy of a work of the father of Ellis Heywood, the author of " Il Moro," another reminiscence of the connection of Sir Thomas White, through William Roper, with the kindred and friends of More?

Of the other treasures, it must suffice to mention a few books which have a special interest in connection with the College.

The large copy of the Second Folio Shakespeare, was given in 1637, two years after its publication, by Henry Osbaston, who was elected a scholar in 1637 from Merchant Taylors', was ejected by the Parliamentary Commissioners, became Rector of Little Ilford, Essex, and died 1669.

A list of the books given, formerly belonging to Laud, to the Library is worth insertion. Probably all came to the College from his own hand.*

De Geographia Universali.   1592.
Ptolemæi Geographia, libri viii.   1546.
India Orientalis, partes iii.–vi.   1601–4.
Francisci Junii De Pictura Veterum.   1637.
Εἰς τὴν Ἀριστοτέλους ῾Ρητορικήν.   1539.
Lucretius.   1514.
Dionysii De Situ Orbis.   1547.
Polybius.   1582.

* This list is probably not complete.

The " Liber Hymnorum Secundum Morem et Consuetudinem Ecclesiæ Sarum.," with the pricked notes for singing, was given by Laud in 1620. It had been one of the Church books of Thame, and had belonged also to Robert King, last abbat and first bishop of Osney.

John Speed's " Σκελετὸς Πολυκίνητος," dedicated to Laud, and the Archbishop's own copy, is in the Library.

Laud's Vulgate, 1566, with his MS. annotations on almost every page, was given by Thomas Earl of Pembroke in 1729. The Thirty-nine Articles, 1571, and another copy 1612, have also Laud's manuscript notes.

The Little Gidding book, given probably by Laud to the College, is the " Whole Law of God, Moral, Ceremonial, and Political, reduced under proper and distinct heads : done at Little Gidding in the county of Huntingdon." It is bound in purple velvet stamped with gold. The illustrations are cut from many sorts of print and engraving, ingeniously fitted to the text, which is a concordance or arrangement of the Mosaic law, formed of verses pasted on to small folio sheets. It is interesting, in connection with this book, to recall that it was Laud who ordained Nicholas Ferrar deacon on Trinity Sunday, 1625, and perhaps this may be one of the books which, in 1640, the young Nicholas and his father brought to Lambeth, when Laud took the lad " up in his arms and laid his hand on his cheek, and earnestly besought God Almighty to bless him and increase all grace in him and fit him every day more and more for an instrument of His glory here upon earth and a saint in Heaven."

Beside the Little Gidding book, in a glass case, are some of the most interesting books, MS. Bestiaries, Wiclif's Bible, two of the Caxtons, Pynson's Hymns and Sequences according to the use of Sarum, the prayer-book that belonged to James I., with Sir William Paddy's MS. account of his last hours, the first prayer-book of Edward VI., and such other treasures as the librarian of the day may think fit to show. Near, in the big bookcase against the east wall, are rare books and fine bindings, specimens of Grolier and of Stephanos, and "a bit of dainty Gascon work, the polished morocco covers, mosaicked in different hues, and bearing intricate designs traced in gold, the leaves painted to exactly imitate the binding." *

Next to the books, on which many more pages might be written, the Laudian relics seem to belong most rightfully to the Library which Laud built. Here are the precious volumes which Sancroft entrusted on his death-bed to Henry Wharton and the giving which, in their ungarbled state, to the world was the last service which that extraordinary young man rendered to learning and the Church. The Diary is a little octavo bound in red morocco. The leaves are brown and singed by Prynne's carelessness or malice, and much of the year 1640 is gone. The open page shows the words:

" The tumults in Scotland, about the Service-book offered to be brought in, began Julii 23, 1637, and continued by fits, and hath now brought that kingdom in danger. No question but there's a great concurrence between them and the Puritan party in England."

* Mrs. Overton in *The Leisure Hour*, October 1893.

Hard by lies the thick volume, the History of the Archbishop's Troubles and Trial. The clear neat close handwriting of the bitter record of injustice, taken down every night in the Tower after the day's baiting at Westminster, shows the extraordinary power and firmness of the old man. These books indeed gave much of its strength to the great Tory and Church movement of the age of Anne.* Near these books is Laud's skull cap, which fell from his head on the scaffold, snipped here and there by irreverent, or too reverent, hands. It is a large red, close-fitting braided *zucchetto*, whose size shows the massive proportion of his head.

Against the wall is a case containing the ivory and ebony walking-stick of the archbishop. It bears the following inscription:

"Hoc baculo dextram subeunte gressus suos firmavit Gulielmus Laud, Archiepiscopus Cantuar., idemque hujus collegii Benefactor insignis, cum ad mortem immeritam ductus esset,

Præsidenti et Sociis Coll. Divi Johannis Baptistæ

D.D.

Gul. Awbery Phelp A.M.

Ecclesiæ de Stanwell

in Com. Middlesex Vicarius

A.D. MDCCCXXV.

The pastoral staff in another case near, which is said to have been found in the College after the Restoration and might have belonged to Laud or Juxon, is by some believed to be merely the ceremonial crozier borne by the heralds at the funeral of Juxon.

* See *William Laud* (Methuen & Co.) second edition, pp. 233-235.

The relics of the Stewart days are completed by the cannon-ball fired into the gateway tower of the College during the siege by the rebel forces. This with the cap and the Laudian manuscripts rest on the case which preserves possessions more ancient and perhaps as precious.

Among the treasures possessed by the College there are none more valuable than the ancient vestments. To these some have been added of later date. As no list of these has yet been printed except in a number of the *Church Times* now out of print, it will be convenient to insert one here.* The vestments now in the possession of S. John's College are as follows :

(i) The orphreys of a chasuble, viz., Latin Cross and pillar with figures of saints and the Virgin and Child, with angels censing.

(ii) The orphreys of another chasuble, also a Latin Cross with figures of saints, and the Baptism of our Lord at the intersection of the Cross.

(iii) The orphreys of a cope. The Annunciation is embroidered upon the hood.

(iv) Two dalmatics of white brocade. The orphreys are of crimson velvet and are simple pillars running down the middle of back and front.

(v) A cope belonging to the same set as No. iv.

(vi) A cope of purple velvet woven with gold. This is a superb vestment. The orphreys are heavily em- broidered with figures of saints, and the hood represents

* This list was originally drawn up by my friend and pupil, Mr. R. F. Cameron Hillman, with the assistance of the Rev. Leighton Pullan, Fellow of the College. I am greatly indebted to Mr. Hill- man for copying it for me. I have made some necessary alterations and additions.

the Coronation of the Blessed Virgin under a canopy of Gothic vaulting. (It is this cope which is popularly supposed to have been worn by Laud, but there is absolutely no authority for the statement.)

(vii) A large fragment of a velvet cope. This is embroidered with the Crucifixion surrounded with exquisite sprays of gold and colours, and with six bells. (The velvet probably shows the real Sarum penitential colour, *i.e.*, not a brown terra-cotta but a soft plum colour.)

(viii) A fragment of a red velvet cope richly embroidered with figures of angels and wheels, representing the vision of Ezekiel. It was used apparently in the seventeenth century as an altar frontal and has a gold fringe of that period.

(ix) Three medieval frontals of brocade much faded.

(x) A frontal of purple plush embroidered with the sacred monogram. This is most probably part of the altar furniture bequeathed by Bishop Buckeridge.

(xi) Two banners of red silk, one painted with S. John Baptist, the Founder's arms and the sacred emblems, the other a banner of the Blessed Virgin. The former has been much mutilated.

(xii) An Italian chasuble of the seventeenth century given recently to the College by the heirs of the Rev. C. N. Robarts, Precentor of Ch. Ch. Cathedral, a devoted member of the College. It is of red silk very heavily embroidered with fruit and flowers.

There are also two altar cushions, on one of which the Presentation of the Magi is beautifully worked. This is not completed. It is of a peculiarly quaint design.

Round the central subject are the four elements, fire being represented by a salamander. There are also ladies in the costume of the early seventeenth century. It has been conjectured that the work was done by one of the many Court ladies resident in Oxford during the wars, when Charles and Henrietta Maria lodged in the city, and that it was made for Laud's College and was unfinished when the Court left. It is a mere conjecture, but a not impossible one.

It will be seen that apart from the post-Reformation work there are the banners made for the College probably at its foundation and used in processions, and the rich and valuable collection much of which is of an earlier date. There is every reason to believe, from the fact that the design of much of the ornament on most of the vestments is of a similar pattern, that these were originally part of the same collection. Whether they were made for the College or purchased, as seems more probable from the architectural details of some of the work which suggests an earlier date than the foundation, by the Founder or others from some dissolved religious house, it is impossible certainly to decide. But that they at one time belonged to Sir Thomas White and were by him given to the College it is difficult to doubt : a note among the College MSS. in the writing of Ralph Hutchinson (President, 1590–1605) confirms this. He speaks of "old superstitious vestments that were conveyed unto me, April 14, 1602, by Mrs. Henry Leech, widow, the Founder's sister's daughter, to be converted to the benefit of some better use for the said College, to which, as is supposed, it some time did appertain." Anthony Wood when he noted this appended the observation which is probably in the main correct. "These I believe being given by the Founder and taken away by him at the Reformation were given to his niece aforesaid." It would seem ·rather that on Sir Thomas White's death they were given, as his property, to his executors.

A robust tradition, which Mr. Andrew Lang has sanctioned in a nodding moment, associates the vestments with Laud. That copes were worn in some of the College chapels in his day is clear from his own remains,* and at S. John's no doubt under Juxon and Baylie, they would be in use. But, though it is probable enough that these very vestments were worn in the College Chapel in the reign of Charles I., there is no proof that Laud wore them.

That Bishop Buckeridge bequeathed some altar furniture to the College has already been mentioned. His gift, further particularised, was "the fronts and cushion of the Communion table, and chalice, and the pall and long cushions, and the clothes belonging thereunto." Much of these cannot be identified. Much certainly has perished.

The Library with its treasures is one of the features which endear the College most deeply to its loyal sons. It combines the two ages and the two Founders that made the College what it is. It looks out on the beautiful quadrangle that Laud's generosity gave, and

---

* *Cf. Laud's Works,* vol. iv. p. 221. A witness at his trial said that there were copes used in some colleges, and that a traveller should say upon the sight of them that he saw just such a thing upon the Pope's back. "The wise man might have said as much of a gown. He saw a gown upon the Pope's back, therefore a Protestant may not wear one," was Laud's reply.

on the gardens which the Society enjoyed from its beginning, and where some of its earliest members lie buried.

The groves have undergone many changes. For some time the College was under obligation to farm them, but in 1612 they were enclosed at the cost of Edward Sprot, Fellow, whose name and work are commemorated in an inscription. In Loggan's print they appear as two separate gardens with a wall between them. In the earlier part of the eighteenth century they were planned out in the most formal style that Le Nôtre and his English followers had made fashionable. A print dedicated to Dr. Holmes shows them in this state. In 1748 they are thus described by Salmon:

"In the first the walks are planted with *Dutch* elms [stunted pollards], and the walls covered with evergreens: the outward garden has everything that can render such a place agreeable; as a terrace, a mount, a wilderness, and well contrived arbours; but, notwithstanding this is much more admired by strangers than the other, the outer garden is become the general rendezvous of gentlemen and ladies every *Sunday* evening in summer: here we have the opportunity of seeing the whole university together almost, as well as the better sort of townsmen and ladies, who seldom fail of making their appearance here at the same time, unless the weather prevents them."

The Oxford guide in 1812 speaks of the transformation:

"They were extensive and were originally disposed in that formal rectilinear taste, which Kent, Brown, and Repton have successively combined to destroy. They now display all the diversity of which the spot is capable, and form a scene of amenity that blends Arcadian grace with academic solitude."

After these descriptions all modern rhetoric must fall flat.   Yet it will be seriously admitted that among the subtle influences which have tended to form the minds of generations of S. John's men the gardens must ever have had a high place.   There is a charming letter of one * whose training in the College led him to great but humble service to the Church, in which he tells how the summer term affected him as a young scholar.

" You have no idea how beautiful at present [April] our groves are : the horse-chestnuts are luxuriantly green, and their dense foliage is a beautiful contrast to the more backward trees, which have not yet flushed into variety along our dazzling white roadways ; while the grass is so soft, and the flowers so sweet, and the college so abbey-like, and the place so cool and so quiet, that I think, with a bell in the distance, dying and swelling, it unites as many conceivable delights as any spot since Paradise."

There seems always to have belonged to the groves the idea of a country seat with its association, and something perhaps in the Fellows' minds of what Mr. Shorthouse has fancifully told of his Dr. Boteraux. "Till he was past fifty he lived entirely in Oxford, in the Oxford of the old school, in that Oxford in which it was a principle of the Presidents of [S.] John's that there should be no houses between their College and the country."   There are all too many houses now, but

* H. W. Burrows (1816–1892), Canon of Rochester, famed for his noble work at Christ Church, Albany Street.   The letter quoted is in Miss Wordsworth's *Life* of him, p. 24.

still the long stretch of garden which begins where Trinity touches the Broad Street, and gradually narrows till it ends in the College property of Black Hall, preserves much of the amenity of a country retreat. There are many birds nesting every year in the great trees, too sadly diminished, of the groves. Within the last few years we have had, and we probably have, tawny owls, ringdoves and stockdoves, jackdaws, blackbirds, thrushes, bullfinches, linnets, the great titmouse and the blue titmouse, the cole titmouse and the chaffinch, nut-hatches and tree-creepers and robins in plenty, hedge-sparrows and wrens; and in summer we have the blackcap, the chiff-chaff, the spotted fly-catcher, and the willow warbler.

Of the cultivation of the garden under the present *custos sylvarum*, save for the bursarially inherited pleasure in cutting down trees, it is difficult to speak too warmly. A recently printed list of herbaceous plants now grown in the groves will speak for itself.

From the gardens we pass back through the quadrangles. Here there are not many changes to note within or without. The handsome rooms at the north end of Laud's Library, by some absurdly called King Charles's, though it is certain he never lived in them— they were doubtless used, with the others between them and the Lodgings, as withdrawing chambers when the king opened the Library—have been of recent years restored to the beauty of their oak panels. It is sad to think that a somewhat earlier taste had painted the panels yellow and blue. Similar barbarities were perpetrated in the most southern room over the western colonnade.

It may be noted that many of our older sets of

rooms still show the original arrangement—the large chamber in which the students slept, and the two rooms off this, the studies where they worked, when they were not in the Library or at lectures.*

The two quadrangles themselves have recently needed considerable external repairs. A large fall of the parapet of the old Library occurred in 1887 during a heavy snow-storm, and on investigation it was found that much of the other parts of the parapet were unsound. Through the generosity of Mr. J. J. Moubray, M.A. of the College, it was possible, though at a time of great financial depression for the College, to undertake a thorough repair. This was entrusted to Mr. J. J. Stevenson as architect and was carried out with the full approbation of the Society for the Preservation of Ancient Monuments. Mr. Stevenson, in an elaborate and valuable record of the work, which he presented to the College, comments severely on the amount of unnecessary restoration which has been done of late years in Oxford. He proves that in most cases the surface only has peeled, and the stone remains generally sound. Thus he was able to use, in the reparation of S. John's, stones which had actually been taken away by the restorer from All Saints' Church in the city. The garden front was put in a perfectly sound condition, without any trace appearing of the

* See Aubrey (*Brief Lives*, ed. A. Clark, ii. 322) who tells also of the old glass he remembers. "When I came to Oxford, crucifixes were common in the glass windowes in the studies' windowes ; and in the chamber windowes were canonized saints . . . and scutcheons with the pillar, the whip, the dice, and the cock. But after 1647 they were all broken—'downe went Dagon!' Now no vestigia to be found."

hand of the restorer. In the Canterbury quadrangle an authentic reproduction was made of the coloured patterns on the rain-water-heads and leaden down pipes. The gateway tower was also found in need of restoration, and it was restored to a close resemblance to its earliest style. Throughout, the old work has been left everywhere where it was possible to leave it, and any new work that is added is clearly shown to be new. The total cost of the work, which was defrayed entirely by Mr. Moubray, was £2020. The architect justly congratulates the College that the building, "unlike most other colleges in Oxford, is handed down to posterity with its venerable appearance and its old features remaining."

In 1881 one side of a designed quadrangle was erected facing westwards, between the President's garden and S. Giles's Street. Mr. G. G. Scott was the architect.

The outside of the chapel has not needed recent restoration. Of the inside more must be said.

At the beginning of the century the chapel remained as it was after the Restoration. A new organ by Byfield had been put up in 1769. It was not to survive. The east window remained, dating from the time of Charles I. till the early Victorian " restoration," when the building was, if the anachronism be suffered, thoroughly grimthorped. The organ screen, says the *Oxford University and City Guide* in 1817, " is of the Corinthian order. . . . The altar is also Corinthian, and decorated by a piece of tapestry after a picture of Titian, representing our Saviour with His two disciples at Emmaus, attended by a servant. The figures are said to be the portraits of the then Pope, the kings of France and Spain, and Titian. The curious observer will not overlook the dog snarling at the cat under the table." This altar-piece, which Queen Adelaide when she visited the College inspected and, being a learned needlewoman, declared to be no tapestry at all, is now in the President's lodgings.

The monuments have been changed from their position many times. Some of the brasses were at one time in the President's lodgings and were restored early in the present century; some were moved from the floor of the chapel when the new pavement was laid down. Those in the ante-chapel are not in a good light, but they can be identified with the aid of Gutch.* Case kneels with a long beard in "formalities," painted "to the life," and near him is Wicksteed similarly attired, and Latewar, bearded and wearing a ruff and a red cassock. There are three brasses of kneeling men in gowns, Glover, Price, Shingleton, and some smaller gravestones. It is much to be wished that these should be removed to the walls of the chapel, where they could be seen. Anything too that would break the regularity of inferior and uninteresting canopy work which now covers the walls would be an advantage. In the Baylie Chapel is the great monument to Sir William Paddy with its coloured "effigies." There too is the urn containing Rawlinson's heart. The other monuments are those of Presidents, Derham, Dennis, Levinz, Marlow, Holmes, and the large tomb with the recumbent figure of Baylie. A marble tablet has recently been

---

* *History of the Antiquities of the Colleges and Halls in the University of Oxford. By Anthony Wood, continued by Mr. Gutch*, Clarendon Press, 1787; where the inscriptions are given in full.

added in memory of Dr. Wynter. The present condition of the chapel is due to the mistaken enthusiasm of the earlier days of the 'Gothic revival' and the Puginesque School.

What the *Ecclesiologist*, a paper which did good service in its day, wrote in 1845 about the chapel, may be worth quoting:

"*The Chapel of S. John Baptist College, Oxford*, dear to all English churchmen as the resting-place of Archbishop Laud, has lately been restored under the superintendence of Mr. Blore in the Third Pointed Style, having after the Restoration been cast into a debased form. The roof, which is open, is of a good character. The stalls, however, are not satisfactory, being low, and their desk-fronts of slight open tracery work ; nor can we praise the screen, which behind the stalls is solid, and in the centre yawns with a large chasm, unfilled up by 'holy-doors,' presenting no one point of resemblance to an ancient rood-screen. But, worst of all, on the epistle side of the altar, the stone arcading is pierced, not for sedilia, though precisely where they should be found, but as a blind and an opening to a comfortable red-cushioned pue for the President's lady and family. The windows would be improved by the insertion of stained glass."

The criticism is in the main justified, though it shows that absurd contempt for the classical work of the Restoration period which has done so much to ruin Oxford, both by the destruction of what was genuine and by the manufacture during the last fifteen years of what is not. But the writer did not take the trouble to observe that the sedilia which he desiderates do exist, and in the place which he points out for them. The criticism of the entrance to the President's "pue" (an invariable feature in some form or other of all the College chapels) is quite undeserved. Before long stained glass was added. Three memorial windows have been given, one to the memory of Dr. Wynter. The east window, within a few years of the alterations in the chapel, was filled, by subscription, with five gaily coloured figures representing the four Evangelists and S. John Baptist, each over twelve feet high. These were replaced in 1890 by glass of Mr. C. E. Kempe's design.

Two years later, in 1892, the reconstruction of the stone reredos and the decoration of the east end of the chapel were entrusted to Mr. C. E. Kempe. Sculptures of the Baptism of our Lord, with angels, and side figures of S. Elizabeth and Zacharias, were inserted. This was done by Messrs. Farmer and Brindley. The whole of the east wall was painted and gilded according to Mr. Kempe's design by Messrs. Powell. The total cost of this work, which was defrayed by subscription, was £329.

In 1897, in grateful memory of the President's sixty years membership, five of the clergy on the foundation of the College had the Baylie Chapel cleared, its monuments cleaned, and glass put instead of curtains behind the screen which separates it from the original chapel, thus exposing to view one of the most interesting architectural and historical memorials of the College.

.The chapel services are now as follows : Holy Communion every Sunday and Holy Day at 7.45, and on the first Sunday of the month after Morning Prayer. Morning Prayer on Sundays at 9.15, with sermons six times a term; on Holy Days at 8.30, and on ordinary Week

THE CHAPEL

Days at 8. Evensong is sung daily at 5.10 (in the summer term on week-days at 6.10). A short service is said at 10 P.M.

The choir is not yet in possession of the full benefit of Sir William Paddy's generous endowment, as the manor of Wood Bevington has not yet "fallen in" to the College. There are six men and twelve boys. The office of Capellanus, created at the foundation of the College, ceased to exist two years ago at the death of the Ven. R. W. Browne, Archdeacon of Bath and Canon of Wells. The duties had long been discharged by deputy, but there seems no reason why they should not now be personally undertaken and the office restored. Two "Readers" (called, in the Bursary books, Precentor and Succentor) are now responsible for the chapel services. The senior was formerly the deputy of the Capellanus, and received apparently on an average about £100 a year. The junior was paid £20 on a benefaction of Dr. Holmes. In 1869 it was resolved to commute these payments for £120 to be divided equally. In 1886 the salary of each reader was reduced to £50. The senior reader is also responsible for the supervision of the choristers. The singing men are paid £150 per annum. The boys have no payment, but receive on leaving the choir a small sum, calculated to average £5, if their conduct has been satisfactory. Against these payments must be set the income from Wood Bevington, and £10 per annum left by Dr. Holmes for extra boys. The income of Wood Bevington is roughly £223. Also one set of rooms in the old Woods building was left for the use of the organist. The site of this building is now occupied by the new

front. The boys' schooling has always been paid for.
An Elementary School was formerly supported in
Oxford by *pro rata* contributions from all the Colleges.
This contribution was raised by imposits on the
resident members. In 1856–8 this school was dis-
continued, and the College applied the imposits to
maintaining a school of its own. This again proving
inconvenient, this sum has been used for educating the
choristers. The imposits in 1884 were £105 2*s*. 6*d*.
Since then the College has sent the boys to the Oxford
High School, where they receive an excellent education.

There are some miscellaneous payments connected
with the chapel which may be of interest. These are
chiefly preaching payments.

1. Case in 1602 left the College £100; with £81
of which was bought a field, called Bradmore. He
charged it with £5 for two preachers. They used
to preach on great festivals; they now (by order
April 4, 1872) preach two sermons a term each, and
are paid for each sermon £1. The residue was left by
Dr. Case to the College.

2. In 1701 Mr. E. Waple left to the College two
sums of £350 each. The first to be applied for paying
four lecturers yearly, who were to preach among them
one lecture in chapel every month on stated subjects.
The second to found a catechetical lecture in chapel,
on the model of that lately founded at Balliol by Dr.
Busby. This £700 together with £200 supplied by
the College was (in 1717) laid out in the purchase of a
farm at Bletchindon. (The College money was part of
the sum paid for Gloucester Hall.) The deed is in the
Register, vol. vi. p. 195, and reserves £8 per annum as

the proportionate share of the College; the rest to go to the lecturers founded by Mr. Waple. At some time afterwards an additional estate at Bletchindon was purchased by the College for £406 5s. 5d. The College share was, no doubt in consequence of this advance, raised to £22 per annum. This sum of £406 5s. 5d. was left untouched till 1817. In that year some repairs seem to have been done, and the opportunity was taken to deduct the residue of the repair fund created by the sale of timber on the farm from the debt. From that time the debt was yearly reduced; at first by sums of varying amount, and after 1822 by £4 every year. The whole (had the account been kept) must have been paid off by this time. In consequence of these charges, the rent was found insufficient for the lectures, and after 1839 the four lecturers were not appointed—the whole being paid to the catechist. (It had been always the practice to appoint Case's preachers to two of the Waple lectures.)

Somewhere about 1860, partly because the President thought the catechetical lectures not so useful as formerly, partly because large repairs at Bletchindon were anticipated, the President (who nominated to the office) allowed the catechist's place to be unfilled, and the surplus was accumulated. In 1868 the sum had risen to £496 7s. 11½d. The present state of things is therefore this: that after deducting from the clear rent £8 for the College, and laying aside a fund for repairs, the residue belongs to Waple's trusts.

At present only £18 is paid out of the two funds, Case's and Waple's, though the income from the estate is about £60. If the full accounts of the chapel are investigated it will be seen that the payments come practically entirely from trust funds, and that the College makes no contribution out of its corporate revenues, if indeed it does not gain by the present arrangement.*

From the chapel we pass naturally to the hall which adjoins it. It has undergone few changes of recent years, the only ones worth noting being the colouring of the walls above the oak, and the barbarous introduction (it is devoutly to be wished only temporarily) of a hideous hot-water table in 1897.† In recent years the *gaudia* have been cut down to vanishing point. The old gaudies of January 30 and April 15, and the Rawlinson dinner on November 1, have disappeared. On Shrove Tuesday the benefaction of Mrs. Holmes is still partaken of, in the form of capons and pancakes. The gaudy of S. John Baptist's Day survives, with all its old heartiness, but is no longer provided entirely by Domus. The College incumbents find their names honoured, and their characteristics enlarged upon. The President happily speaks ; the Fellows, as happily, are silent.

From time to time, as old records and guide-books show, the pictures in Hall have been changed. At one time a picture of S. John Baptist, rashly ascribed to

---

* For all that relates to the financial aspect of the question I am indebted to a paper prepared by the President in 1885, the words of which have in most cases been followed.

† The intention is, of course, that undergraduates should see their meat cut and get it hot. The Fellows are content to have their dinner brought as of old from the kitchen, only a few feet away from the hall door. The College halls are better as dining-rooms : it is ridiculous to try and turn them into restaurants.

Titian, and by another writer to Guercino, given by John Preston, a Fellow (M.A. 1715), was over the chimney-piece. Towards the end of the eighteenth century it was replaced by a painting on marble (in *scagliola*, it is called) from Raffaelle's beautiful picture of S. John preaching, now in the Tribuna of the Uffizi, executed by Lamberto Gorio, and presented by John Duncan, D.D., a Fellow, " ex Italia redux," in 1759.

Over the high table, in the middle hangs the portrait of the Founder. It was given to the College by T. Rowney, Esq., sheriff of the county in 1692, sometime gentleman-commoner. That of Laud, on one side of the Founder, was the gift of Baynbrigg Buckeridge, A.B. 1695, of North Hall, in Hertfordshire, who had been a gentleman-commoner also, of the family of Bishop Buckeridge, and of the Founder's kindred. It is clearly a later copy of the familiar Vandyke. That of Juxon, on the other side of 'the Founder, was given by William Rollinson, or Rawlinson, Esq., of the county of Oxford, also a gentleman-commoner. Opposite, over the gallery, hangs a great picture of George III., painted at his coronation by Ramsay. It was given to the College in 1779 by the dowager Countess of Lichfield, whose husband, a S. John's man, had been Chancellor of the University. The other portraits are Bishop Buckeridge, Bishop Peter Mews (in the robes of the Garter, and with the black patch over the wound on his cheek, on a background, perhaps intended to represent the fight at Sedgmoor), Sir James Eyre, Chief Justice of the Common Pleas ; William Gibbons, D.M. ;* Dr. Holmes, and Mrs. Holmes ;

* See p. 187.

Rawlinson ; Edward Waple ; * Dr. Woodroffe, a Fellow
of S. John's, and Sir William Paddy. The last is full
length, taken in the black gown of a Doctor of Medicine,
with a great gold watch on the table beside him—an
impressive figure, but artistically less interesting than
the other portrait in red robes which hangs in the
President's house. A third picture of Paddy is in the
Library, and was given by Dr. Gibbons. Three pictures cannot certainly be identified. One, of an Elizabethan in black, with a ship, is traditionally said to be
Hudson the navigator ; and, indeed, it is quite likely
that the association of the earlier College benefactors
with the expansion of English trade may account for
the gift. Another is a handsome man in the robes of
a Doctor of Law or Medicine, and a wig of the era of
William III., given by John Dorrill, gentleman-commoner. A third is a small picture of a gentleman of
George II.'s day. This, an old Oxford guide leads me
to think, may possibly be George Scott, D.C.L., of
Ingatestone Hall, Essex, a benefactor to the Library.
The most curious of all the pictures, by some imitator
of Holbein, is the portrait of Dr. John Case. He
stands between a skull and an hour-glass, with the
skeleton of a monkey before him. Mottoes of mortality—

"What earst I was is gone and past,"

and

"The flitting streme not halfe so faste,"

are at each side, and below, after his title : " Joh. Case,
Philos. Oxon.," quaint lines of funereal import. It

* See p. 188.

may be added here, that there are many pictures of interest in the President's house, including a charming oval of Charles I., perhaps by Old Stone, and in the Bursary there is an early portrait of Sir Thomas White, one of Rawlinson, and one of Dr. Adams (Bursar, 1871–76).

From the Hall to the Common Room is but a few steps. This is an entirely separate building, with rooms above and below for servants. It was built under Charles II., Wood says in 1676. " Handsomely wainscoted," says Ingram; and the piece of fine carving over the fireplace is attributed, like so much Oxford work, to Grinling Gibbons. The ceiling is more curious than beautiful, but it is certainly much more attractive since its recolouring (1898). Tradition makes it, in its earliest form, of the same date as the room, and the shell-work in stucco is attributed to one Roberts. The inner Common Room, whose ceiling, with its Latin and Greek mottoes, was designed by Mansel, was built shortly before the beginning of the present reign.

The fine silver sconces in the outer Common Room lead us to another subject. Since the College loyally surrendered the whole of its plate to Charles I., making only the exception which has English precedent at least as early as the Saladin tithe of 1188, nothing now remains of an earlier date than the Great Rebellion, save only some of the vessels for the Holy Communion. These are worthy of separate mention.

There are two large chalices of silver gilt, the one dated 1572, London, the other closely resembling it, but having the date mark obliterated, and with a cover. The second, which bears an engraved figure of the Good Shepherd, was, perhaps, a ciborium. There are two plain patens, silver gilt, also dated 1572, which fit the top of the chalice. There are also two larger Elizabethan patens, or alms dishes, with fine arabesque work. Two other large covered chalices closely resembling each other are dated, the one 1601–2, the other 1624–5; the latter is "donum Joannis Page, filii natu maximi Richardi Page, Armigeri in Com. Middlesex." There are two large flagons for wine and water, dated 1633–34, a flagon of Irish make, given by Latewar (who was it will be remembered, chaplain to Lord Mountjoy in Ireland), 1605–6, and another by Keblewhite, 1685–6. Lastly, there is a large silver gilt alms dish, dated 1664.

Much of the plate in ordinary use is of great interest and value. Only two cups date from earlier than the Restoration, but from then the College, and since the eighteenth century the Common Room, have received many generous gifts. There are a large number of fine covered quart pots, several magnificent loving cups and some fine candlesticks and sconces. It was at one time a custom of members of Common Room, on vacating their fellowships to give handsome presents of plate, or other tokens of regard. One of the last of these, a handsome and very modern clock, the Common Room owes to Lancelot Lambert Sharpe, B.D., the last of the Fellows elected from Merchant Taylors' under the original statutes.

Customs as old as the plate, some perhaps older, still survive. The graces before and after meat are certainly of the sixteenth century. The former is simply the brief petition for blessing usual in the Oxford Colleges, with the Lord's Prayer.   The latter is worth quotation, though it of course follows older models.

POST CIBUM.

Agimus Tibi gratias, omnipotens et sempiterne Deus, pro his et universis beneficiis : dignare, Domine, misereri nostrum, et manere semper nobiscum, ut auxilio Spiritus Sancti mandatis Tuis sedulo obsequamur, per Jesum Christum Dominum nostrum. *Amen.*

Agimus Tibi gratias, omnipotens et sempiterne Deus, pro THOMA WHITE, milite, Fundatore nostro defuncto, ac pro AVICIA et JOANNA uxoribus ejus, reliquisque quorum beneficiis hic ad pietatem et ad studia literarum alimur, rogantes, ut nos, his donis Tuis ad gloriam Tuam recte utentes, una cum illis ad resurrectionis gloriam immortalem perducamur, per Jesum Christum Dominum nostrum. *Amen.*

Vers. Benedicamus Domino.
Resp. Deo gratias.

In Common Room there is still one toast every night : "Church and Queen," given by the Vice-President or senior Fellow to the next senior. The custom, too, which survives in only two or three other Colleges, of "taking wine" with a guest at dinner, still lingers, though it is clearly at the point to die.

When the "grace of the House" is asked for the degree of any Bachelor of Arts he is still described as "Sir" on the notice, the old title of Dominus still surviving at the Universities.

Till quite recent times the College kept up, as some Colleges do still, the formal progresses round the estates. The President with some of the Fellows travelled in great state, held the manorial courts, and was received everywhere with 'bated breath and whispering humbleness. Formal fishing too of the College waters was preserved till recently, not always it is said without mishap to those who were more expert with the knife and fork than the rod. Modern customs, the new statutes which do so much to destroy security of tenure,* have tended sadly to sever the connection of the Society with its old estates. The first blow was struck when the Bursarship ceased to be an annual office. Tenants' dinners, at a time when the Fellows in residence are at their wits' end to find time for all their teaching obligations, do not help much. Happily the visit to Wasperton, or at least to Warwick, is still an annual event: and the bicycle perhaps may do wonders. Round Oxford at any rate the Fellows may easily go,

> "Crossing the stripling Thames at Bablockhithe,"

or

> "Where once the gipsies pitched their tents
> In autumn on the skirts of Bagley Wood,"

and indeed the frequent absence of some from High Table and Common Room may even suggest that they do not disdain

> "to dance around the Fyfield Elm in May."

What more shall be said of the College to-day?

---

* My own Fellowship was once renewed for two years only, when it was (apparently) feared that I might marry and doubted whether I should not have a right to retain my Fellowship if I did. No Fellows are now elected for more than seven years. It may be said that the present arrangements give to the Fellows under the new foundation the disadvantages of both systems: they may not marry and yet they have no security of tenure.

Athletics might claim longer mention from a more competent writer. Here it shall only be told that S. John's certainly holds its own in all sports, and that, as is known to all whom it concerns, the College has for many years held a much higher position on the river than its numbers would warrant. If numbers are any test of the strength of a College, the continued increase tells its own tale. S. John's, whether wisely or not, is becoming one of the larger Colleges of the University. The strength that comes from unity of feeling is even more marked. These are matters which it were idle to trumpet forth, but certainly no College can boast to-day of a more complete and thorough harmony between those who are taught and those who teach.

No changes have impaired the old loyalty to the College. It draws to itself as readily the attachment of those who have come to it from other Colleges as it retains that of its oldest, its hereditary, members. How much all this owes to the wise rule the College has now enjoyed for twenty-seven years is known to all its members, and the best wish but one that its most loyal sons can express is that that rule may long continue. The best wish of all is that the Founder's intentions may ever be more fully realised, and that within the walls of Chichele and White and Laud, true Religion and sound Learning may for ever flourish and abound.

INDEX

June 1898

SOME BOOKS PUBLISHED BY

F. E. ROBINSON

20 GREAT RUSSELL STREET

BLOOMSBURY, LONDON

TIMES.—"We are glad to welcome the first two volumes of what promises to be an excellent series of College Histories. . . . Well printed, handy and convenient in form, and bound in the dark or light blue of either University, these small volumes have everything external in their favour. As to their matter, all are to be entrusted to competent men, who, if they follow in the steps of the first two writers, will produce records full of interest to everybody who cares for our old Universities."

Universities of Oxford and Cambridge

Two Series of Popular Histories of the Colleges

To be completed in Twenty-one and Eighteen Volumes respectively

EACH volume will be written by some one officially connected with the College of which it treats, or at least by some member of that College who is specially qualified for the task. It will contain: (1) A History of the College from its Foundation; (2) An Account and History of its Buildings; (3) Notices of the Connection of the College with any Important Social or Religious Events; (4) A List of the Chief Benefactions made to the College; (5) Some Particulars of the Contents of the College Library; (6) An Account of the College Plate, Windows, and other Accessories; (7) A Chapter upon the best known, and other notable but less well-known Members of the College.

Each volume will be produced in crown octavo, in a good clear type, and will contain from 200 to 250 pages (except two or three volumes, which will be thicker). The illustrations will consist of full-page plates, containing reproductions of old views of the Colleges and modern views of the buildings, grounds, &c.

The two Series will extend over a period of about two years, and no particular order will be observed in the publication of the volumes. The writers' names are given on the opposite page.

Price 5s. net. per Volume

These volumes can be ordered through any bookseller or they will be sent post free on receipt of published price by the Publisher.

Oxford Series

COLLEGES		
University . . .	A. C. HAMILTON, M.A.
Balliol	H. W. CARLESS DAVIS, M.A.
Merton	B. W. HENDERSON, M.A.
Exeter	W. K. STRIDE, M.A.
Oriel	D. W. RANNIE, M.A.
Queen's	Rev. J. R. MAGRATH, D.D.
New	Rev. HASTINGS RASHDALL, M.A.
*Lincoln	Rev. ANDREW CLARK, M.A.
All Souls' . . .	C. GRANT ROBERTSON, M.A.
Magdalen . . .	Rev. H. A. WILSON, M.A.
Brasenose . . .	J. BUCHAN.
Corpus Christi .	Rev. T. FOWLER, D.D.
Christ Church .	Rev. H. L. THOMPSON, M.A.
Trinity	Rev. H. E. D. BLAKISTON, M.A.
*St. John's . . .	Rev. W. H. HUTTON, B.D.
Jesus	E. G. HARDY, M.A.
Wadham. . . .	J. WELLS, M.A.
Pembroke . . .	Rev. DOUGLAS MACLEANE, M.A.
Worcester . . .	Rev. C. H. O. DANIEL, M.A.
Hertford	S. G. HAMILTON, M.A.
Keble	D. J. MEDLEY, M.A.

Cambridge Series

Peterhouse . . .	Rev. T. A. WALKER, LL.D.
Clare	J. R. WARDALE, M.A.
Pembroke . . .	W. S. HADLEY, M.A.
Caius	J. VENN, Sc.D., F.R.S.
Trinity Hall . .	H. T. TREVOR JONES, M.A.
*Corpus Christi .	Rev. H. P. STOKES, LL.D.
King's	Rev. A. AUSTEN LEIGH, M.A.
Queens'	Rev. J. H. GRAY, M.A.
St. Catharine's .	THE LORD BISHOP OF BRISTOL.
Jesus	A. GRAY, M.A.
Christ's	J. PEILE, Litt.D.
St. John's . . .	J. BASS MULLINGER, M.A.
Magdalene . . .	W. A. GILL, M.A.
Trinity	Rev. A. H. F. BOUGHEY, M.A., and J. WILLIS CLARK, M.A.
Emmanuel . . .	E. S. SHUCKBURGH, M.A.
Sidney	G. M. EDWARDS, M.A.
Downing. . . .	Rev. H. W. PETTIT STEVENS, M.A., LL.M.
Selwyn	Rev. A. L. BROWN, M.A.

* Ready.

The Oxford and Cambridge volumes will be
succeeded by the following:

University of St. Andrews.

J. MAITLAND ANDERSON, *Librarian, Registrar, and
Secretary of the University.*

University of Glasgow.

Professor W. STEWART, D.D., *Clerk of Senatus.*

University of Aberdeen.

ROBERT S. RAIT, M.A. Aberdon., *Exhibitioner of
New College, Oxford.*

University of Edinburgh.

Sir LUDOVIC J. GRANT, Bart., *Clerk of Senatus, and
Professor of Public Law.*

University of Dublin.

W. MACNEILE DIXON, Litt.D., *Professor of English
Language and Literature, Mason University
College, Birmingham.*

**University of Wales and its Constituent
Colleges.**

W. CADWALADR DAVIES, *Standing Counsel of the
University of Wales.*

SELECTIONS FROM THE BRITISH SATIRISTS

With an Introductory Essay by Cecil Headlam, late Demy of Magdalen College, Oxford

Crown 8vo, cloth gilt, 6s.

" His book was a decidedly good idea, which has been well carried out. The Introductory Essay is a scholarly performance."—*Athenæum.*

" The introduction is long and elaborate; it proves that the writer is a sound student of our literature."—*Times.*

" . . . is a book to be welcomed and commended—one specially to place in the hands of the young people who show a taste for literature. . . . In his introductory essay Mr. Headlam supplies a readable and useful sketch of the history of English satire."—*Globe.*

A HANDSOME GIFT-BOOK

Fcap. 8vo, in gilt morocco cover specially designed by E. B. Hoare. 5s. net.

PRAYERS OF THE SAINTS

BEING A MANUAL OF DEVOTIONS COMPILED FROM THE SUPPLICATIONS OF THE HOLY SAINTS AND BLESSED MARTYRS AND FAMOUS MEN

BY

CECIL HEADLAM, B.A.

" His book is a welcome addition to our devotional literature."
Glasgow Herald.

" The volume contains many of the finest extant examples of the petitions of the great and the good of all ages."—*Dundee Advertiser.*

SCORES OF THE OXFORD AND CAMBRIDGE CRICKET MATCHES FROM 1827

Compiled, with Index and occasional Notes, by

HENRY PERKINS,

LATE SECRETARY OF THE M.C.C.

Fcap. 8vo, cloth boards, 1s. net,